MOON DUSTERS

To The Town
Hall Gang-

BY

MOLLIE VOIGT

God's Blessings ♡

Mollie Voigt

www.TotalPublishingAndMedia.com

ISBN: 978-1-937829-32-2

Acknowledgements

I am filled with gratitude for all those who contributed their wisdom, expertise, and heartfelt stories as I wrote, rewrote, and edited this story.

Mom: Thank you for reading my first copy, believing writing was my career before I believed it, and buying me "Writer" t-shirts so I would see my dream every time I looked in the mirror.

Dad: Thank you for running the many errands of printing and sending multiple copies of the manuscript around the country.

Josh: I'm a lucky gal to call you my brother.

To my family, friends, and critics of my baby: Thank you for encouraging, believing, and hanging with me on my journey.

Tyson Manning: Thank you for many detailed responses and for helping me figure out the time-consuming life-consuming rewritten-a-thousand-times scenes. My gratitude for your help is beyond words. You are a brilliant and beautiful soul.

Pete Schantz: For being the first person to heavily critique my work, several times, and for knowing how to inspire me to dig deeper and fully commit to writing my best work...thank you. You are an amazing friend and I'm eternally grateful.

Jim Stovall: Thank you for believing in my work as a writer and for always supporting my work with the troops and veterans.

Thank you for your service to our country and for sharing a part of your world with me:

Jason Actis
Joe Aguilar
Butch Armstrong, KOW
Curtis Armstrong
Steven Armstrong
Shane Bretza
Richard Boettcher
Anthony Chandler
Joshua Clark
Matt Cooper
Catrina Dorsey
Stan Doty
James Dunn
Joel Fehl
Cheryl Foston
Claudia Fuller
Jonathan Fuller
Mark Hamilton

Paul Harrison
Russel Scott Hawkins
Heath Hayes
Walt Henry
James Hobbs
Timothy Hodges
JP Hogan
Jacob Janes
Zackery Kalinauskas
Jason Krivda
Cory Lawrence
Michael Lippert
Damon Mancuso
Tyson Manning
Micheal McGee
Douglas McGlothlin
Eric Muniz-Rivera
Alejandro Ramirez

Rich Rodriguez
Mike Orban
Will Parzyszek
Jonathan Patton
Jeffrey Powers
Jay Sachetti
Cynthia Shuler
Michael Stiles
Will Stuart
Mark Sward
Joshua Tourdot
Jason Ware
Daniel Wilden
David Winn

Thank you for freely sharing your wisdom:
Douglas Andrew
Heather Chandler
Kristin Gillingham
Becky Gordon
Brennan Hussey
Chuck Sasser
Lynn Simmers

For inspiring me…thank you:
Sheryl Duncan
Danny Gokey
Fred Kunkel

_____ (Please insert your name here if I missed listing it above):
Thank you.

May you be blessed on your journey as you conquer life's challenges and emerge victoriously, proudly carrying torches of peace, hope, healing, and love.

God's Blessings,
~Mollie

A note from the author:

Difficulties during my own life blessed me with the realization of the power of our mind and how we can change our world by changing our thoughts. I wanted to share this "amazing discovery" which has been around for many years so I began writing a book to emphasize we alone define our purpose.

Through experiences with troops and veterans, I was encouraged to highlight combat Post Traumatic Stress Disorder, which I renamed WARE in the story for Warrior Readjustment, to sanction the reality of a combat veteran adjusting when returning home.

The most rewarding part of writing this novel was communicating with the troops and veterans...the honor of being trusted with the stories of the beautiful souls that served in our Armed Forces.

CHAPTER 1

Give me a lever long enough and a prop strong enough. I can single-handedly move the world.
–Archimedes

Each day is a game: you live, you win. Play again tomorrow.

Iraq...

Sgt. Drew Manning kneels in front of the small computer screen to check his email. A new message from his wife, Wyla, pops into his inbox.

Drew, Happy Anniversary. Three years and you've been deployed for two of them. I got your flowers and the necklace...reminded me of our honeymoon, not the disaster part, the fun part. I reconnected with Steve, you know him, he's my old debate friend from high school...don't worry, we are just friends, but it's nice to talk with someone who is here. Love, Wyla

"Asshole Steve," Drew remarks with disgust before replying.

Wyla, Happy Anniversary. Our honeymoon...I remember...missing flights, flooded hotel room, lost luggage...but endless food, beaches and sunsets...good times. Three more months then I'm leaving this sand pit. Can't wait to see you. Love, Drew

Drew pushes the computer screen down to sleep mode and walks over to Jasper, who is on the floor futzing with his mouse trap invention.

Jasper carefully places peanut butter on a piece of cloth.

Outside the razor wire are terrorists threatening their lives with mortars, rockets, and other weapons of choice. Inside their tent is a four legged threat; teeth are his weapon; stealing food is his game.

"How's Wyla?" Jasper asks, still focusing on his project.

1

"Fine," Drew says.

"Who's Asshole Steve?"

"Some friend from high school."

"Same dude she left you for last time?"

"I don't know. It doesn't matter," Drew says.

"That's shit man. We're out here for nine months, our lives are on the line…and she's with Asshole Steve. Well, guess what? Asshole Steve wouldn't last a minute out here."

"Roger that. How's the mouse launcher?"

Jasper grins. "The newly designed Pressure Plate Activated Electronically Fired Mouse Launcher is about to go," he sings the last word, "money!" He stands up. "Awww, yeah! Come on, Drew, do the dance with me."

Jasper breaks into his victory dance, a mix between the sprinkler, the salsa, and an NFL end zone dance. He looks at Drew in disapproval. "You didn't do the dance, man."

"I need beer to dance."

Tucker Reiss, former marine now Army medic, chimes in as he passes by. "I need beer to watch you dance."

"Did you hear something?" Drew asks Jasper.

"No, sir, but you know Sgt. Manning, the Marines are just a department of the Navy," Jasper taunts, loud enough for Reiss to hear.

Reiss belts out, "Yeah, the Men's Department!"

Jasper turns his attention back to the mouse launcher. "This trap…is epic. It took me four months to design this bad boy."

"What happens when the mouse eats the peanut butter, again?" Drew asks.

Jasper shows off each piece of the metal, wire, and wood contraption as fine art. "The mouse smells the peanut butter, and is like, 'Oh baby, my favorite snack.' When he steps on the cloth, the victim operated pressure plate presses the lever attached to this electronic switch," he points. "The switch turns the motor, which snaps the first trap, which pulls the string. The string pulls the nail loose that is holding the second trap open. Wham! The second trap snaps, picks up the mouse in the cloth, and launches it at the sticky pads on the wall. Bam! Mouse on the wall…and cue the victory dance music."

"Where did you get the motor from?" Drew asks.

"Sadie Gallagher…the only gal who sends care packages to us arrogant bastards!" Jasper hoots. "She sends boxes every month…and has never met any of us!"

"Probably for the better…" Drew grins. Wyla had sent Drew a care package when he first arrived overseas…and never again. He doesn't know why. "I'm just glad the guys get something from someone. Makes for better days out here."

"Roger that," Jasper agrees. "Oh, Sadie sent an air freshener so I used the motor from the mini fan that was part of it. And the battery pack powering the mouse launcher is from a flashlight."

"Is it ready?"

Jasper slaps the final sticky pad on the wall. "Sgt. Manning, my diabolical mouse launcher is ready for battle."

Drew looks at a beat up brown box on the floor. Big black letters mark the box *Teddy Bears.* In a baby's voice he taunts, "Aww, Nina sent something to help you sleep at night?"

Jasper glances at the box. "Sleep? Who needs help sleeping when we have mortar lullabies? Nah, she sent toys for the kids here. Said I should hand them out for Edison's birthday. My little man turns two today."

"Edison is two already?"

"Yeah, I know, right? He's a little tornado, too. Nina keeps this diary of crazy stuff he does each day…then tells me. It's funny. Oooh, I should teach him the victory dance when I get home. Nina said she wants to escape somewhere warm and feel the sand on her feet. I told her Iraq is such a place…if you blast fifty hair dryers in your face to simulate the wind and toss in some sand. She said Iraq doesn't meet her paradise requirements," Jasper laughs.

"I don't think my sister would appreciate the smell either."

"I can just see Nina's face as I'd describe the nasal cocktail of burning trash, rubber, plastic, human waste, and a splash of diesel."

Reiss passes by again. "And burnt flesh...and fuckin' rockets...and fuckers trying to kill us...yeah," Reiss yells back toward them as he walks out, "it's a fuckin' paradise!"

"Does anyone ever talk directly to Doc Reiss? I think he just enters and exits random conversations," Jasper smirks. "By the way, Drew, Nina says you owe her big."

"Owe her for what?"

"I'm just the messenger, man."

"Tell her she owes me big."

"What for?" Jasper asks.

"I'll think of something."

"I'm not getting in the middle of you and your sister."

"You're already in the middle."

"Dang. Well, I'm not getting any more involved. Hey, when is Sgt. Cooper going on leave?"

"Two days."

Jasper glances around then says quietly, "Tension is higher today."

"Because of what happened yesterday?"

Jasper nods.

"Did any of our guys know that kid?"

"Not really. I guess he had some rough stuff going on back home..."

"Our guys here are solid."

"True that," Jasper holds out his knuckles to Drew.

Drew knuckle bumps Jasper. On his way out the door, Drew motions toward the launcher. "I wanna be the first one to know when that thing gets a mouse."

*

United States...

Country music rolls out of the vintage stereo. The late morning air floats in through the open garage door; it smells like fresh cut grass in the shop.

In faded blue jeans and the gray baggy sweatshirt she wears on days she feels exhausted, Sadie leans on the door jam, quietly smirking. Jake is under Candy...where he has been for the last three hours. He is talking to himself in "car language." All the terms are unfamiliar to Sadie...oil pan, crank shaft, drive train. Intermittently, Jake sings along to the music...hearing him sing is her favorite part of secretly observing him in his element. "How's the work on Candy coming?"

Startled, Jake slams his head into a crossbeam on the undercarriage. "God bless America..."

"Are you okay?!" Sadie bends to look under the car. Her dramatic worst case scenario imagination pictures him knocked out by some large piece of metal or pinned under the car paralyzed forever. She stares at him underneath the car, her long blond curls lightly sweeping the floor.

"I'm fine, babe." He slides out on the creeper.

Sadie stands, folding her arms and leaning against the bumper of the car. "Remember our third date, somewhere around ten years ago, when you sliced your hand on a knife hiding in the dishwater...blood was all over, but you were *fine* and only in need of a quick stop at the emergency room so your mom could stitch up your hand before we went to dinner?"

Jake starts to say something, but Sadie bends down, her face close to his. "Eleven stitches later, you were *fine* in a less blood, bandaged hand, awkwardly eating dinner with your left hand sort of way." She whispers, "Are you that kind of fine?"

He grins. "No emergency services necessary this time."

"Want me to get an ice pack?"

"No, I'm good."

"How was lunch at your mom's house?" Sadie asks.

"Good. My mom and sisters say hello." Jake wipes his hands on a rag, wincing as he sits up. "How are you feeling?"

"I'm okay, just tired. I'm sorry I didn't go with."

"It's okay, love. Some days you can play more, and some days you have to rest more...we all get that."

Taking the rag from Jake's hands, Sadie wipes the grease from his forehead, then kisses the red mark. "Better?"

"I think I have a bruise here," pointing to his lips with a face of innocence.

She purses her lips playfully. "Hmmm…we'll blame your recent cranial wound for that fib," she smiles and kisses him.

"Much better. Did I ever tell you the story about Candy?"

Sadie has heard the story a million times. "Tell me," she puts down her purse and plops into an oversized blue velvet butterfly chair facing Jake.

"So there I was, eight years young, falling in love with this car Gramps bought from an old war buddy of his. When I first sat in Candy, stroking her white leather seats, soft as butter, I closed my eyes and imagined speeding down an open road…"

CHAPTER 2

No individual is so insignificant as to be without influence.
–William George Jordan

Iraq...

"Changeover was complete yesterday." Sgt. Cooper nods into the phone. "Correct. In two days I'm headed to see Germany, drink beer, and see the wife." He chuckles at the response on the other end. "Yes, Lieutenant, I think I'll rearrange that order when I talk to my wife," he hangs up the phone.

Sgt. First Class Mike J. Cooper, a 38-year-old platoon daddy, gears up and grabs his sunglasses, heading into another dust storm in its eerie haze of yellow. A black bandana with the phrase *I'd rather be fishing* covers the lower part of his face, blocking the majority of the moon dust, nasty microsand, attempting to invade his very soul. Buzzing around his head, a fly taunts him, sparking another mental venting session. *Damn flies, an irritating pain in the ass like this rat hole country...*

Cooper smirks when he sees the thermometer outside the company supply tent pegged at its max point of 120 degrees. "One-hundred-twenty degrees my ass," he scoffs. Today, 120 would be a cool summer breeze. "Two more days," he mumbles. "Two more days."

*

United States...

Sadie resumes her normal spot in the garage, sinking into the blue butterfly chair. "When did your grandma name the car Candy?"

"Day three," Jake slides out from under the car. "I can still hear her yelling at Gramps from the kitchen." In an old woman's voice Jake screeches, "'Earl, you light up when talking about Candy, spend countless hours under her, and brag about her when company comes over. She's your mistress!'"

"I can't imagine your grandma yelling...how did Gramps respond?"

"He asked her what she wanted so she would know she was his girl."

"And?" Sadie asks.

"Fresh Flowers. Every Sunday. And a fresh coat of paint every month."

"Paint?"

"Her nails."

"Smart girl," Sadie laughs. "They made it through seventy years of marriage."

"After grandma died, Gramps covered Candy with a tarp and never worked on her again."

"Maybe Candy was the key to their seventy years?"

"Maybe," Jake looks with admiration at the '72 Nova. "And now this fire orange chassis is my baby." In a deep husky voice he adds, "A powerhouse with a Chevy 350 and all sorts of potential."

"I thought I was your baby," Sadie stands, stretching her hands toward the ceiling.

"You, are my babe...there's a difference."

"Oh yeah?"

"A baby requires work to sustain her beauty; a babe is always beautiful."

"Ah, points for that one." Sadie yawns loudly. "Okay, I gotta leave before I decide to stay and take another nap."

"Where are you going?"

"Just to mail a few care packages."

"I can mail the boxes for you."

"Nah, there are only four and I need some fresh air. I've been so tired lately, and just sitting around the house makes me feel like a bag of lazy bones."

"Then I'll load the care packages into the car." He stands up. "It's time for my liquid break anyway."

"Thanks, babe."

Jake heads inside while Sadie walks toward her car in the driveway, unhooking her keys from the ring in her purse.

Sadie stops, attempting to brace herself on the car as her world starts spinning.

She silently requests, *No, God please give me more time.*

Her knees collapse; her body drops to the cement.

Care packages for the troops fill Jake's arms as he walks through the garage toward Sadie's car humming a country tune.

Turning, he sees Sadie's lifeless body on the driveway.

*

Iraq...

Sgt. Cooper rubs his eyes in frustration at the fact that his wife, his beautiful wife, won't be meeting him in Germany.

Sophia reiterates, "Mike, my mother broke her hip. I know she's awful to you, but she needs my help."

Cooper wants to say, *I haven't seen you for nine months...the old bat's hip will still be broken when you return from Germany.*

Instead Cooper says, "If you feel you need to be with your mom, Sophia, that's fine. I support your decision."

His mother-in-law is a witch of exceptional proportions. When Cooper first met her, he gave her a pink rose; she asked him if he stole it from the cemetery. On his wedding day, Cooper told his mother-in-law that she looked beautiful; she said she would be happier if her daughter were marrying a cement block...because then at least she'd be crazy not stupid. The only time Cooper's mother-in-law held her tongue was at his son's funeral...the one time Cooper was looking for her to say something inappropriate...something to distract his grief...someone to be a target for his anger.

"I've been counting down the days, Mike," Sophia sighs. "I miss you. I started making a necklace with tiny glass beads…and every day I add a bead. Ninety more beads and you'll be home."

"Ninety more beads, Sophia. Ninety more beads. I love you."

"I love you too, Mike."

Cooper shakes off the emotions as he hangs up. *I've still got Germany and beer,* he silently coaches himself.

"Sgt. Cooper!" Breathless, sweat pouring from the specialist's face, "the convoy was hit!"

Adrenaline surges through Cooper's veins. At the Tactical Operations Center he reads the 9 line and MIST report.

Two of his men are Category A with extensive burns.

CHAPTER 3

Freedom is not the right to live as we please, but the right to find how
we ought to live in order to fulfill our potential.
–Ralph Waldo Emerson

United States...

Tubes and wires connect Sadie to several machines as she waits for her fifth heart surgery. A beeping noise accompanies the snug hug on her arm from a blood pressure cuff; terror tightens its grip on her gut every passing minute.

Jake looks up at Sadie, a car magazine open on his lap. "You okay?"

"Yeah," her voice crackles.

Jake points to her hand, a white knuckled fist with fingernails carving moons into her palm. Sliding his chair forward, he rests his open palm on the bed.

She fits her hand into his and closes her eyes for a good ten seconds, saying a silent prayer. With each surgery the probability of dying is higher...this reality strips hope from her mental toolbox.

The surgeon pops his head into the room, flashing two thumbs up. "Any questions?"

Sadie asks, "What is the plan if this doesn't work?"

"The plan is this will work," confidence oozes from the surgeon's words. "You're in good hands, Sadie." He points toward Jake. "We'll see you after surgery, Jake," he pats the doorframe twice and rushes out.

"Jake, if I..."

"Sade," Jake cautions.

Sadie brings his hand to the side of her face. "I..."

"I know. Me too."

11

"For sickness and in health?" she asks, this question now a tradition before every surgery.

"For broken and when fixed."

"I'm sorry," Sadie whispers.

"For what?"

"For being a mess."

Jake crawls into the small hospital bed. "It's all good, love." He wraps his arms around her. "We'll just take one day at a time. Plus, you look pretty hot in this hospital gown...we should steal one for home."

She laughs. "We should steal two for home. These faded blue swirls would really bring out your dark brown eyes."

Rita, Sadie's nurse, walks into the room eyeing them suspiciously.

Sadie models her gown, sliding her hand from her shoulder to her knee. "Don't tell me you don't have one of these gowns at home for special occasions, Rita."

"Girl, you know how many old flabby bodies have worn that gown?"

Sadie's face scrunches in disgust.

"I think that one was washed after the last hairy, hairy, person," Rita says with a mischievous grin.

"Stop!" Sadie pleads.

"Now I know I won't have to search your bag before you leave." Rita points her finger at Jake in a scolding manner. "You buy Sadie a nice gown for home...something silk...and cute."

Jake nods. "Yes, ma'am."

Rita glares at Jake, hands on her hips and eyebrows pinned high on her forehead.

Jake repeats, "Silk and cute, got it."

Motioning for him to get out of the bed, Rita turns to Sadie. "Okay girly, we're ready to roll."

Sadie forms a heart with her hands as Rita unlocks the wheels of the bed.

Jake returns their heart signal, his anxiety consumed eyes betraying his reassuring smile.

*

Pre-surgical chatter erupts from a swarm of blue scrubs adding to the chill of the operating room.

One thought runs through Sadie's mind. *Did I make a big enough difference?*

Seeing the anesthesiologist reminds Sadie of a recent television episode of *Medical Mistakes*, where the patient was awake and felt the excruciating pain of the surgery but was unable to speak or move—a horrific experience of being trapped in one's own body.

Sadie demands from anyone who will listen, "I want to live. I want to wake up when this is over!" Her heart rate accelerates as she begins to panic, upsetting numerous machines in the room.

A warm hand hugs her shoulder. The surgeon's kind eyes twinkle above his surgical mask. "Sadie, I have my magic cap on today—the one with the hearts—the one I wore for your last four surgeries. You will live today. You will wake up, darlin'."

Magic? An acronym comes to Sadie's mind. *My Awesome God In Control…MAGIC.*

Sadie relaxes, likely due to the potion they just injected into her IV port. "Okay, doc, you work with MAGIC to fix me." Sadie starts counting backwards. "One hundred, ninety-nine, ninety-eight, ninety…seven, nin…."

*

Iraq…

Drew stares at Jasper's helmet, rifle, and boots on the memorial stand, still unable to grasp the fact that outside the wire today was their first KIA in nine months…a father, a husband…his brother-in-law.

CHAPTER 4

To stay locked in that dark time is to surrender the opportunity to enjoy life as it continues.
—Michael Orban

Three and a half months later: United States...

Wyla shoves the last of her belongings into a purple zebra bag, a bag so big she could fit inside. Slinging the straps over her shoulder, she stares at the door and sighs. "I'll always love you, Drew..."

A faint slurred response, "Tell Asshole Steve I say 'Hi.'"

Wyla's eyes narrow as she turns toward Drew, her jet black hair frames an acid glare. "Asshole Steve? That's real grown-up, Drew! You came home two weeks ago and I've tried every day. But that bottle is all you care about. And if Steve is the asshole, what does that make you?!" she storms out, slamming the door.

A lone bottle sits on the table. Drew empties it as Wyla's heels click loudly down the cement walkway.

The shrill voice of his neighbor, Gigi, shouts a bubbly "Good morning, dear!" to Wyla.

Cracking the seal on a new bottle, Drew remarks, "If Steve is the asshole, what does that make me? Why, I'm a medal wearing, boozed up, dysfunctional sergeant...and on my way down divorce lane thanks to Asshole Steve." He takes a swig from the bottle. "And I'll drink to that, Jack."

*

An anatomical heart model sits on the surgeon's desk. Jake reaches over Sadie to pick it up, the moveable pieces dumping into her lap. "I

14

guess it comes apart." He puts the anatomical puzzle back together, placing it in its original location. Seconds later, the model breaks apart, the pieces bouncing off the desk and onto the carpet. Jake gathers the pieces and lays them in a little pile on the desk.

Emotionless, Sadie stares at the wall; the possibility of needing another surgery threatens her nerves. Anxious energy bounces her knee at an impressive speed. "I don't think I can do it again."

Jake puts his hand on her knee. "Let's just see what the doctor says, Sade."

"The thought of another surgery…a sixth surgery…I can't…"

"Maybe the last surgery was the last surgery."

"I'm just so tired of it all, Jake…and the longer the doc makes me wait in here, the more I'm freaking out, like he's trying to figure out how to tell me the bad news…I don't think I can do this anymore!"

"Okay, Sade? Let's just wait. Maybe he got stuck in surgery and he's running late." Jake kisses her forehead. "Maybe your heart is good to go."

"Maybe." She takes a deep breath, her mind still bracing for devastation.

*

The phone. The ringing. The earsplitting noise.

Drew hits the bedside table, picking up the phone.

"Drew? It's Nina."

He hates how she annoyingly identifies herself, as if he doesn't recognize her voice or have caller ID. "Yah."

"Are you awake?"

"No."

"Wyla called me. She said she left." Nina's washing machine thuds in the background like a clothing filled rocket about to launch.

"She left three days ago," and he emptied three bottles of Jack…a large portion still residing in his bloodstream.

"Drew, I'm going to make cookies. Want to come over?"

"Not now. I'm trying a liquid diet," he laughs, then winces from the pain in his head.

"Not now. For lunch."

"You eat cookies for lunch? That's funny."

Nina sighs with extra effort. "You coming or not?!"

"Yah, sure. Cookies for lunch." Drew hangs up and buries his head in the pillows.

*

Snow lightly frosts the trees of the cemetery. Sadie places flowers on her brother's grave then wraps her arms around Jake.

Jake pulls her in close.

Sadie repeats the surgeon's words. "'Welcome back to your life Sadie.' I could have kissed him when he delivered the good news about my heart."

"Yeah, you and me both." Jake pauses. "But…I'm glad I just shook his hand."

"Me too," she kisses him. "This is our brand new life." Sadie starts laughing. "The surgeon's face when he saw the model in pieces on his desk…that was funny."

"Maybe he shouldn't have made us wait," Jake defends.

"Or put the model out of reach."

"Or had some little sandwiches or snacks available."

"And tea!"

"Smoothies would be acceptable too."

"So what you're saying is it's his fault."

Jake's eyebrows rise in agreement. "Yeah, he pretty much forced me to mess with his heart model."

Driving home, the radio station announces try-outs for the American Rockstar Competition.

Sadie shrieks, "Try-outs in Chicago?! Jake, you should audition…you so have to audition! You have to…Jake, you have to! For me…for humanity!"

"You want me to audition for a singing competition on television?"

"Not just any singing competition…for American Rockstar, where ordinary people rise to stardom as America votes each week…you'd receive a recording contract and perform in concerts around the country…wouldn't that be amazing?!"

"Yeah."

"So you will audition?"

"Probably not."

"Okay."

Jake narrows his eyes at her response. "That's it?"

"For now."

At home, Sadie calls Jake's best friend, Devin, placing her phone on speaker. "D, don't you think Jake would make a good contestant for the American Rockstar Competition?"

Jake shakes his head. "Here we go…"

"Heck yeah, sista!" D puffs in-between breaths.

"And don't you think we should encourage Jake to try out?"

"Heck yeah, sista!"

"Are you working out?" Sadie asks.

"Yeah, my newest program." D adds in a deep voice, "Hard core abs for hard core men."

Jake mocks, "Hard core men…"

"Is Jake listening to our conversation?" D asks.

"Yes," Sadie replies. "And giving me a disturbing look."

"He's probably picturing his own abs…" D laughs. "Forget him girl…you and I can audition and when we win, we'll travel the world together. Hey Jake, maybe you could be our butler…our flabby abs butler…"

Jake grabs the phone and cancels the speaker mode. "No, I'm not telling her that. Actually she can't come to the phone right now…she's busy."

Sadie attempts to snatch the phone.

Jake turns away from her, still talking with D. "Isn't there a soccer ball you could be pumping air into or something?" He laughs. "I see why all the ladies are after you, man, with that charisma." Grinning at D's response Jake adds, "Later, coach." Ending the call, Jake looks at Sadie.

She pats his abs, "I like my man's abs."

He grins. "That won't make me do the singing competition."

"Do what you want, babe…" Sadie shrugs her shoulders, grabbing her phone from his hand. "But I'll have to get a new gown to wear on the red carpet when we dazzle Hollywood…maybe a blue one to match your swanky blue tie…ooh, or silver to match the silver tie…maybe a blue dress with silver heels…"

*

The smell of freshly baked chocolate chip cookies greets Drew as he opens the front door.

Two-year old Edison races over and holds up a red miniature truck. "Fruck."

Drew grins. "Oh, I bet your momma likes that word. Nice truck, buddy. How's my favorite nephew?" He picks him up, carrying him like an airplane into the kitchen. "I brought sandwiches for dessert."

Nina's eyes are bloodshot and swollen.

"Why don't you go play, buddy," Drew puts Edison on the ground, rolling his truck into the hall. He leans against the counter and waits for Nina's burst of problems.

"My cupboards are bare…and piles of laundry…and bills…and…you!"

"Me?"

"I don't know how to help you, Drew!"

"I'm fine."

"And how many bottles does it take for you to be fine?"

"This is an intervention lunch?"

"Jasper didn't come home, Drew."

Drew's blood pressure spikes. "Let's not do this again, Nina."

"But you did, Drew. You did. And I don't know why he didn't. But you did."

Drew's anger explodes, mental steam escaping like a cover removed from a boiling pot. "I fuckin' ask that question every day, every night, every moment!" he catches a glimpse of Edison peering around the corner. Drew tosses the bag of sandwiches onto the counter and walks out.

"Drew!" Nina pleads as the front door slams.

*

Sadie strolls over to their garden and bends down, admiring a lone baby oak tree. "Remember when I planted the acorn here?"

Jake pauses from busting up ice on their sidewalk with a shovel. "I remember."

"Inside an acorn, a massive tree sleeps."

Jake curiously looks at her.

"This baby oak tree has a tiny, thin, unstable trunk, but his leaves are the same size as a full grown tree's leaves because he's growing into his big leaves. The oak knows deep in his little tree soul that he will be a tall tree one day. He constantly ponders this truth, producing leaves today that are the same size of a fully grown tree. This tree is just like us."

Jake flings a shovel load of ice into a pile of snow. "How so?"

"We have to align our thoughts not where we are but where we want to be…nurturing our dreams until they become reality."

"Which dreams do you so poetically speak of?" Jake asks.

"Well, you could try out for American Rockstar, but you don't see yourself as a rockstar. You just see a little trunk like this oak tree." Sadie pauses, blowing a few snow flakes off of the tree's crisp winter leaves. "Someday, you may feel deep in your little tree soul that singing is one of your great talents. And if your talent becomes a passion, you'll nourish the dream until it becomes reality."

"We're still on the singing competition, huh?"

"We all start out ordinary and then choose the size of our dream leaves. You can have bigger leaves any time you want to."

"And what are your big leaves?"

"I don't know. I have a new life now. I'm learning how changing my thoughts can change the way I see the world. And I want to capture my new thoughts in a journal. Want to come with me to the bookstore?"

"Sure," Jake chops the last bit of ice on their sidewalk. "Their coffee shop has good smoothies."

"A smoothie when it's thirty degrees outside? I'm thinking more about tea. And maybe one of my big leaves is getting you to have bigger leaves."

Jake puts his arm around Sadie as they leave the bookstore. "Do I get to read this journal?"

"Nope, but I might let you smell the leather." She inhales deeply with her nose pressed against the journal. "Mmm...leather."

"You're bold having no lock on the journal...nothing to deter me from examining your secrets."

"A lock would be an irresistible invitation for you to try and pick it...or break it."

"It only took me a few minutes to jimmy the lock on my sister's journal in grade school...that provided hours of entertainment. Grace lit up when she saw me reading it, crying and screaming at the same time," Jake laughs. "My parents established privacy laws in our house after that. I," he beams, "was the inspiration."

"Sounds more naughty than inspirational but good for you, babe, already making a difference in grade school."

"Now can I read your journal?"

"Maybe...if you try out for the singing competition," Sadie's eyes sparkle.

"Never mind."

*

People scurry in and out through the glass sliding doors, exiting the store with carts full of groceries. They are all in a hurry to get somewhere. Where...Drew doesn't know...or care. Their destination is as unimportant as they are.

In Iraq, sandstorms race through the desert with moon dust invading every crack, crease, and space. Nina's words irritate Drew more than Iraq's nasty ass moon dust...as if she needs to remind him of Jasper's death.

She lives with knowing he died, Drew fumes, slamming the car door and heading toward the liquor section of the store. *I live with knowing how he died...the IED...the fire...the cries from the Humvee as flames melted his flesh. I live with being too late.*

20

CHAPTER 5

*The quest, then, is not to stabilize that wave and make each one
exactly alike (our environment) and predicable by all, but rather to
perfect your own adaptability to an ever-changing situation and make
it through to the other end. If you can survive, great.
If you have executed it with style and grace, even better.*
—Tom Barrack

Jake consumes the last swallow of his caffeinated morning fuel, a
dark Italian brew, and hands Sadie a letter with *Free Mail* written
in the upper right hand corner of the envelope. "Another note from
overseas."

"Ooh, fun!" Sadie slits open the envelope and begins reading the
note.

Meg, the only makeup-free girl Sadie and Jake know, knocks three
times on the back door and walks in, sporting her normal attire under a
black wool coat: baggy camouflage pants, an old t-shirt marked with
splotches of paint, a ball cap with her red ponytail partly hanging out
of the back of the cap, and high heels.

"Meg!" Sadie greets her with a hug.

"Nuchu, Sadie."

Sadie grins and bows. "Nuchu, Meg. I'm almost ready to go. Give
me five minutes."

As Sadie leaves, Meg says, "Nuchu, Jake."

"Bless you."

"I didn't sneeze. I'm greeting you in Vietnamese."

"Why?" Jake teases.

"Because…I can. Does greeting me back in Vietnamese make you
uncomfortable? Threaten your manhood maybe?" Meg asks.

"I don't actually know if you're greeting me…you could be
swearing or calling me something inappropriate."

21

"Me? Inappropriate? Why, I'm sweet as pie," Meg bats her eyes.

"Like the tart cherry kind, right…the sugar free stuff?"

"You're mean."

"Thanks," Jake smiles sweetly.

As Meg removes her coat, the strap on her purse unsnaps, the items spilling out midair. A small mirror busts in half as it hits the floor.

Jake reaches to help pick up the pieces but Meg puts out her hand. "I got it," she bends down. "This means seven lucky years, right?"

"Sure, seven lucky years," Sadie walks back into the kitchen. "I'm ready to go Miss Lucky."

Meg sweeps her purse contents into a little pile with her hands, dropping them into her purse in no particular order. "Then we shall vamanos to be care packageatorians."

"English, Vietnamese, Spanish, and a Meg word…all in one morning…impressive," Jake nods. "You watching the game tonight, Meg? You know who your football team will lose to, right?"

Meg's eyebrows rise. "A declaration of war on my football team…you should have tissues readily available, my feathered friend. Your team will be sporting big L's on their foreheads after the game."

"That's precious. If only your team was as tough as their three fans."

"If only your team had three fans."

Sadie steps in-between them and kisses Jake. "Have a good day at work, babe."

"See you girls later." Jake whispers to Meg, "That's what my team will be saying to your team at the end of the game."

On her way out the door, Meg smiles at Jake, itching her forehead with her middle finger.

"Ah," Jake says. "I see it now…sweet as pie."

*

Drew reluctantly knocks on the door.

Surprise lines Nina's cloud of sorrow expression. "Since when do you knock?" Nina leaves the door open and walks back to the kitchen, plunging her hands into dish water.

Drew walks in, setting bags of groceries on her counter.

"Drew, I never wanted to be an Army wife because I never wanted to be a single mom."

He unloads the groceries. "I know."

"And here I am...crashing and burning as a single mom," Nina sighs. "You went shopping for me?"

"I saw this little kid asking his mom to buy him a bag of taffy, promising he'd be happy forever if she would just let him have it. I figured if the taffy is that powerful, I should buy a bag." He holds up the bag of candy. "Shall we see how happy it makes us?"

"Let's," Nina dries her hands. "My hips could use more sugar," she smirks at the pile of cookies on her kitchen table.

Opening the bag of taffy, Drew says, "I'll uh, I'll help you...with whatever."

Nina stretches a piece of the stringy candy in her fingers. "Care to stay for breakfast?"

"Sure," he pulls off his hooded sweatshirt and drapes it over a kitchen chair, his t-shirt revealing muscular arms.

"We're messed up, aren't we?" Nina plops into a kitchen chair.

"Yeah," Drew pops a blue nugget of taffy into his mouth. "Pretty much."

*

"Hard to believe we used to pack these boxes in your basement, Sadie," Meg says, laying a baggie of drink mix packets inside a care package. "And your kitchen table was only available for meals once a month...right after shipping the boxes out. It was sweet of Bobby to let us use this space."

"Bobby called me the other day," Sadie finishes filling a box. "Said she's moving and putting this place up for sale."

"Huh," Meg calmly replies. "Didn't see that coming."

"I was freaking out...I don't know what we'll do or where we'll go." Sadie begins taping a box and adds, "Maybe we'll strike it rich and we can buy the building."

"There you go. Problem solved," Meg says.

"Speaking of problems, how have you been feeling lately?"

"Oh, just swell."

"Swell as in grand or swell as in inflammation?"

Meg lets out a brief chuckle. "Desire for the former while dwelling in the latter."

After a minute of silence Sadie comments. "And you don't want to talk about it."

"Right. Instead of focusing on it, I try to block out my pain. It's a denial type of therapy."

"Okay...how about painting. How's that going?"

"I was invited to an art show to display my work."

"Oh my gosh, Meg! How fantastic!"

"I haven't accepted the invitation yet."

"Why?"

"I don't know if it's worth the time and effort of driving all the way down to Chicago...and I don't know the people...my grandpa knew them...so it's kind of a pity thing I think."

"Who cares?!" Sadie exclaims. "It's a chance for exposure, for people to see your work...your amazing work! I'll go with you if you want. I think you should go...what a great opportunity!"

"Always the optimist," Meg grins.

While loading packages onto the shipping cart at the post office, a white-haired man with a face full of wrinkles approaches them. "Golly, you ladies have been busy! Are those all for family members and friends overseas?"

Sadie shakes her head. "We don't know many of these guys and gals. Most of them don't receive anything from home."

"While stationed overseas, I didn't receive anything from home except one day...I got a package. It felt like Christmas," a smile spans his entire face as he recalls the memory. "Hearing my name called for mail—I thought they made a mistake!"

Sadie loads the last package onto the cart. "In what branch of the military did you serve?"

"Coast Guard. And boy, support from home makes a big difference." After mailing his letter, the man tips his hat. "It was a pleasure to meet you both. Keep up the good work."

Sadie smiles. "Nice to meet you. What is your name?"

"Bill."

"I'm Sadie, and this is Meg."

Meg says, "Pleasure to meet you, Bill. Thanks for your service."

"Ladies, thank you. It might not seem like a lot to you, but oh boy, it's a lot to them when they see that box with their name on it."

Sadie and Meg wave goodbye to Bill, then start loading their care packages onto the counter.

The gal behind the postal counter asks, "How many boxes?"

Meg answers, "Fifty box-a-roonies."

"This will take me all day," the postal gal complains. "Wow, you use a lot of tape on these. Probably could use less tape in the future."

Sadie suppresses her annoyance. "My troops don't want moon dust in their packages...the tape keeps out the moon dust."

"I'm not calling you out or anything...I just think it's a waste. I see boxes in here all the time with less tape."

Sadie whispers, "Moon dust...it's the bloody moon dust."

"I just think you could use less tape."

Meg responds in her typical matter-of-fact style. "Oh, I know. Our guys and gals overseas like extra tape. So we give them extra tape. It's all about them. Now if you were in the desert, in uniform, willing to die for our country, and I was sending you a box, I'd use a little teeny tiny piece of tape, because I know you don't like tape. But our pals are tape wanters. So tape we give them...because that's how we roll."

Back in the car, Sadie glances at Meg. "She complains every time we bring in boxes...every time!"

"She's a slinky, Sadie, and likely can't help her bad behavior."

"A slinky?"

"She'd put a smile on our face if pushed down stairs."

Sadie bursts out laughing.

A song lights up Meg's phone. She briefly dances with her arms before answering. "That works, I'll bring him in today."

Sadie's facial expression asks the question.

"Just something with my dog. It'll be fine. I've got seven years of luck on my side after busting my mirror today."

"Well, if you need anything..."

"Thanks." Meg holds her fist out toward Sadie. "Done for another month."

"Thanks for your help, hon," Sadie knuckle bumps Meg. "Another set of care packages headed overseas."

CHAPTER 6

To truly enjoy the good in life you have to know the worst. To really enjoy freedom, you should understand what it takes to preserve it.
–Joel Fehl

"Sgt. Cooper?" Drew opens Nina's front door, wishing he hadn't just downed a shot of whisky from his flask.

"Manning," Cooper nods. "I am looking for Mrs. Jasper."

Nina steps around the corner, carrying a wide-eyed Edison on her hip. "Afternoon, Mrs. Jasper…"

Drew motions toward his head, drawing Nina's attention to three clips designed to close bags of potato chips holding up her hair.

Nina quickly removes the clips, frantically running a hand through her hair.

"I'm Sgt. Cooper. I was Jasper's platoon sergeant."

"We've met before, Sgt. Cooper," Nina nods. "Come on in. I'm sorry…the house is a mess. You want coffee or tea or anything?"

"No thanks, ma'am."

Nina hands Edison to Drew, and through one look conveys her concern regarding his recent lip-lock with liquid Jack.

Cooper disregards the look between them and follows Nina into the living room, the star in the window catching his attention.

Nina defends, "Jasper gave me that little red and white flag when he left. Said he'd take it down himself. His body came home but my husband never returned. I'm keeping the flag up. I don't care what you all think."

"I have one in my window…for my son," Cooper says.

"He's over there now?" Nina asks.

"He was. Died two years ago in combat."

"Then you know…" her eyes fill with emotion, "how it is."

27

Cooper nods. "Ma'am, did you know about the mouse trap Jasper built in Iraq?"

"He was trying to describe the mouse launcher to me over the phone…but I'm more of a visual person so after a few attempts he said he'd send a picture when his invention was finished. He never…" she wipes a tear. "He never sent one."

Cooper pulls out his phone and scrolls down to a picture of Jasper's mouse launcher. Turning the screen of his phone toward her, he explains Jasper's invention.

Nina soaks in his words, tears cascading down her cheeks.

Around the corner, Drew listens to every word with his back against the dividing wall. Edison sits on Drew's lap, gently touching each tear as it runs down Drew's face, a face wet with memories.

"Were you close to your son, Sgt. Cooper?" Nina asks.

"Very close, ma'am."

"Then you know how Drew is. My Jasper was Drew's best friend."

After drying his eyes, Drew grabs a colorful foam book from the kitchen table and holds it up.

Edison growls, "Rarsur!"

"Race cars." Drew sniffs deeply and plops Edison on the counter. Standing beside him, Drew reads aloud as Edison points out each car in the story.

Cooper walks into the kitchen. "Manning."

"Sgt. Cooper," Drew nods.

Nina enters behind Cooper and says to Edison, "Let's go play outside, honey."

As the door shuts, Drew follows Cooper into the living room. "Is it my turn to cry?"

Cooper ignores the sarcasm and motions for them to sit.

"I didn't know about your son."

Cooper pulls a laminated photograph from his pocket, handing it to Drew. "He was nineteen."

Drew looks at the picture, then hands it back, attempting to avoid Cooper's gaze.

"Indirect fire hit the medical tent. I held my son for the last fifteen seconds of his life…the worst fifteen seconds of my life." Cooper places the photo back into his chest pocket. "Jasper was a hell of a soldier, Drew."

"Yeah," Drew shakes his head and folds his arms across his chest. "There was this little Iraqi kid who always wore red pants with blue stripes...and he always had to talk with Jasper. Jasper would let him stand on his boots when talking so the kid's feet wouldn't burn on the sand." Heartbreak blends with disgust as his eyebrows knit together. "And...they killed him." Drew mutters, "I keep seeing it, hearing it, and the smell...and his son, Edison, is only two...it just, uh," he looks at Cooper, "is fucked up."

"You saved Reiss."

"A KIA trumps a save."

"Not when you're the one that's saved." Cooper leans forward and gives the speech his sergeant gave him after his son died. "To truly enjoy the good in life you have to know the worst. To really enjoy freedom, you should understand what it takes to preserve it. So we carry on for our country and for those lost protecting it." Emphasizing his point, he taps his index finger on the coffee table. "We're still here, Manning. Over there, we'll die for those next to us...but here, we live for those taken from us."

Drew unfolds his arms and stares out the window. "That little kid with the red pants came looking for Jasper the next day."

"You're one of my best leaders, Manning. A bottle won't make anything make sense. How long is your leave?"

"I'm back on base in ten days."

As Nina closes the front door, Edison bolts through the living room and jumps into a pile of stuffed animals, belting out a word only he understands. "Surisuro!"

Cooper stands, reassuring Drew with his eyes. "See you in ten days, Manning." He turns to Nina, "I'm sorry for your loss, ma'am."

"Thanks for coming...I'm sorry I just sat and cried. I'm still a mess!" Nina laughs in embarrassment. "He respected you, Sgt. Cooper. He told me," she chokes back tears, "he'd follow you anywhere."

"Thank you, ma'am. It was an honor to serve with your husband."

Cooper climbs into his vehicle, nodding to Drew as he backs out of Nina's driveway.

He takes the first right turn exiting the subdivision, pulls over, and parks his truck.

Cooper rests his arms on the steering wheel and lowers his head as an explosion of emotion shakes his body.

*

Jake crashes through the door, his arms full of groceries. "How's my care packageatorian?"

"Packages are on their way overseas," Sadie closes her journal and hooks her pen through the elastic loop on the journal. "I wonder sometimes."

Jake sets brown paper bags on the counter. "What about?"

Sadie walks to the kitchen and starts emptying one of the bags. "If a care package really makes a difference."

"Some of the troops send you messages of thanks for the packages...so they must make some kind of difference."

"But how much of a difference does jerky or a package of cleansing wipes or a bandana for sandstorms make? They say, 'I'll die for you' and we say 'Great, here's a toothbrush.'"

"Don't forget about your letter, Sade."

"And my letter...why would they care about my life and the goofy stories I write in the letters?"

"Same reason people watch television...to escape their lives for a while. If I was overseas, I would want something from home—anything to distract me."

"I guess so. Me too. I wish I could do more."

Jake says while kissing her, "Amazing describes how you care for them."

"Mmm...I love kissing you."

Jake smiles. "We have the whole night."

As they make their way to the couch, Jake's phone rings. He answers the call with, "Abs of steel model, Jake speaking." Jake laughs and turns toward Sadie. "D wants to know if we want to go to Sydney's Café for karaoke tonight."

Sadie looks at him with a sparkle in her eyes. "I thought we were busy tonight...kissing." She concedes, "Sure, you guys are always entertaining to watch on stage."

A mischievous smile crosses Jake's face after he hangs up.

"Uh oh. What are you thinking?" Sadie backs away from him.

"Are you going to get on stage with me tonight, love?"

"I prefer blending into the background."

"Please, Sade! D is an okay singing partner, but you...you have a great voice. If we sing together, we can win the prize."

"I do love Sydney's famous cinnamon rolls."

"Is that a yes?"

Sadie holds up her finger. "One song."

Jake puts his arms in the air as if he just scored a touchdown. "Sweet!"

*

Meg shifts Ruger's weight to her left hip as she unlocks her door. She walks inside, pushing the door shut with her right foot and dropping her keys onto the kitchen counter.

"There you go, Ruger," Meg lays the black dog on an oversized suede couch. "You're too young to leave me, baby. Tomorrow will be better with the pills we got."

When Meg was 15, she asked her parents for any firearm from the Ruger collection for Christmas. They instead bought her a puppy in hopes she would grow out of her desire to spend time at the shooting range.

Meg sits on the floor and rests her head on the couch. Pain shoots across her temples, an intense pressure tempting her to poke a hole into her skull...if only that would relieve the pain.

Ruger moves his head to touch hers, the cool of his nose brushing against Meg's cheek.

"We'll figure out what's wrong and everything will be okay." Meg wraps her arms around him and stares at the grandiose painting of the

Colorado Rockies transforming her living room wall: a sunset of purple and pinkish-orange clouds, white snow caps on dark chocolate mountains, and a valley of pine trees, all casting a mirror image in a lake below.

Willing her way to the kitchen, Meg makes a cheese sandwich, wraps a blue starry fleece blanket around her shoulders, and plops back on the couch next to Ruger, flipping between the football game and the National Geographic Channel.

*

Outside Sydney's Café, a pink neon sign boasting "Best Cinnamon Rolls in the World" buzzes as Jake opens the door for Sadie.

"That sign looks like it is about to fall and decapitate someone," Sadie glances up at the sign before walking inside. "I just hope I won't be the one to break its fall."

Inside the café, Jake takes Sadie's coat. "I'll protect you so the sign doesn't slice off your head."

"Always my gentleman," Sadie pats his arm.

D walks toward them showing off his tango dance moves. "Whassup?! Sade, you look…fantastic," he hugs Sadie.

"Thanks!" Sadie twirls in her golden heels, modeling her emerald striped chocolate brown dress.

"Uh, Sadie, I said you look fantastic and you didn't say anything about how I look." D steps back without letting Sadie answer. "Wait…are you going on stage tonight?"

Sadie holds up her finger. "One song with Jake."

"What? What about me? Where's my love at, girl? I'm even wearing my silver vest tonight."

"I love that silver vest."

"I know, sista!" D spins to model his own attire.

"Okay, I'll sing one with you and one with Jake." Before D can celebrate, Sadie adds, "Because you'll encourage Jake to audition for the singing competition, right?"

"And here I thought you just found me irresistible…but yes, I'll nag him. Hop on stage with me and I'll be a singing competition drippy faucet for you."

Sydney saunters over to their table, using his belly to balance a tray of waters. "Halo, my regulars," a bit of his Australian accent sneaks out. "Evening, Sadie. More beautiful tonight…" slight affects from his stroke still evident as he concentrates on correctly speaking each word, "than a queen's crown of diamonds."

"Thank you, Sydney," Sadie beams.

"You boys back to compete again, eh?" Sydney distributes the coasters and glasses.

Jake clears his throat. "Back to win, Sydney."

"Yah, yah. Of course ya are."

Jake says, "Sadie's coming on stage with us tonight."

Sydney's eyebrows rise. "Oh, well then you have a shot at winnin'," he winks at Sadie as he leaves.

Sadie bursts out laughing as she takes Jake's hand and steps off stage. "You were sooo funny!"

"That was fun," Jake agrees, still breathing heavily. He escorts her to their table. "I'm going to…"

"I know, babe…go talk to the world my social bug."

D slides out a chair for Sadie to sit down. "Our duo was top notch sista…but your husband takes insanity to a whole new level on stage."

"I know! Put a mic into his hands and he takes off like a rockstar…that's why I keep saying he should…"

"Audition," D finishes her sentence. "He will. Oh, what did the doctor say?"

"My heart is strong. No more surgeries!"

He holds up his fist and knuckle bumps Sadie. "Right on, sista. That news is as hot…as me," D grins.

Sadie laughs. "You're not going to show me your abs now, are you?"

"Nah, Jake is staring over here…and the view of my steel six-pack might spiral him into a jealous rage."

"Talking about staring, D…quite a few gals are staring your way."

"Yeah, and I can't even ask one out without her instantly planning our wedding and how many kids we should have."

"And what's wrong with marriage and kids?"

"I fully support marriage…as long as it's other people getting married. I'm a best man kind of a guy." D faces Jake and pats his abdomen.

Jake rolls his eyes and makes a hand gesture toward D.

"And after your husband's…" D clears his throat, "sign of appreciation, I must go engage in some good ol' guy talk."

"Also known as verbal abuse?" Sadie asks.

"Right," D grins. "Guy talk."

Looking at the empty stage, Sadie imagines Jake performing his own songs.

"Hi, Sadie."

"Addison!" Sadie stands to give her a hug.

"Oh my gosh, you were so cute on stage. And Jake was so funny sliding across the stage and belting out lyrics." Addison touches Sadie's arm. "How are you?"

"My doctor said my heart is good to go…no more surgeries!"

Addison hugs her again, a barely-there baby belly brushes against Sadie. "I'm so happy for you."

"Add, it's like a weight has been lifted from my mind. I just feel like living…really living…and not being afraid anymore. We're too young to be afraid…we should just be happy."

"You so deserve to be happy, Sadie."

"As do you. What brings you to karaoke night?"

The light in the café highlights the dark circles residing under Addison's eyes. "I've been thinking about the baby and about Nathan leaving…and I needed to laugh at people being silly on stage." She twirls a strand of sandy blond hair around her finger. "I'm starting a baby class to get ready…a part of me hopes Nathan comes back…so I don't have to do this alone."

"Oh, hon. I'll go to baby classes with you if you want."

Jake slides toward the table. "Hey, Addison!"

"Hi, Jake."

Jake holds out his hand to Sadie. "Dance?"

Addison motions for Sadie to go and dance. "It's way past my bedtime. It was fun to see you both."

"Let me know about the baby classes, okay?" Sadie insists.

"Okay. See you later," Addison waves.

"Good night, Add." Sadie grabs Jake's hand. "I'd love to dance."

Jake spins her once. "Baby classes?"

D puts his hands on Jake's and Sadie's shoulders. "I'm heading out. I'll see you kids later."

Jake nods. "Later, D."

D whispers to Sadie, "Thanks for being my stage partner. I'm glad they ruled it a tie. I'd hate for Jake to be jealous of our Broadway talent."

"I think you both should try out for American Rockstar."

"I'll be a dripping faucet." D pats Jake on the shoulder as he walks away.

Jake smiles at Sadie as they float across the dance floor.

Music accompanies Sadie's world like a pleated paper umbrella in a tall drink. She whispers to Jake, "This is perfect."

"It is," he draws her closer.

"I'm starting to freak out."

Jake pulls slightly back to see her face. "Why?"

"Because this is perfect...and the only way to go when life is perfect...is down."

"But we paid the bad times forward, love...so that's why we get perfect now. Those are the rules."

"So perfect is our new normal?"

"Right," Jake confirms.

"So I shouldn't freak out."

"Nah, save it for some other time...otherwise, you're just wasting good freaking moments."

"True," Sadie grins. "I wouldn't want to be wasteful."

*

Sitting on his porch step with his flask in hand, Drew studies the beam of a street light as Cooper's words trail through his mind. *Here, we live for those taken from us.*

CHAPTER 7

Nothing can resist the human will that will stake
even its existence on its stated purpose.
–Benjamin Disraeli

A light drizzle drums against the window as the Saturday morning storm moves south to drench another city.

"Drew! It's Nina!" she half screams and half cries into the phone. "Water's everywhere and Edison's puking and the smoke from the stupid toaster is setting off the stupid alarm!"

"Who is this?" Drew teases.

"Don't even start…can you come over?!"

"Now's not a good time." Dried blood decorates his hands, arms, and blankets. A bottle of Jack lies shattered on the floor, glass shards garnishing the bedside.

"Drew! The toilet is shooting water! Shooting!"

"Okay! I'll come." He hangs up, contemplating the most efficient way to clean up the latest mess of blood and glass. "Damn nightmares."

*

Jake and Sadie intentionally walk through every puddle they encounter as they make their way toward a lone bench in the middle of the park.

Jake runs his fingers over the symbol carved on the bench.

Sadie smiles. "I remember our third date every time I sit here."

"J hearts S." Jake adds, "or J defaces public property with S."

Sadie laughs.

An older man in a wool coat and black Stetson hat waves at Sadie, his arm around a grinning gal with a head full of crazy white curls.

"Bill!" Sadie smiles. "How are you?"

"Oh, golly, just fine. Sadie, this is Gigi. Gigi…Sadie."

"Hi Gigi, Bill and I met at the post office." Sadie pats Jake's arm, "And this is my Jake."

"Nice to meet you, Bill," Jake shakes Bill's hand.

Gigi's greeting bubbles out. "Sadie, Bill said you send packages overseas. How wonderful!" Gigi turns to Jake. "She's a real sweetheart."

Jake nods. "She is."

"Well, we'll see you kids later," Bill tips his hat. "We have to keep our legs moving so we can make it home for our nap!"

*

The house smells like burnt toast.

Drew walks in and looks at Nina's short brown hair sticking straight up from her head with the assistance of three chip clips. "Fancy hair."

Nina meets his sarcasm with a dirty look. "Edison's still throwing up…ugh, I've got enough laundry to last me for a month." Towels line the bathroom and hall. "It's a mess, and the toilet is shooting water, and I don't know who else to call…"

"Nina!" Drew interrupts, hoping to stop her rant before she brings up Jasper and somehow pisses him off. He calmly adds, "I'll fix it."

*

Hot pink, melon orange, sunflower yellow, and lilac purple paint the evening sky outside their front window.

Jake holds up a letter. "Another note for you, Sade…from San Diego."

"San Diego? Oh, Gail! I send her Encourage Cards."

"Cancer?"

"Yeah, she's been battling breast cancer for several years." Sadie opens the note. "Oh, she sent me a picture…wait a minute…oh my gosh…she died?" She sits down and stares at the picture. "Beautiful…I didn't know she was so beautiful."

38

Jake glances at her. "Didn't you know what she looked like?"
Sadie shakes her head.
"You never met her?"
She shakes her head again.
"Why did you send her cards if you didn't know her?"
"Most of the people I send cards to begin as strangers. Meg designed the cards and named them Encourage Cards. I fell in love with the pictures and messages of hope. One gal received fifty-seven cards from me. She's cancer free now…hearing her say those words after seven years was…a magnificent moment." She holds up Gail's picture for Jake to see. "She died so young."
"Who sent the note?"
"Her husband."
"Did you know him?"
"No. Oh, wow…she died five months ago?"
"How long ago did you send a card?"
"I send cards every six weeks. It's a weird feeling."
"What is?"
"Gail dies, and I don't even know about it. What was I doing? Did I even pause at the loss of her life?"
Sadie looks at a website created in Gail's memory. "Nine-hundred people attended her funeral…nine-hundred people! I wonder how many people would come to my funeral."
Jake shakes his head. "I'll be in the shop."
"Jake," Sadie says as he's walking away. "This woman dies and we just go on with our lives?"
"Sade," he replies before closing the door between the shop and the kitchen. "A lot of people die and we go on with our lives."
"Yeah, but," Sadie says to an empty kitchen, "Gail was significant to nine-hundred people that day. Nine hundred!" She walks to the counter and writes a note in her journal.

Jake is under Candy, but the radio is off.
Sadie stands in the doorway of the shop. "Are you mad?"
"No."
"Jake…" she sighs.

"I'm fine…just thinking."

"Because I talked about my funeral?"

He remains under Candy. "Every surgery, I wondered if you would make it…hours wondering what I'd do without you." He pauses. "Without you, I have nothing. If you die…so will I."

"But I feel like I finally have some clarity in my life."

He rolls out from under the car. "Clarity about what?"

"Doing something greater with our lives…a transition."

"Like what?"

"I don't know. Fear used to rule my life…the question of if I'd live for another year or even a week was always on my mind."

"Our minds, Sade. Our minds," Jake sits up, leaning his back against the bumper.

"And when I talk about dying it's because I can. I'm not afraid anymore, Jake."

"Our future…that's what I want to think about. Not how to get nine-hundred people to your funeral."

"My point is not about getting nine-hundred people to visit me when I'm dead…but I want to focus on making such a phenomenal difference…influencing nine-hundred lives."

"Sade, you send cards to strangers. You strike up friendships in the post office with old people. You send care packages to the forgotten troops."

"I just want to do the things I'm meant to do, and be the things I'm meant to be."

"Then be…not talk about not being," Jake pleads.

"I know," Sadie says in almost a whisper, closing the shop door. After a few steps into the kitchen, tears stream down her face. She grabs the picture of Gail and softly says, "I'm sorry I didn't notice when you died…I'm sorry I didn't pause."

*

Drew stares at the midnight sky, attempting to identify various star formations.

Nina slides open the balcony door carrying two mugs of tea. "Edison finally fell asleep," she hands a steaming cup to Drew.

"Good. That little man had a rough day."

"Just like his momma." Nina hugs the hot mug to her chest as steam floats past her face. "You know, when Jasper was overseas, I did everything on my own. Plus I worried about him every second of the day. He wasn't here, but I got to talk with him…vent to him." She laughs but sounds like she wants to cry. "I'd complain and he'd make me laugh. And then I was good. I was set…knowing he was okay. Now, everything I do, which is everything I did before, seems so much harder…" she sighs. "I wake up every day thinking I'll hear from him…and I lose him every morning…all over again. I miss him."

"Me too," Drew sends the emotion packed words into the darkness.

"I saw the cuts on your hands and arms, Drew."

"It's not what you think."

"I wasn't thinking anything. What happened?"

"A nightmare, a smashed bottle, and me."

"Sounds like a mess."

"Yeah."

"Thanks for helping me today."

Drew takes a sip of the tea, which tastes more like honey with tea than tea with honey. "No problem."

"Drew, I…I uh…"

He waits for her question.

"Would you consider living here? With us?"

Drew sets down his mug, digesting the question along with the sweet spiked tea. "I'm still figuring things out…"

"We can move my stuff into the guest room so you can have the master with the bathroom…the good bathroom."

"It's not about the space."

"I know, but with Edison…and the house…and everything, it would be nice to have you here for a little while…til I figure things out and maybe while you figure things out."

"This might be me all figured out," Drew smirks.

"I'm not saying it will be perfect."

"I'll think about it, Nina."

"Good. It's an open invitation…for whenever you decide."

"I'll think about it."

Thanks to clouds floating across the black sky and hiding the moon, she cannot see the soul churning angst her question sparked. *Nina needs someone, I get that…but I'm not that person.*

CHAPTER 8

Let us consider the way in which we spend our lives.
–Henry David Thoreau

Sadie's eyes narrow as she points her red pen toward Jake. "I can see you watching me write in my journal."

"Actually, I'm sleeping," Jake's lips curl into a slight smile.

Sadie bites the end of her pen. "Addison just found out Nathan married the girl he was cheating on her with."

"That's rough."

"Four months ago, Nathan found out Addison was pregnant with his baby…so he left. Two months ago he found out his new girlfriend was pregnant with his baby…so he married her."

He opens his eyes. "The new girlfriend's already pregnant?"

"He made two moms and two kids…two months apart."

"Nathan's a talented guy," Jake jokes.

"Something like that…" Sadie laughs. "Jake?"

"Yeah?"

Raising her eyebrows she hesitates. "I want one."

"A baby, huh? Don't hate me for asking this…"

"What?"

"Is it safe to have a baby with your heart?"

"I think so. I hope so," her stomach knots. "What if I can't, Jake?" Panic builds as she processes the world-crushing possibility. "What if I can never have a baby! Never be a mother?!"

He replies in his typical calming manner. "It's probably fine. Let's just ask in case you need to take extra precautions."

Sadie stares at him as emotional distress caves her body into the plush chair.

He adds, "Not if we can have a baby…how to safcly have a baby."

Sadie bites her pen. "Okay, I'll ask the doctor."

Jake drifts off to sleep as Sadie continues writing.

Sadie exclaims, "I've got it! Jake, I've got it!"

"You've...got...what?" Jake asks, in a sleepy voice.

Sadie bounces to the couch and sits on him, straddling his body between her legs. "I know how our lives will change!"

He puts his hands on the side of her hips. "How?"

"You'll quit teaching music and audition for the singing competition!" she lightly hits his chest with both hands. "Jake, I can see you on that path! I know it's the right move!"

"I'm not in a good position to negotiate right now."

"I'm serious! It's time for us to take risks and make a difference and...do something crazy and perfect!"

Jake gives her a quizzical look. "You're serious?"

"Yes!" she hits him on the chest again, this time a bit harder.

"Quit teaching?" he uses his hand to block her next hit.

"Yes!" she refrains from hitting him.

"I don't know. Each time you talk about this crazy idea, I get closer to considering it."

"Just think about it. I won't mention it anymore. Well, I'll try not to mention it anymore." She slides on the couch next to him, patting his chest lightly. "You can finish your nap now."

*

Edison races through the restaurant's playroom, jumping into the plastic ball pit and flying down the tubular slides.

Nina sucks the last drop of soda through her straw making a slurping noise. "So, I had to clean up your mess the other day."

"Oh yeah?"

"Mom and dad called."

"How nice for you," Drew's sarcasm evident.

"Drew, if you recall, a few months back I had to drop the deployment bomb and cover you for the shocker that you left for your second deployment without telling them. Yesterday, mom and dad asked me when you were getting back from Iraq." Nina leans in with a look of exasperation. "You didn't tell them you were home?!"

"Guess not." Recalling useless conversations with his repulsive parents makes Drew want to break or throw something.

"If you deploy again, maybe you could just send them a note…a note only takes a minute."

"Sounds like a waste of a good minute."

"Fine, forget it. I'm changing topics," Nina uses her hands to scramble the air. "Are you going to move in with us? I asked you a month ago and you haven't given me an answer."

"Probably not."

"Drew! Is it that big of a deal to live with us?"

Drew stands up and drops some bills on the table to pay for the meal. "I should get going."

*

Grace knocks twice then explodes through the back door wearing a gray suit. "Sadie, can I borrow a pair of your heels for tonight?!"

"Sure," Sadie nods.

Jake's facial expression after seeing the suit almost makes Sadie laugh out loud. He turns to Grace. "Hey, sis."

"Hey, Jake. Something is messed up with mom's computer…you think you can stop over there?"

"I was just there yesterday and she didn't say anything about the computer."

"You want me to take a picture, write a report, and overnight it to you?"

Jake laughs. "No, counselor, I'll check out mom's computer."

"Good." Grace looks at Sadie. "What's that look for…you don't like my suit?"

"I'm thinking about an outfit with a little less attorney and a little more sugar with spice for your blind date."

Jake grins. "Another blind date?"

Grace speed talks, "I'm on number six for this year! Number one and five had peculiar attributes—unusually large ears, an

45

unidentifiable odor, unusual eyes. Number two," she rolls her eyes, "proclaimed his love for me upon meeting…something about soul mates. Number three didn't show up…twice. Number four, talks only about himself…and everything I say, he first answers with 'No,' and proceeds to tell me how he is correct. He is a real delicacy. I marvel at his single status," she adds with disdain. "I had to cancel my date with number six twice already because of work…but he's still interested. Maybe he will be intelligent and polite…I know, call me Miss High Expectations."

"Follow me, Miss High Expectations," Sadie motions toward the bedroom.

"Sadie, you really don't approve of my suit?"

"The suit needs to be put away until you are eighty years old or older, when your lipstick is outside the lines of your lips and even a little on your teeth. Then, the suit will serve as a nice distraction."

"Fine, no suit."

Sadie chooses three items from her meticulously organized closet and hands them to Grace. "Sugar with spice."

Grace returns wearing a sleeveless black dress, a silver silk scarf wrapped loosely around her forearms, and coral pink heels. She looks at her reflection in the mirror.

Sadie nods. "Amazing is the word you're looking for."

"Okay," Grace takes a deep breath. "Here's to meeting Mr. Right."

"I'd say good luck but you don't need luck with coral heels."

"I love the heels," Grace smiles. Heading back through the kitchen she says, "Jake, you'll check mom's computer, right?"

"Yeah, Grace, I'll check mom's computer…right after I get that report and picture from you."

Grace sends an evil glare his way then hugs Sadie. "Thanks, Sade! See you later!"

As Grace leaves, Jake glances at Sadie. "Nice work. She's wired. Really wired. And that was the dullest grandma suit I've ever seen."

"I told her not to wear the suit until she is eighty."

"I would have gone with wearing the suit when the world goes blind…but eighty is fair."

*

Drew's own scream awakes him from what was supposed to be a relaxing afternoon nap on the couch. Sweat soaks his clothes.

His phone flashes a missed a call from Nina.

After changing into some dry clothes and avoiding the urge to pick up his clothing filled laundry basket and smash it against the wall, mainly because his hand still is sore from last night, he dials Nina's number.

"Drew!" she whines. "You punched someone?!"

"This is why I was supposed to call you?" Drew takes a swig of Jack. "Moron was being a total jackass to some sorry sap who wouldn't defend himself. So I did," he calmly explains.

"By punching the guy?!"

"I didn't hit Moron as hard as I could have hit him. I should have beaten the stupidity out of him...although I'm not sure that would be possible, but I'd be willing to try if I see him again."

"Drew! He could have pressed charges!"

"He didn't press charges."

"It doesn't matter! You could have killed him!"

"I didn't kill him. How'd you hear about that anyway? The cops weren't called."

"A friend was there...she saw you!"

"What friend of yours goes to that bar?"

"Not important..."

"Who told you, Nina?" Drew demands.

"Wyla."

"She's in town?"

"She went there to find you, Drew."

"Why...did Asshole Steve find someone else's wife to...?"

"Drew, I'm not going there. Point is, you hit some guy!"

"So Wyla calls you instead of knocking on what, six weeks ago, was our front door?"

"She's worried about you..."

"I gotta go, Nina."

"I have a bunch of cookies for you…that's why I called earlier. Want to swing by and pick them up later?"

"Sure."

Nina sighs. "I'm sorry."

"For making me fat with your cookies?"

"For not being able to help you…I just…"

"I know. I'll see you later," Drew hangs up.

CHAPTER 9

No one fully understands the extent of the
sacrifice for serving in our military
until they are in that position.
–Mike Stiles

J ake and Sadie walk into the hospital, rolling a cart loaded with red, white, and blue gift boxes for the veterans.

Jake inquires, "Do you know all the people we're giving these boxes to?"

"I know one of them…well, I've never actually met him…but we're friends." Sadie whispers, "He was injured overseas. He sustained significant burns on the left side of his body including his face."

Concern and frustration fill his eyes. "What's his name?"

"Reiss. He sent me a picture when he was overseas…he's cute in a tough as nails kind of way…a real ladies man."

"So him and I are alike, is what you're saying."

"Sure, babe, that's exactly what I'm saying. This is the first time I'm meeting him." Sadie squeaks, "I'm so excited!"

A nurse directs them to room 230. Sunlight beats against the blinds attempting to pierce the room's darkness with its late morning message of cheer.

Stale air meets Sadie's face as she peeks into the room. "Reiss?"

Reiss opens his eyes, a brown knit hat concealing everything above his eyebrows. "Miss Sadie," a grin bends his cheek. With the press of a button, an overhead light turns on. The right side of his face is handsome and expressive; the left side looks melted, scars scattered in a disfigured pool. A thin leather rope around his neck dangles a piece of metal in the middle of his chest.

Jake, expressionless upon seeing Reiss's face, puts his hand lightly on the back of Sadie's shoulder.

"Reiss," Sadie drenches his name in compassion.

He turns off the light. "Is that better?"

"No, I want to see you," she walks to his bedside and turns the light back on.

"This is me," a huge dimple sinks his right cheek.

"Will I hurt you if I hug you?" Sadie asks.

"It will be worth the pain," Reiss lifts his right arm as Sadie hugs him. Reiss turns to Jake, "Hey man, I'm Reiss."

Jake shakes Reiss's hand. "I'm Jake."

"Wait...Jake, as in the Candy Man?" Reiss looks at Sadie. "The Nova, right? What year is it again?"

"'72," Jake replies.

"Color?"

"Fire orange."

"Chevy 350 is what Sadie told me."

"Yeah," Jake shoots Sadie a quizzical look.

Sadie grins. "That's the extent of my car knowledge."

"Dude, Jake, I've got this guy that can get spinners real cheap." Reiss extends and contracts his left hand several times.

"I'll keep that in mind...but I want to keep the Nova looking stock...not like it belongs in a rap video."

Reiss laughs. "Keeping it clean, I get that."

"You'll have to come by sometime to see the car."

"Don't have to invite me twice, Jake. Tell me the time and place and I'll be there."

"Aw, it's so cute you two are planning a date," Sadie teases.

A country tune lights up Jake's phone. "I'll be right back," he walks into the hall to answer the call.

Sadie sits on left side of Reiss's bed. "So, how are you?"

"Burned out, ma'am."

"That's not funny, Reiss..."

"It kinda is..." he grins.

"I'm sorry you have to go through this...it's all so awful. Are you doing okay? For real?"

He touches the piece of metal hanging from his necklace, his eyes studying Sadie for a split second. "A fuckin' infection is running through my veins." Reiss shakes his head. "Survive a firefight, almost get burned alive in an explosion...then get some infection? I'm a fuckin' shit magnet."

"A chick magnet?" Sadie intentionally changes his words.

Reiss again extends and contracts his left hand. "Yeah, right. A guy missing some brain cells may be date-worthy, but a melted face?"

Jake walks back into the room.

Reiss continues, "I see some pretty hot women with some dumb ass guys." He glances toward Jake, "And I'm not saying you're in that group, man."

"Wow, okay, thanks," Jake laughs.

"Yeah, no problem," Reiss grins.

"What about attracting the perfect gal with your wit and kindness?" Sadie asks.

"I forgot you are studying that mind stuff. Fine. I intend to attract a hot honey...my personality will have to be enough."

"Oh, trust me," Sadie says with a spark. "Your personality is more than enough, Reiss."

"I think that's a compliment." Reiss asks Jake, "Is that a compliment?"

Jake nods in amusement. "Sure, man. Sure."

"The right gal won't care about your war wounds. In fact, I'll tell you a secret..." Sadie leans closer. "Chicks dig scars."

"Chicks dig scars?" Reiss laughs. "That's good. You should be a shrink or somethin'."

"You want me to let some sunlight in here?" Sadie asks.

"Are you changing the subject because I started talking about how great you are?" Reiss teases.

Sadie fires back, "Are you changing the subject because I asked about opening the blinds?"

"Jake, you gonna help a brother out?" Reiss asks.

"Maybe Sadie could be great and open the blinds halfway...then you both would win."

Reiss looks at Sadie. "Candy Man says we both should win."

"Okay!" Sadie opens the blinds halfway. "I brought you a little care package."

"Thanks."

Sadie gives him a hug. "Let me know if you need anything, okay?" She nods to someone in the hall. "Oh, I have to catch one of the nurses." Sadie smiles and waves, walking out the door. "Later, Reiss!"

"See ya, Sadie."

Jake shakes Reiss's hand. "Reiss, thanks for your service."

"Just doing my job," Reiss nods. "I do want to see the Nova though…"

"Anytime, man. Anytime." Jake pats the door frame as he leaves, "Later, Reiss."

"See ya, Jake."

Sadie smiles as Jake comes into the hall. She runs her hands along his face and kisses him.

"Some things we take for granted," he gently touches her face. "Oh, my mom called…mind if we run over there after this so I can look at her computer?"

"No, that's fine."

Rolling the cart down the hall, the pile of care packages dwindles, with one box left for Room 299.

Sun streams through the doorway reaching its warm fingers into the hall. Sadie hears a voice softly counting, "thirty-two, thirty-three…"

A wheelchair sits idly in the corner of the room. This patient, who looks to be in his early thirties, is missing both legs.

Sadie's heart breaks. She takes a deep breath and whispers to Jake, "I hate what war does to my boys."

"I know, love," Jake subtly nods in encouragement.

Sadie knocks on the door. "Hi, my name…"

"Sadie," the patient answers. "I know. Morning, ma'am. I heard you're some kind of angel."

Sadie blushes. "I'm not any kind of angel."

Narrowed eyes analyze her, the same emptiness present as in Reiss's eyes.

"If I were an angel, I'd be walking down these halls healing people, and they'd be following me out of the hospital with big ol' smiles. This is my husband, Jake."

"Morning, Jake. Do you both want to stay for a minute?"

Everything in the room is neatly stacked, perfectly folded, and in its proper place. Opposite the bed is a rose colored couch with a black diamond pattern. A thin white blanket, edges immaculately matched, sits on the edge of the couch.

"Just toss the blanket on the bed," the patient says.

Sadie carefully moves the blanket to the edge of the bed and sits next to Jake. "What's your name?"

"Roy. But you can call me Gunner," the right side of his mouth opens more than the left side when he speaks.

Sadie says, "This is the most organized hospital room I've ever been in."

"Everything has its place."

"Are you married?" Sadie asks.

"Nah," Gunner shakes his head.

"Dating?" Sadie pries further.

"No."

"Would you consider dating a single mom?" Sadie smiles.

Amusement spreads across Gunner's face. "Uh…maybe."

Jake grins, shaking his head. "How long are they keeping you here, Gunner?"

"I'm here until tomorrow…that's the plan anyway. Do you guys have a lot more packages to drop off?"

"You are our last stop," Sadie answers.

"Thanks for what you both do for our military."

Jake points to Sadie, "It's all her. I just tag along sometimes."

"Well, we appreciate the support. No one fully understands the extent of the sacrifice for serving in our military until they are in that position."

Sadie shifts on the couch, leaning forward. "You would go back overseas in a second, wouldn't you?"

"I would," Gunner nods. "I spent years with my marines—living together, eating together, hating life at the same time—"

A nurse walks into the room.

"Morning, ma'am," Gunner greets the nurse.

"Well, it was nice talking with you, Gunner," Sadie walks to the bedside and gives him a hug. "Thanks for your service."

"Thanks for yours."

Jake shakes Gunner's hand. "Thanks, Gunner."

"You bet."

Sadie turns before leaving Gunner's room. "Do you want to come over for dinner when you get out of here?"

Gunner's picture-perfect teeth make an appearance with a brief smile. "That sounds good."

After exchanging phone numbers, Sadie waves, "See you soon, Gunner!"

"Take it easy," Gunner nods.

As Jake and Sadie roll the empty cart to a storage room, a smile breaks out on Jake's face. "Gunner and Addison, huh?"

"Maybe," Sadie hooks her arm through his.

Plush deep purple chairs contrast yellow walls in the lounge near the exit of the surgical floor.

A young nurse swiftly passes Jake and Sadie in the hall, heading toward the empty lounge. Facing away from them, she sits on the back of a chair and begins to sob.

Sadie's stomach protests in hunger as she looks at the nurse, then back at Jake.

"I'll get the car," Jake gives her hand a gentle squeeze.

Sadie sits down in the chair next to the gal and quietly asks, "What's your name, sweetie?"

"Laina," mascara paints emotional chaos beneath her eyes. "I'm okay...just need a minute, you know?" Strands of hazelnut hair partially cover her face as drops of water mark her baby blue scrubs.

"I'm Sadie."

Time moves in slow motion as they both stare ahead.

"Are any of your family members in the military?" Laina asks.

"My brother was." Sadie chews the end of her thumbnail, hoping she won't have to say anything more.

"He got out?"

"He…died…in a helicopter crash."

Why did I have to disturb this girl? Sadie scolds herself as the torturous memories of her brother's death return.

"My dad…" Laina pauses, shifting her lower jaw sideways as emotion creases her forehead. "My dad…killed himself."

Sadie's eyes fill with tears.

"PTSD," Laina says. "You know what that is?"

Sadie nods. "Post Traumatic Stress Disorder. Was your dad a veteran?"

"My dad said serving his country was his greatest contribution to the world right beneath having me…said I was his reason for making it home, for surviving." Laina's eyebrows draw close together in anguish. "I found a box of his medals and was going to put them all into a display box…I was just so proud of him, you know? But he said that with every medal he could clearly see the face of a brother who died." She looks up, "Your brother, was he in the Army?"

"Air Force."

"He died overseas?"

"Yeah," Sadie bites the edge of her lip. "He joined the Air Force at eighteen. I was the proudest sister at Sterling's graduation ceremony," she smiles, recalling when he held up his diploma and blew a kiss to her in the audience. "Shortly before he was scheduled to return home, the helicopter crashed."

"How did you make it okay in your mind?"

"What do you mean, hon?" Sadie asks.

"He died for all these people," Laina motions toward the hall. "Yet none of them know that. They laugh, make jokes, some crude, talk about parties, or complain about something, you know? So how do you make it okay that your brother died for them, and they aren't even grateful for his sacrifice?"

"My brother loved what he did. He chose the Air Force…not for all these people," Sadie motions toward the hall, "but for himself…to make his contribution…for his future. A month after Sterling died, this guy, Kurtis, showed up at my door. He said that Sterling took the flight in his place because his wife was delivering their first baby back home. Sterling insisted Kurtis call and find out if it was a girl or boy. Sterling told Kurtis to repay him with a beer when he got back. Kurtis brought beer and a picture of his baby boy, whose name is Sterling, to my house. We sat on the porch as he told me stories about my brother," Sadie takes a deep breath. "My brother gave a baby his father that day. The little details count in death. It's not about who doesn't notice…but about who does notice, and what they do with that knowledge. We're not all going to change everyone…but if we can change one life while we're here…that's something."

"That gives me goose bumps," Laina rubs her arms. "My dad couldn't keep a job, and ever since coming home, peace was nonexistent. So he spent his time trying to help other veterans. He was a wreck…but he was my wreck, you know?"

"I'm so sorry, Laina."

"I was going to get him a puppy. Have you heard of the Puppy Rescue?"

"I haven't."

"When puppies cannot stay in their current home, the Puppy Rescue takes them and places them into a new home. The owner, Izzy, places half of their puppies with veterans…something about veterans bonding with animals better than people after combat."

"Do you have a large family?"

Laina shakes her head. "Just an aunt in California. Were you visiting a friend here?"

"My husband and I were dropping off care packages. One of the soldiers here received care packages from us when he was overseas. I finally got to meet him."

"You don't know the people who receive your care packages?"

"They start out as strangers."

"I'm sure they appreciate it. You're probably their hero."

"What your dad gave to our country…is the real sacrifice. I just send care packages. Your dad is the inspiration behind what we do."

"I'm so mad at him, you know…isn't that stupid?" Laina wipes a few tears.

Sadie shakes her head. "No."

"I spent my days trying to make his better...obviously, I failed. I don't get how some come home and they are okay...and others, are not. Our world was disturbing and distorted and stressful...but we both were part of it...like a team...a messed up dysfunctional team...now, it's me...in pieces, you know?"

"I wish I knew the answers, hon. I wish I knew the reason for your heartbreak...but I do know your fight is not in vain...and neither was your dad's."

Laina nods, wiping her swollen eyes. "Thanks." Her pager alarms. "I have to go."

"You take care of yourself, Laina."

"You too, Sadie." Laina briskly walks back toward the surgical ward.

Sadie stops at a nursing station before exiting the hospital.

A pair of eyes, full of attitude, wander from a computer screen over to Sadie. "Yeah?" rolls from plump lips decorated with too much bright pink lipstick.

"Can I ask you a question?"

The chubby gal pushes off with her feet, sliding on her chair across the small cubicle toward Sadie, an action she has clearly mastered with repetition. "You just did. But go ahead and ask another question, Sadie."

Sadie smiles, unsure of how people she doesn't know, know her name. "Do you know if the suicide rate is high among veterans?"

"Very high."

"Why?"

"PTSD. Some won't admit they are struggling; some don't know there is treatment; some are embarrassed...when there ain't no reason to be," slight passion creeps into her voice. "I mean, we all got issues...and if we ain't embarrassed for all the crap we do or say...they don't need to be either."

"So...how do we fix it?" Sadie asks.

"Fix what?"

"The suicide rate. How do we solve this problem?"

"You one of those happily ever after people?" she drones, rapidly clicking her pen. "That ain't gonna happen."

"Why can't happily ever after happen for America's heroes?"

"Happily ever after don't happen for no one. Not us, not them…no one. Everyone struggles. And everyone's gonna die. But thanks for handing out presents today…gave them all a moment…and it's those moments that keep em' all goin'."

"They are certainly worth it. Have a nice day."

"I plan to," the gal pushes off and glides back to her computer.

Cool damp air greets Sadie as she exits the hospital. Sliding onto the car seat, she looks at Jake. "I'm sorry you had to wait."

"It's all good…is that girl okay?"

"Not really. I never even thought about what our veterans go through once they come home. I never thought PTSD could lead to suicide."

"What is PTSD?"

"Post Traumatic Stress Disorder."

"The gal crying…is PTSD related to that?"

Sadie tells him about her conversation with Laina. "I don't know how it would be to lose a dad, a true dad. It sounds like Laina's father really loved her…but not enough to stay."

"It was tough when my dad died," Jake says. "Maybe more so for me than Grace or Beth with my older brother running around the world playing doctor. But you know what it's like to lose a parent…both your mom and dad left you."

"Yeah, but my father left when I was two years old and my mother moved to Canada with her boyfriend when I was seventeen, leaving my brother and me. I was used to being the caretaker for Sterling, so my mom's departure was more of a relief, one less person for me to care for."

Jake pauses. "You have that look…"

"Some of our heroes come home and struggle…so how are we helping them? We brush it off like they did their job and we all move on…but for Reiss or Gunner…they can't just move on. Maybe I was just meant to listen to Laina and not get involved in something I don't really understand?" Sadie sighs. "I don't know. It kind of freaks me out…jumping into such an unknown."

"Everything is unknown."

"I know," questions race through Sadie's mind. "I'm excited to see your mom; I haven't talked to her in a long time."

"A long time? We had dinner with her last week."

"Seven days of not talking…that's almost a record for us."

An evening breeze tangos with a flag branching off Phoebe's yellow house. *How can I bring awareness to something that mentally plagues veterans?* Sadie wonders. *But if not me, who?*

CHAPTER 10

There is none so obscure that he cannot make the lives of those around him marvellously changed, brightened and inspired if he would merely progressively live up to his expanding possibilities in the way of kindness, thoughtfulness, cheer, good-will, influence and optimism.
–William George Jordan

Sadie puts her journal aside and hugs a pillow as she stares at Jake. "Good morning, love," Jake opens his eyes and smiles. "So," he sits up, stretching his arms toward the ceiling. "You think I'd make it?"

Sadie quickly sits up. "For real?" She hops into his lap and drapes her arms around his neck. "You're going to audition for the singing competition?!"

"I've been thinking about it."

Sadie squeals and kisses him. "America will love you! Maybe I could stand on the side of the stage and flash you…"

"You're going to flash me?"

Sadie hits him on the chest. "I was going to say that I would flash you our heart signal before you sing."

He puts his arms around her. "Either one works. Or both."

*

Yellow, sky blue, royal blue, and black gracefully explode to all edges of the canvas. In a shooting-star motion, Meg lightly sweeps the blues into the yellow with her brush, a soft green emerging.

"What do you think, Ruger?" Meg holds up her paintbrush and steps back from her latest creation.

The dog's eyes open at the sound of his name. He stretches his skinny black legs before burying his head back into the corner of the couch.

A knock interrupts Meg's contemplation on naming the new piece. "Who is it?"

"Sadie!"

"Come in!" Meg yells.

Sadie peeks in the door. "I just came by to…ooh, you're painting!" she studies Meg's first finished piece leaning against the wall. "This is insanely good! What's this guy's name?"

Meg looks over. "*Instrumental Chaos*…and he's waiting for me to finish his eight comrades for our Gallery Group Exhibition in Chicago in three months."

"For real?! Is this the gallery owner who knew your grandpa?"

"Yes."

"You accepted the pity invitation?!"

Meg grins. "I did. I'm the only art virgin invited. And hopefully, the universe won't flip me the cosmic bird on this adventure."

Sadie laughs. "We could make a weekend of it…we could go shopping in Chicago!!"

"I hate shopping."

"Then…we could check out the museum…Chicago's buildings and parks are so pretty!"

"I actually hate Chicago," Meg extinguishes Sadie's excitement. "I find it dirty…and the people annoy me."

"You find all places dirty, Meg…and all people annoy you."

"But other than that, I'm a real treat to be around, right?" Meg winks. "Speaking of my pleasantness…you said you came by to…?"

Sadie pulls a note from her purse.

"From one of the troops?"

"No, from Joel!" Sadie beams.

"As in Jake's brother?"

Sadie hands Meg the note. "He sent the note to Jake's mom. You should have seen Phoebe's face…she was so excited to hear from Joel! She called a special family dinner with Jake's sisters and us so she could read the note out loud. I thought you might want to read the note."

"Sure," Meg reads the letter then hands it back. "I'm glad Joel finally wrote."

"Grace and Beth were thrilled." Sadie tips her head, "But it's hard for Jake. Joel didn't come to his dad's or grandpa's funeral and this is the first time he's contacted anyone since he left years ago." Sadie shrugs, "It was hard on Jake when Joel left...and then he finally writes and everyone gets all excited and loves him just as they did before...but Jake figures Joel will disappear again...and he despises him for messing with their hearts."

"Do you think Joel is messing with their hearts?"

"I don't, but I'm the happily ever after girl," Sadie studies Meg's Colorado wall while talking. "Jake and I grew up with very different families. His family had dinner together and went to each others sporting events...my parents left, I raised my brother, and then I lost my brother. The way I see it, everyone has a sweet spot...for some you have to dig deep to find that spot...but there's always a spot." Sadie looks at Meg. "What do you think about Joel?"

"He's sincere."

"Is it hard to talk about him?"

"Because of my brother?" Meg asks.

"And because he was your boyfriend..."

"Oh yeah," Meg grins. "Nah, him and I are cool. Joel blames himself for my brother's death..."

"Do you?" Sadie asks.

"Blame Joel? No. When my brother died, we were all shocked and...it was awful...but no one's fault. And we all dealt with it in our own way...my parents split...I moved in with my grandpa...and Joel immersed himself in college and then ran away to save the world. That's life. Unpredictable." Meg scribbles an "M" into the lower right hand corner of her latest painting.

"I like the blast of color," Sadie looks at the painting Meg just marked. "What's this guy's title?"

"Painting number two is named *Rhythmic Spark*."

"That's a perfect name! Well, I better get going. I just wanted to share the news that Joel is alive and well!" Sadie opens the door to leave. "Later, Meg!"

"Adios, Sadie."

As the door closes, Meg looks at Ruger, still lying on the couch. "Don't look at me like that," she tells the dog. "I promised Joel I wouldn't say a thing…and now it's almost too late to say anything. I'm just glad the bum finally sent a letter to his family! I guess I can stop nagging him now…"

*

"Jake! You'll never guess what just happened!" Sadie busts through the front door. "Meg and I were invited to the Annual Military Ball! We're being awarded a Hometown Heroes Award…nominated by people who received our care packages!"

"Sade, that's phenomenal!"

"It's insane!"

"When is it?" Jake asks.

"Three months…March fourth. I'm kind of freaking out though…I have to give a speech! I get so nervous standing in front of people!"

"Have Meg give the speech."

"Her first art show is that same day in Chicago…so she can't come!"

"You'll do great, love. Where is the event?"

"Milwaukee Art Museum. Quite a few people are attending—several who received our care packages while overseas."

"Looks like you'll be famous before me."

"They will all forget me by the end of the night, but when you sing your songs on national television…they'll not only remember you, they'll play your music over and over." Sadie pledges, "But since I'll be famous first, I can coach you on how to deal with the press and massive amounts of raving fans."

"I appreciate that. Can you autograph my shirt?"

"Sure!" Sadie picks up a marker and signs Jake's shirt.

"You did not just do that…" Jake looks down and sees the ink on his shirt. "Sade, this is my dress shirt!"

"I signed on the part you tuck in…"

"You got pen on my shirt!"

"No," Sadie manages to squeak out while laughing hysterically. "I signed with permanent marker!"

"Permanent marker?!"

Sadie falls onto the couch, unable to stop her laughter.

He storms off to the bedroom. "I can't believe you wrote on my shirt!"

"You tuck in that part anyway!" she defends.

Gunner's phone call distracts Sadie.

"Hey, Gunner! Do you want to come for dinner tonight?"

"Uh, tonight, ma'am?"

"Yeah. Jake and I would love to have you over."

"And it would be rude for me to decline your invitation."

"6:30 PM?" Sadie asks.

"I'll be there."

"Gunner, I've been thinking about putting together a program, shedding light on what veterans go through when they come home, specifically their struggles with PTSD."

"Interesting project."

"I need a military guy to work with," Sadie hesitates.

"Are you asking me?" Gunner asks.

"Yes."

Gunner pauses. "I'm game."

"Really, Gunner? You're on board?"

"Consider me on board."

"Maybe we can brainstorm some details at dinner tonight?!"

"Sounds like a plan."

"See you later, Gunner," Sadie hangs up and throws her fists in the air. "Yes!" Her enthusiasm diminishes when Jake walks out of their bedroom. She bites the side of her lip, unable to analyze his expression.

"I still can't believe you wrote on my shirt."

Sadie does her best to stifle a grin. "I'm sorry."

Jake's eyes narrow.

"Jake," she starts laughing. "No one will see the writing because it's where you tuck in the shirt. But," she covers her mouth so he can't see her smile, "I'm sorry."

"Worst apology ever…"

"Babe, that shirt will be worth millions when I'm famous!"

"I'm sure." Jake leans against the wall and stares at her.

Sadie wraps her arms around his neck, with her face a few inches from his face. "You're going to love that shirt."

*

Tears sting the latest open wound on Carter's cheek.

"Ah, kid, I don't know why she hits you," Theo puts his hand on Carter's shoulder. "You're a good egg, you hear me? You're a good egg. You remember that."

Carter giggles every time Theo calls him an egg. "I'm gonna be better, Theo. I'm gonna be better."

"Going to, kid, not gonna. You're going to make it, kid, but you got to be talking right. An' that foster momma of yours…well, you can come by me any day, though I can't offer you much. These legs of mine just aren't working like they used to. A soldier's knees only last him so long."

Except for the bruises, Carter's skin is white. His foster mother, who insists Carter call her Momma, has white skin too. But Theo has creamy brown skin, like a chocolate bar.

"I brought this for you," Carter proudly hands Theo a loaf of bread.

"Oh, and it's still soft. Where'd you get this from?"

Carter shrugs. "It don't matter."

"Doesn't matter, kid, it doesn't matter. And it does matter! You don't have to be stealing for me. You hear me?! No more stealing for me! You hear me?!" he raises his voice, his yellow tinted eyes a mixture of frustration and concern.

Carter bursts out, "It don't matter! Ya can't walk…and ya sit here on the street…if there's a bread to give ya, I'm gonna, going to, steal it for ya!"

Theo's facial expression softens. "Okay, son, it's okay. I love you like my own, you know. Wish I could get on over to that house and beat the life out of the woman that beats on you, or have her locked up. But no one's going to believe a man on the streets. We're not too high up on the respect list…years ago…ah, never mind. I'm okay here, kid. You, now you," he points an arthritic finger at Carter, "are going places. I can tell. When's the last time you had something to eat?"

"My neighbor had a party outside a few days ago…so I took some of her food."

"Days ago? Is that Momma still making you throw up to prove you didn't eat anything all day?"

Tears spill down Carter's cheeks. "Cuz I'm the ugly one."

"Why would you say something like that, son?"

"Momma says ugly don't deserve food but she don't make me dress up."

"Not don't, kid, doesn't. She doesn't make you dress up. And who does she make dress up? I haven't heard this story."

"The cute boy, Momma calls him, has to wear dresses and dance in front of her. He can't cut his hair neither…she braids it. She says only the cute one can play dress up with her."

"Is that the twelve-year old?" disgust and anger drive Theo's hands into fists.

Carter nods.

"Well, you, son, are a fine young man…that Momma is the ugly one. An ugly soul she has…and it's the soul that counts in life, son. You got a good soul, kid." Theo points to Carter's heart, "Right in there."

An empty cigarette box tumbles past them as rain pours off the overhang they crouch beneath.

"I used to hate the rain, kid…all my joints getting all sore…now I kind of like when it rains."

"Why?"

"Because I know you might be coming to visit me…that you might escape that bad egg Momma," wheezing mixes with Theo's laughter, triggering a bout of coughing.

"Bad egg Momma," Carter giggles.

"You'll get out of there one day, kid. You're going to have the life. You'll be eating like a king. What will you eat first? Steak? Lobster? Chocolate cake?"

"I don't know," Carter shrugs.

"I say we celebrate today…for the day you will live like a king."

"Okay. How should we celebrate?"

"My friend brought me a bread today…you hungry?"

"You're my best friend, Theo."

Theo grins, a few teeth missing from his smile. "And you're mine, kid. Only one I ever had."

"One day, Theo, I'm gonna, going to, have me a house. And you and me will live like kings together."

Theo rips a piece of bread off of the loaf with his cracked worn out hands and passes it to Carter. "You and I kid, you and I will live like kings…and that sounds like a mighty fine way to live."

CHAPTER 11

We don't really create, but we assemble what has been created for us.
-Donald Trump

G unner arrives precisely at 6:30 PM, freshly shaven and wearing a white shirt and a blue tie.

Sadie opens the door as Gunner wheels himself inside.

"I brought chocolate," he scans each part of the room. "I hope you like chocolate."

"I love chocolate," Sadie nods. "I consider it a vitamin."

"I thought I was the only one," Gunner's crooked smile appears for a split second. "Need any help with dinner?"

"Nope, dinner is almost done." Sadie notices Gunner's white shirt and smiles as she recalls Jake's expression when she wrote on his shirt.

Gunner looks down at his shirt, then back at Sadie.

"No, there's…" Sadie shakes her head. "Your shirt just reminded me of something that happened this afternoon." Sadie shares the story with Gunner and ends with, "In my defense Gunner, I signed the part Jake tucks in."

"Did Jake appreciate this…thoughtfulness of yours?"

"Shockingly, he was unappreciative," her eyes widen in playful astonishment.

"Hey, Gunner! How's it going?" Jake walks in. Seeing Sadie's facial expression he adds, "She told you the shirt story, didn't she? You know," Jake points at Gunner, "Sadie could sign that white shirt of yours before you leave…"

A laugh escapes Gunner. "Tempting, very tempting, but I'm good, though I appreciate the offer, Jake."

Polishing off the last of his lasagna, Gunner asks, "Why did you hand out those care boxes at the hospital?"

Sadie says, "A friend of mine was injured overseas and is in that hospital…so I got to meet him for the first time. And instead of just bringing a present for him, we figured we'd bring one for everyone."

"Admirable."

Sadie is about to protest when Jake says to Gunner, "Sadie may say 'we' but in most instances she's the one who does the work and has all the compassionate ideas. I just tag along." He reaches out toward Gunner. "If you're finished, I'll take your plate."

"Great lasagna, Sadie." Gunner hands Jake his plate. "Thanks, Jake."

"Thanks, babe," Sadie says to Jake as Jake grabs her plate and takes the dishes into the kitchen. Sadie turns toward Gunner. "I want to know more so I can do more. I'm shocked that the suicide rate is so high among veterans. I always thought that when troops come home, the hard part is over. They are with their family and friends…and life goes back to normal. But is it that the brain goes through training and then sometimes trauma…so it needs to be untrained?"

"It's hard to explain to someone who hasn't been there," Gunner strokes his chin.

"Please try," Sadie smiles sweetly.

A brief sparkle enters and quickly exits Gunner's eyes. "Uh, battle lines were present in previous wars, so there was a safe place for guys to go. Now, wars lack a safe place. So down range, we get off the street from a patrol, and even behind razor wire the damn terrorists are still firing mortars, rockets, and other craziness. Some of the complications of readjusting to civilian life come from this reality, because our bodies are always alert. It's constant tension."

Jake sets cookies and Gunner's chocolate on the table. "I ate way too much dinner to be able to fit dessert in me…but I'm going to try."

"Me too," Sadie smiles at Jake and fires another question at Gunner. "How do you get rid of that instinct, or feeling, of always being in danger?"

"Uh, good question. We do the best we can."

"Do all the guys and gals returning from combat suffer from PTSD?"

"Everyone experiences some kind of an adjustment, but it all depends on what you did over there, what you experienced, and how things changed at home or at your command when you were gone…and if you were part of those changes. Some guys get home and are shocked with all the changes that happened without 'em."

"Can I ask one more question?" Sadie bites the edge of her lower lip.

"Yeah," Gunner's crooked smile emerges.

"Is PTSD a forever thing?"

"It might be…it might not be…it depends," Gunner shrugs. "Everyone deals with loss in a different way and no one can say that death doesn't affect them, because it's too real, but some people make a happier memory of the tragedy and others lock it inside. A lot of guilt is carried around…wondering why you lived and the guy next to you didn't. Guilt locked up causes problems. There's just a lot that happens over there."

Jake clears the dishes from the table.

"Sorry, Gunner, for having so many questions…" Sadie frowns. "I bet you won't want to come back ever again."

"If you make lasagna again…I'll be back," Gunner grins.

"You're still willing to help me with my project?"

"Yeah, though I'll probably put on a few pounds eating Sydney's cinnamon rolls," Gunner pats his abdomen. "Those things are dangerous."

Jake calls from the kitchen, "Sadie helped win some of those famous rolls with karaoke…are you a karaoke fan, Gunner?"

"Not a fan of the stage, but I'm a fan of laughing at others on stage." Gunner begins wheeling himself toward the door.

Sadie puts her hand on Gunner's shoulder. "You should come to karaoke with us sometime!"

"Maybe. We're meeting tomorrow at eleven, right?"

"I'll see you at eleven," Sadie opens the front door.

God, Sadie silently marvels, *you took Gunner's legs…so what did you give him?*

*

Theo hands Carter the last piece of bread.

"No, you eat it, Theo."

Theo rips it in half and holds out both pieces.

Carter chooses a half and gently places the light brown treat into his mouth. "Yesterday, Momma made me throw up to prove I didn't steal no food from her kitchen. She was real mad, so she made the other kids watch me eat my vomit. The other kids laughed. I tried not to cry," he looks up at Theo. "My yesterday wasn't so good."

"Oh, kid…" anguish frames Theo's eyes. "We have to get you out of that place. She still making the oldest boy buy drugs for her?"

"Sugar…" Carter corrects. "The oldest boy is always getting into trouble with sugar. Sometimes he steals Momma's sugar. Then he gets punished. He's big enough to hit her but he says he's too close to leaving."

"He ain't stealing no sugar, kid. When you get your chance to get out of that place, you take it. You hear me? You best be getting out of that place."

"Like…run away?"

"I'd keep you here with me but the streets aren't for a young man like you. I'm going to figure out how to help you."

"I'd be in real trouble if Momma knew I told ya, Theo! Ya won't go tellin' her, will ya?"

"Nah, kid, I won't get you into trouble. I'll make sure you're safe." Theo rubs his hands together, pausing to blow a lung-full of warm air into the middle of his palms, then continues rubbing them together. "My today is better than my yesterday," he puts his arm around Carter's shoulders.

Carter leans against Theo's side. "Mine too."

*

Meg presses her palms inward against the side of her face, adding pressure to her already pounding head. Releasing her hands she hopes for relief, her efforts are in vain.

With such intense head and neck pain, every position is uncomfortable. Meg sits up in bed, waiting a second for the dizziness to subside. "Thank you doctors," she converses with the darkness. "You ran all sorts of tests and found that nothing is wrong with me. The trouble is that something is wrong, just nothing you can find."

Meg laboriously pulls on her silk robe and Vegas dice slippers. In the kitchen, she presses the coffee button and inhales as the heavenly French vanilla aroma fills her favorite mug…the finger mug.

A year ago, Meg acted upon an out-of-character useful suggestion from her boss that she retire immediately from her short lived coffee shop waitress gig. Her boss had an extraordinary talent for giving loads of useless advice…so it was not a shock his practical retirement comment was followed by a dim-witted remark suggesting she refrain from any activity involving communicating with humans. Despite his lack of love for her, or maybe due to his intense hatred for her, her boss gave her the finger mug when she left. This particular mug had been collecting dust on the shelf since it arrived ten years earlier.

The finger mug is a hand with the palm, thumb, and most fingers forming the cup. The middle finger sticks out as the handle of the mug. Meg gladly accepted the finger mug, as it was and still is a fine representation of how the universe acts toward her.

Meg grabs the steaming finger mug and turns on the only light her head can handle, an old fashioned microphone with a faint red light peeking out through silver lattice.

The microphone sheds faint light down the hall, revealing the jazz musicians she painted years ago. Meg closes her eyes and tries to hear music in the disturbing existence known as her life.

CHAPTER 12

Even the helpless victim of a hopeless situation, facing a fate he cannot change, may rise above himself, may grow beyond himself, and by so doing may change himself. He may turn a personal tragedy into a triumph.
—Viktor Frankl

Gunner chose the back of the café for their meeting spot, an exit sign casting a slight orange hue over their table.

Sadie announces "Day one" as she approaches Gunner, placing her mug of tea and cinnamon rolls on the table. "I got you a cinnamon roll...you need more coffee or anything?"

"Morning, ma'am. I had one cinnamon roll already, but I can be forced to eat another one...and I'm good with coffee. Thanks."

"I read something interesting the other day. Want me to share?"

"Yeah," Gunner cuts the cinnamon roll into equal size pieces and begins eating the icing drenched bun.

Sadie sits down, opening her blue notebook. "Only ten percent of what someone says comes from what they say. The real message comes from what they are doing when they are talking—their pitch, expression, tone of voice. And when listening with the intent of understanding, we won't always have a response to someone's story. We just let their story *be* without judging or giving them advice...because it's not about us...it's about them when we're talking about them!"

Gunner straightens a napkin on the table. "Allowing them to share their reality without clouding theirs with ours."

"When you came home, did people allow you to share your story without clouding your reality?"

"Nah," Gunner smirks. "It's better to not rely on others for confirmation you did the right thing."

"What do you mean?"

"Uh, just that others are going to disagree with certain decisions you make…maybe because of beliefs or maybe because they don't understand the details of what really happened."

"Why it is so hard to explain what happens overseas?"

"Combat cannot be explained…it can only be experienced."

"So if combat cannot be understood well by civilians…then the emotional challenges from combat would be difficult to explain as well, yes?"

"Maybe not the symptoms…but the reasons behind them, yes."

"I just…" Sadie wrestles with finding the right words. "I want to know the stories and struggles not in a sick way of enjoying the drama but…many civilians seem to take military service too lightly. Many don't understand, maybe because they don't take the time to or maybe because they don't want to, but I do. I want to know because I want to know how I can help."

"I don't see civilians as not caring about veterans. Everyone has their life and they're constantly running, doing what they have to do. We know what we do and how it affects our country. That's all that matters."

"I'm new with talking about this kind of stuff, Gunner. I usually email my troops and then I can read my message three times before sending it to make sure it sounds right…"

"I've been through a lot of worthless therapy, Sadie, and you wouldn't believe some of the questions that were thrown at me," Gunner shakes his head in disgust. "Some of those people asked the stupidest questions, things that shouldn't be asked…and things they had no place asking…" he curses, recalling an unpleasant memory. "But you're asking for a reason…so we're good. I'll try to answer your questions."

"What was the worst part of coming home for you?"

"Uh, returning home alone was the worst part. And facing the families…the questions of why I lived and their brother, husband, son…didn't. I had no answers for them. I saw what happened to their guys but I was not going to tell the family about a dead body or some sick stuff like that. I just told them he was a hell of a man and he didn't deserve to die…but bad things happen over there."

"They asked you why you lived and their loved one didn't? That's awful!"

"It was, uh…challenging," Gunner answers expressionless.

"If I lost my legs for our country," Sadie's hands lift off the table in outrage. "I'd be angry, and I'd expect some kind of payment for what I gave up…but what payment would be enough? I don't know what I'd do if I lost my legs…so I wonder how you get up each day."

"Well, very carefully so I don't fall out of bed," Gunner teases for a moment before his unreadable eyes return. "Uh, did I expect something from our country? Just medical treatment. When I came home, all I wanted was to be with my guys, so yeah, I was pissed, because they were still out there and I was in some hospital. All I could do was wait by the phone and hope they would call, which they did. But expecting payment? Nah. I knew what the risks were when I signed up. We all do."

"How did you transition…how do you process such a loss…such a life change?" Sadie asks.

"Uh, it is what it is. People are quick to label things impossible. Maybe it's the therapy or how I grew up or just life, but I don't see anything as impossible. Especially now."

"Can I ask you a personal question, Gunner?"

"Aren't these all?" his smile appears. "Sure."

"At the hospital I heard you counting."

"I count to…calm the nerves."

Sadie hesitates, "You were nervous at the hospital?"

"It's okay; I don't mind your questions, Sadie." He pauses. "Uh, public places…are mentally demanding."

"Even here?"

"That's why we're in the back near the exit; it's easier to stay if I have a fast getaway plan. When I first got back, I wasn't able to sit in coffee shops…just wheeling in and out was a success for me. Then I made the goal of wheeling in, getting coffee, and wheeling out…little steps."

"You seem so…calm."

"Good."

"Gunner, the more I learn, the sadder it seems, yet the more I feel like this story has to be told; the awareness has to be increased."

"We are somewhat of a forgotten bunch when we return home from overseas, so I agree with increasing the awareness." Gunner finishes the last of his cinnamon roll. "I'll have to wheel a few extra miles to get rid of the rolls I ate today. Are we on for tomorrow?"

"You still want to meet with me after I bombarded you with questions today?"

"Yeah, I'm still game. Same time, same place?"

"Deal. Thanks, Gunner."

"You bet. I'll see you tomorrow, Sadie."

*

Gigi closes the tin door on her mailbox, a stack of envelopes and magazines tightly in her grasp.

Drew walks past Gigi carrying several boxes to his car.

"Oh," Gigi's happy venom seeps out. "You're moving?"

"Yeah," Drew answers, directing a sharp glare toward his cheery neighbor.

Damn happy maniac, Drew comments to himself.

"Be nice," Nina hits the side of Drew's arm as she passes by him and drops a box into her trunk. Nina walks over to Gigi. "I'm Nina, Drew's sister."

Gigi shifts the mail to one hand with a bit of effort. "I'm Gigi, Drew's neighbor."

"Please excuse Drew," Nina apologizes.

Gigi leans closer to Nina and speaks softly. "Honey, we've been his neighbors for years…and I've excused him ever since he returned home from his first deployment. Bill, he's my husband, he knows what it's like, and he tells me, 'Just be friendly, Gigi, but don't be expecting him to show he appreciates your salutations,' so that's what I do. Drew's a special boy, but I was sorry to see his wife leave."

"He's coming to live with my son and me. Well, we'll see how long he stays…you know how he is."

Gigi puts her hand on Nina's arm. "Everyone wants to be loved. They may not say it, but everyone wants to be loved. It's nice you're doing that for him."

"I think it's selfish. My husband," a few tears escape, "was killed overseas. He worked with Drew. And I can't seem to be okay by myself. So if I can worry about Drew or help him…it takes my mind off not being able to help me." She wipes tears and fans her face with her hands. "I can't do this right now. I uh, I'm a mess. Maybe more of a mess than Drew," Nina laughs.

"I'm sorry, dear. And if being selfish is asking for help when you need it, then by golly, be selfish. Most don't know you need help unless you ask because we're busy in our own world."

"Sorry for gushing my emotions on you, Gigi!"

"It's quite alright, dear. I like a girl who isn't afraid to gush," Gigi's laughter bubbles out.

Nina hands her a slip of paper with her address and phone number. "In case you need to contact us…or me."

Gigi takes the piece of paper. "Sure, dear. We'll keep an eye on the house. It was nice to meet you."

"Thanks, Gigi. It was nice to meet you, too."

*

Carter uses the darkness to escape Momma's drinking because at night she cannot see him crawl out his window and tiptoe along the house.

Theo's normal street corner is empty.

Carter sits down where Theo should be.

"Yo, kid."

Carter freezes in terror at the unfamiliar voice.

"You shouldn't be here, boy. Whattya doin' down here?"

"Waitin' for Theo."

"Speak up boy," the shadow barks.

"Waiting for Theo," Carter says louder.

"Theo?" The broken street light flickers long enough to reveal a boy's face with a look in his eyes only living on the streets can create. "He dead. Yeah, little man, Theo dead."

A faint whisper, "Dead?"

"Yeah, like, ah, gone to Jesus, kind of dead, kid. He gone. You betta be leavin' too kid. This place ain't for little men."

A crusty voice shouts from a block up the street. "Whattya doin' Tag? Someone down der'?"

Carter stands, cautiously eyeing Tag.

Tag spits. "A rat! And quit yellin'! I'll come when I come!" He turns toward Carter. "Can ya hear boy? I said run along. Get otta here." Tag's voice softens. "Go that way," he points the opposite direction of the crusty voice.

Noises seep from the darkness as Carter walks to the park.

His real mother left without saying goodbye.

Now Theo, his only friend, left without saying goodbye.

Carter crawls into the middle of a bush alongside a park bench and wraps his sleeves, wet with tears, around his knees.

CHAPTER 13

Optimism is the armour of brave souls who
fight conditions and never surrender
to domination by the darker side of
life that dares to daunt them.
–William George Jordan

S adie smiles as she approaches Gunner. "We should get a sign or something marking this as our table."

"We have been coming here for a month. It would only be appropriate for Sydney to honor such dedicated customers." Gunner briefly winces in pain.

"What's wrong?" Sadie sets her notebook on the table.

"Nah, it's nothing."

"Okay, we're not going to talk about it. That's fine."

Gunner narrows his eyes in the silence. "Phantom pain."

"Your legs hurt?"

"The bliss of missing limbs. Pain that's air."

"So...what hurts?" Sadie asks.

"My right foot."

"Oh...well, move your foot...maybe put it up on a chair," Sadie pulls a chair next to Gunner.

Gunner stares at her in disbelief.

"Maybe it's cramping or something."

"You sound serious..."

"I am serious, Gunner. Your brain says your foot hurts...so tell your brain to move your foot so it stops hurting. Close your eyes and mentally put your foot up on the chair. Maybe when your brain doesn't receive any pain signals back from moving your foot...it will hurt less."

A second passes as they stare at one another while the idea dances in the middle of the table.

Gunner's lopsided smile appears. "That's the most ridiculous suggestion I've ever heard...I'm game to try it."

Sadie stands. "Maybe it will work? I'll get us some cinnamon rolls. You put your foot up."

Sadie returns to their table with cinnamon rolls and tea.

"That was a strange suggestion and a strange activity...even stranger that it eased some of the pain," Gunner sips his black coffee. "Where did you hear about moving a limb that's gone?"

"From a friend of mine...who is also one of the most brilliant physical therapists I know," Sadie sits down.

"Thanks. One thing before we start talking about PTSD."

Sadie lifts the lid on her tea, a cloud of steam escaping the cup. "Shoot."

"I don't like the label of PTSD."

"What label would you prefer?"

"Warrior Readjustment."

"And the military likes acronyms...so, WARE?"

Gunner nods. "WARE on the warrior's mind...I like it."

Sadie opens her blue notebook and clicks an orange pen on the table. "Okay, what should the world know about WARE?"

He smiles at her readiness. "Uh, WARE is...not a mental illness or a disease. It's a transition from combat that we make, in our own time, when we return home."

"You have to somehow process what you experienced."

"And that process is different for everyone," Gunner adds.

"But easier to process when talking with other veterans...because they understand what civilians can't, right?"

"Civilians don't know the circumstances for which we act and how we handle certain things...some even think PTSD, what we're calling WARE, is a BS way for us to get more money or disability, when it can be an actual problem."

"So what is the secret, Gunner? Is there something the warrior who learns how to live with WARE can teach to the warrior who struggles every day?"

"Why one person relives events and has nightmares while another doesn't, isn't a question I can answer...there are too many factors and unknowns to say that a simple solution exists. Why someone like Laina's father would seem okay but then commit suicide forty years after returning home from combat...is beyond me."

Sadie bites the edge of her lip. "I haven't seen Laina since that day at the hospital...but that's the day I figured I had to do something with bringing awareness to WARE. I wish it wasn't beyond my realm...that there was some way I could help. It's tough because I'm not a warrior, so I can't say to someone, 'I know how you feel, or I know what you went through.'"

"You wish for something that sometimes I wish I didn't have," Gunner nudges the napkin holder on the table so it sits at its proper 90-degree angle.

"The curse of understanding, right?" Sadie shoots him a look of compassion. "Yesterday, I was reading a book and came across a graphic scene of a rape, something completely disturbing for any sane human to think about, but the author had this strange way of ending the scene. The character, instead of being horrified or ashamed or sad, didn't shut down or announce to the world that she had been violated; she turned instantly to plan revenge. So this atrocious thing happens, this violation, and the response is genius...instant planning to avenge the sin imposed upon her body and mind. And though war is not rape, it's a type of mental violation, don't you think?"

"It's a type of mental violation...and physical. And it's personal when someone blows your legs off."

"Gunner, what if a warrior's point of view when coming home would be to seek revenge for surviving? Leaving behind the notion that they are a prisoner of what they saw, did, or didn't do? What if they come home and focus on a revenge they deem appropriate...revenge along the lines of purpose?"

Deep thought fills Gunner's eyes.

"Would this be an appropriate approach? I'm not a warrior so I can't say..."

"It's good, Sadie. It's really good." Anguish replaces the emptiness that once occupied Gunner's eyes. "Losing my legs was more than just my legs…those bastards took…everything. Being a marine was my life…that's who I was…that's who I am. But I can't lead my guys with fuckin' wheels…and it's something I have to accept, and something I have accepted most days, but to get revenge…and a day job won't satisfy what I still got inside…it's hard to explain."

Gunner continues, tracing the rim of his coffee cup with his index finger. "Sometimes we tell our horror stories to other vets just to get them out…maybe so it's known that we did what we could…or to let 'em know that we get what they are going through…but I think the secret is how we make it through certain points in time—how we escape the darkness that attempts to destroy us. The inspiration behind the warrior…not what knocks us down, but what makes us get back up again."

Gunner pauses. "You are giving me a strange look."

Sadie beams, "Gunner, you just titled our program: *Inspiration Behind the Warrior*! You should be a motivational speaker."

He looks at her, denial spiced with curiosity.

Sadie reiterates, "Others need to hear that leaving their darkness is a choice and is possible."

"I'm not in a position right now to be leading anyone."

"You inspire others to be their own leader, Gunner, not to follow you."

Gunner narrows his eyes, entertaining the idea. "It's possible."

Sadie grins. "Anything's possible, right?"

*

Meg unhooks Ruger's green leash as they walk in the front door. She hands him a black rubber cone filled with sweet potato. "Nice walking with you, Ruger…see you in a few hours."

Ruger saunters away with his prized potato treat while Meg shuffles through the stack of mail. "Vet bill, electric bill, junk mail…ooh, a letter from Joel."

She tosses the other letters onto the counter, taking Joel's handwritten note to the couch.

"Okay, my traveling doctor, where have you been this past month?" Meg unfolds his letter and sets the pictures Joel enclosed aside.

Dear Meg,

I was at a clinic in Ecuador. I walked into our doctor's hut (a fancy title meaning the only place with clean drinking water) for lunch. A local had brought some fish for us (his payment) because we helped his sick wife. Ten minutes after eating this fish, I started feeling really tired and was sweating like mad. Our nurse, Cheyanne, (Remember? She's the biker, and only girl, to beat me in an arm wrestling match—again, I should stress I let her win because of her good looks!) said my face was red and that I felt very hot. She walked out of the hut and then came running back inside. Doc Rivers (I beat him in the arm wrestling competition!) had also eaten the fish. He had passed out in the clinic with the same symptoms I had. Rivers was carried into the hut and just when they laid him on a cot, he started vomiting. I, on the other hand, do not throw up—gift or curse?? As I was lying there, my body started hurting...all over. The room started spinning and I blacked out. We were taken to a hospital. I remember being told that I was about to get a shot that would hurt...and it hurt a lot!

I slept for four days straight. I guess the town was quite worried I would die. Rivers threw up, so he had a faster recovery from the food poisoning. It took me a bit longer. Anyway, it was a close call but I'm still here. I just don't eat the fish in Quito anymore...lesson learned!

I got a little scared because I almost died from something as lame as food poisoning. They now have on record that if I die from something 'not sexy,' to tell people I died heroically being mauled by a lion while rescuing a child...crawling up steep rocky hills with no shoes...haha! If I'm going to die, I'm going to be a frickin' hero!

And to let you know how crazy medical costs are here...my four day stay at the hospital...or what they call a hospital...was a whopping $7.45.

Hope you are doing well. I'm waiting to hear about the paintings you've finished for the Chicago event...don't forget to include pictures. And yes, I finally sent a note to my mom to let her know I'm fine...so you don't have to 'come to the jungle and kick my axx' as you said in your last letter...which entertained and terrified me all at once. I didn't know I had an axx but I'm afraid now that I know you know where mine is.

Meg smiles, recalling her threat.

But...my family doesn't know that I've been writing to you since I left...so this is still our secret.
Lots of love, Joel.

Meg reads the note a second time. "Dysfunctional, yet lovely, darling," she says to the empty air, studying Joel's photos of Ecuador.

*

An ambulance speeds past the park.
Jake nudges Sadie. "You're quiet today."
Sadie traces their love symbol carved on the park bench with her finger. "Veterans experience more trauma in a few months than many of us experience in a lifetime."
"What exactly is PTSD?" Jake asks.
"A response to an event where someone fears for their life, or feels helpless due to a lack of control over their life."
"So it's not just a military thing?"
"Nope, anyone can suffer from it. The mind replays the event so the same feelings resurface as if the event were reoccurring. And the body responds in the same manner as it did during the actual attack...making it difficult to distinguish between perception and reality."
"It's not like war is new though...shouldn't programs already be in place to help PTSD?"
Sadie nods. "Yeah, but PTSD is not well understood. Some veterans who served twenty, thirty, or fifty years ago are still struggling. Gunner said some of his veteran friends reached out for help and were told their mental issues were not from their military service...but stem from their life before they joined...only, if they had

mental issues before they joined, the service wouldn't have allowed them overseas…at least, not in the capacity they were serving." Sadie shakes her head. "It's disturbing. Gunner looked at me with his super straight teeth and said, 'Awareness and strength in numbers, that's all we need.'"

"He does have amazingly straight teeth," Jake puts his arm around her.

"I know, right?!" Sadie laughs, inching closer to him on the bench. "And, we are referring to it as WARE not PTSD."

"Why WARE?"

"Warrior Readjustment. Because PTSD can happen to anyone…but war is a different type of trauma. Different trauma, different name, different treatment."

"It's not just about being separated from us lowly civilians?" Jake challenges.

"Some have that special attitude…but we all have an attitude sometimes…and these guys and gals are the only ones who are willing to die for us because we belong under the name of the United States. It's amazing that one man and one group have offered to die for freedom…Jesus, who died for eternal freedom, and the military, where many have died for our country's freedom. But I don't see the relabeling of PTSD as a need for them to be better than us. I see it as a need for them to be better for themselves…to be able to come home and enjoy the freedom they had a hand in preserving. But it's easy to forget."

"What they did for us?"

"What they may be going through. We can't see the mental part. Gunner said war mentally changes everyone."

"And to different degrees I imagine, based on their experiences," Jake adds.

"And their support system. Some are willing to talk about their struggles, others are embarrassed they have such struggles. The sad thing is that many veterans don't realize other vets are struggling with the same challenges."

"Well, admitting that you're struggling mentally or seeking counseling could jeopardize any career, love."

"That's why our program for WARE encourages warriors to ask for help so they can remain strong, not because they are weak. Instead of slapping on the label of PTSD and saying that someone is screwed up, Warrior Readjustment is neutral…all the warriors returning home go through some kind of an adjustment, making the label more of a transition, instead of a disease, erasing the stigma of struggling once returning home. With PTSD there is something wrong, reactions unacceptable to society and to ourselves. With WARE, there is an adjustment to be made…not right, not wrong, just…there."

"A less stressful approach…"

Sadie faces Jake. "Hope…which is something."

CHAPTER 14

A mighty flame followeth a tiny spark.
–Dante Alighieri

Sadie knocks on Reiss's hospital room door. "You're in the hospital again? You know, I'd come visit you even if you weren't in here," Sadie teases.

"I like the atmosphere…sick people, white walls…"

"Your description on the phone of why you're here was a bit vague: bad drivers. What does that mean?" Sadie asks.

"I believe I said shitty drivers," Reiss clarifies.

"Yes, you did. Care to expand on that explanation?"

"Not really."

"Okay, what would you like to talk about…car rims?"

"My car hit a rail."

"For real? How's…the car?"

"The car?" A dimple deepens his cheek. "Minor repairs. Thanks for asking."

"Why did you hit a rail?"

"I was bored. Nah, an idiot driving behind me failed to stop. So my car stopped him. And a rail stopped my car." Reiss adjusts a stack of pillows behind his back. "What's going on with you?"

"I'm still meeting with Gunner. You should come sometime. And…" she analyzes his expression. "Is everything okay?"

"I'm fine."

"Okay," Sadie agrees to disagree.

Reiss shakes his head, looking toward the ceiling.

"How is your hand?"

"Working less. I was out with my girlfriend the other night and my hand went numb but I didn't notice until I reached for my glass and fuckin' knocked it over…" fury lights Reiss's words. "She was so embarrassed…she always is now because of," he smirks, disappointment in his eyes, "everything. So am I. I ended us."

"How did she react?"

"Cried. I didn't exactly use gentleman-like words."

"Reiss…"

"You're lying if you tell me this is anything but fucked up!" he points to his melted flesh.

"Of course it is fucked up!" Sadie explodes. "It's a disturbing reality of war! Being a soldier is not just a job; it's a bloody life commitment!" Sadie's voice softens. "I'm sorry she left."

"No worries…got any hot friends?"

Sadie shakes her head. "You and hot girls."

"Did I tell you I'm getting out?"

"Of the Army? What are you going to do?" Sadie asks.

"You mean who am I going to do?" Reiss grins.

Sadie's face scrunches. "No, I definitely don't mean that…"

"Oh. Well, my car needs to be fixed…and I don't know what else. Maybe modeling." Reiss's phone rings. "This could be a modeling agency seeking my services."

Sadie laughs. "Go ahead, I'm leaving. And those scars are a sign of strength, Reiss. If a hottie can't see that…she's no friendie of yours."

Reiss nods. "Thanks, friendie."

As Sadie walks out of Reiss's room, crazy white curls pass her by. "Hey, Gigi, right?"

Gigi turns around. "I'm sorry, dear, I've forgotten your name."

"I'm Sadie. My husband and I met you and Bill at the park."

"Oh, yes, you are the gal that sends packages to troops."

"That's me. What are you doing here?"

"My Bill is sick. What brings you to the hospital?"

"One of my friends is here. Is Bill okay?" Sadie asks.

"He's had a good life. We've had a good life together." Gigi's lips quiver. "Cancer."

"Cancer?!" Sadie gasps. "Do you want to get coffee?"

"I'd like that, dear," Gigi nods, her words unsteady.

The hum of vending machines fills the silence as empty seats surround them in the cafeteria.

Gigi says, "You never expect it, dear."

"Death?" Sadie asks.

Gigi nods.

After a moment, Sadie says, "The soldier I talked with today sustained burns when he was overseas. He just broke up with his girlfriend. And he crashed his car."

"Oh my."

"I'm not sure why I just told you that. Maybe because I don't know what to say to comfort you...and I didn't know what to say to comfort him," Sadie bites the side of her lip.

"You don't have to say anything to comfort me, dear. Just sitting here is nice. My mind is a bit busy for advice." Gigi takes a sip of her coffee. "Tell me more about your friend."

"He seems different from when I talked with him when he was overseas. Did Bill suffer from PTSD?"

"Oh, yes. At a bar one time, someone said something he didn't like. He nearly killed the man."

"What stopped him?"

"Some of his friends dragged him outside. PTSD was not advertised, talked about, or understood back then...many just buried it with alcohol, endless work, or abuse. Bill formed a group with veterans...that's what helped him."

"So veterans talking with other veterans helps?"

"Oh, yes. They understand and comfort each other in ways we can't, dear."

"I'm working with a marine on a program that encourages veterans to seek help if they are having difficulties adjusting...or reach out to help other vets who are struggling."

"That's wonderful, dear. My neighbor returned home from his second deployment, and his wife left him two weeks later. And last month he moved in with his sister. She lost her husband in combat...and her brother saw the whole thing...he was there. It's a shame. Such a young soul. Drew is a nice young man, though. I can tell the good ones from the bad ones and he's..."

"Do you know his last name?"

"It starts with an M...let's see..."

"Manning?"

"Yes, I believe that's right."

"I sent care packages to him!"

"I probably shouldn't be telling you all this. I do tend to stick my nose where it doesn't belong...but I'm old enough to get away with it," Gigi laughs, then notices a change in Sadie's expression. "What is it, dear?"

Sadie pauses. "All of this effort in trying to make a difference...ah, I'm fine. It's nothing."

"That look is anything but nothing, dear."

"I feel like what I'm doing now isn't enough, Gigi..."

"Just be the best you can be with who you are right now, dear. Your best right now is always enough."

"Thanks," Sadie grins.

Gigi puts her soft wrinkled hand on Sadie's. "Thank you. These past few minutes took my mind off my Bill."

Sadie writes down her phone number. "Call me sometime. We'll make another coffee date."

"I might just take you up on that offer. I'd like to give your number to Drew's sister in case Drew wants someone to talk with."

Sadie writes down Gunner's number. "We're happy to help."

Gigi holds up the piece of paper. "I'm going to give this to Nina...and stick my nose where it might not belong."

Sadie laughs, making a toast with her last drink of coffee. "To sticking your nose where it doesn't belong."

Gigi raises her paper cup. "This is the first time I've toasted a bad behavior, dear. How fun!"

*

"Dirty pants!" Edison hands Drew his blue stuffed hippo and a diaper.

"I'm supposed to put a diaper on him?" Drew hands the hippo back to Edison. "Yuck! You do it."

Edison squeals with delight. "Yuck! You!" he hands Drew the hippo and runs away giggling.

Nina walks into the living room and hands Drew a phone number. "This is the number of a veteran who knows some gal that used to send you care packages…he talks with other vets…so maybe he can help."

Drew stands, his blood instantly boiling. "Maybe we should take out an ad in the paper and tell everyone how fucked up I am…or a blimp 'Here lives a freak!' Seeing a bunch of moronic therapists isn't enough? Damn, just leave it alone, Nina!" he tosses the paper into the garbage as he walks out, slamming the door.

Nina retrieves the paper from the garbage and dials the number.

CHAPTER 15

Often opportunity involves a great deal of work and a willingness to take a chance on something, the outcome of which may be uncertain. Eventually you reach a point when you must either accept an opportunity with all of its unknowns or else turn your back on it. No one can tell you when you have reached that point; you alone know when it's time to make your move, to have the courage to take a chance.
—Napoleon Hill

S he should be sleeping with the silence of midnight, the cool air drifting around the house, and the warmth under the covers. Sadie whispers, "Are you awake?"

Jake moans in a deep crackly voice. "Sure."

"The doctor says I should wait, but I don't want to wait."

"Wait?" Jake sighs and turns toward her.

"To be a mom." A tear hits Sadie's pillow. "I don't want to wait."

"Are you crying?" Jake leans on his elbows to see her face.

"No...maybe a little."

"Sade..."

"I want to have a baby, Jake."

"What did the doctor say?"

"To wait a few months to make sure my heart is strong enough. And that other mothers with heart issues get pregnant and everything goes fine."

"So in a few months, we'll try for a baby...that's not so bad, is it? A few months?"

"Ninety days...is a long time."

"We have a lot to do if you're going to get pregnant in three months."

"We do?" Sadie says.

"Well, we have to clear out the guest room so we can fit a crib in there. You'll have to research those mothers who did get pregnant and see what special precautions they took."

"Plus I have to get my warrior project up and running."

Jake kisses her forehead. "Good thing we have some time."

"Now I'm kind of panicking...wondering if we'll get all that stuff done," Sadie crawls close to him.

"Ah, we'll be fine, love. It's not that much."

*

With one paintbrush secured between her teeth and one in her hand, Meg billows blue around a setting sun on canvas.

The last brush strokes for this piece are in pink; a color Meg never wears yet secretly admires due to God's fascination and frequent utilization of pink when He paints the sky and flower petals.

The painting's name, *Secret Admirer*, floats into Meg's mind as she adds puffs of cotton candy to the sunset.

*

Nina walks onto the balcony in her pajamas and robe, carrying two mugs of coffee. "You're up early."

"Yeah," Drew stares at the sunrise.

"How long have you been out here?"

"A while."

"More coffee than sugar this time," Nina hands him a mug.

"Thanks," Drew gives her a brief smile.

"Thanks for fixing the front door...and the squeak in the stairs. My car runs now without all those lights going on...that's a relief. What are you doing out here? It's cold." She pulls her robe tighter around her.

"Thinking. Or not thinking. Both."

Nina sits on the porch swing, the chains loudly announcing the extra weight.

"I'll fix the swing tomorrow."

"You move in and my whole place gets a makeover. It's nice. It's so quiet out here...and peaceful." Nina sighs loudly. "Drew, it doesn't bother me."

"How can it not? It squeaks when you sit on it."

"Not the swing, Drew. I'm talking about...you know what I'm talking about."

"I didn't sleep much, Nina, so maybe you can just tell me."

"You don't have to avoid sleeping just so..."

"So I don't wake you up screaming from nightmares at 3 AM?"

"It's okay. I mean, not for you, but I'm okay with it. Just sleep when you want to sleep and if you wake me up...I'll go back to sleep."

"Wyla called me last night."

"What did she say?"

"Said she misses me," Drew shakes his head. "Bitch."

"Maybe she does miss you."

"She ran away with Asshole Steve three months ago."

"She left the drinking, Drew. Not you."

"Yeah, well. It's part of the package."

"So, stop."

"Without it, I remember...too much."

"And you don't want to remember."

Drew shrugs. "Or forget."

"How do you not remember without forgetting?" Nina asks.

He holds up his flask. "And no, I'm not drunk, or even close."

"Don't you want more?"

"I didn't know you had Jack here."

"Not Jack. Don't you want more from life?"

"It doesn't matter."

"It does matter, Drew."

"I'm an alcoholic...I can fix everything but myself...how fuckin' shameful!" Drew stands to leave.

"No! Drew, no. Stay. Alcohol is a strategy for your battle. I get that."

Drew curses, sitting back down. "I need a new strategy. I could beat Asshole Steve. That might be fun."

"Or you could stop the alcohol."

"I don't know."

"I don't know either, Drew. But we'll figure it out. Just like we did last time."

Drew looks at Nina unconvinced. "I ended up drinking again and Wyla ended up leaving again…not an impressive track record."

Nina nods. "We're messed up…but all we can do is try."

Drew feels dead inside, but maybe time will take away the horrors…or maybe this dark hole is all he gets.

*

A car pulls in front of the café.

"There he is," Sadie announces to Gunner.

Reiss smiles briefly when he sees her, looking around the café.

Sadie walks over and hugs him. "I'm glad you could come."

"Sure." Reiss scans the café, a few strangers beginning to stare at his face. Reiss swears under his breath. "This was a bad idea."

Sadie motions to their table. "Gunner, this is Reiss. Reiss, this is Gunner."

"What's up, Gunner. So you're a marine?" Reiss asks, still scanning every inch of the café.

Gunner nods. "And you're former marine and Army medic?"

"Yeah, as a marine I was doin' all sorts of shit and nothing ever happened. Made the switch to medic and all sorts of shit happened…concussions, burns, shrapnel…" Reiss curses.

"I think shit happens in every branch, man," Gunner points to his wheels.

"Damn. Iraq?"

"I fought there, but this was in Afghanistan."

"Ah, yes, Trashghanistan…I was there before Iraq. IED?"

"Pakistani anti-tank mines. Triple stacked, detonated with a pressure plate."

Reiss winces. "Those bend Humvees like paper clips."

"I was ejected," Gunner looks toward Sadie then back at Reiss. "Stuff happens in every branch."

"True that," Reiss flexes and extends his left hand several times.

Gunner looks at Reiss's hand but doesn't say anything.

Sadie begins telling Reiss about *Inspiration Behind the Warrior*.

The sound of busting dishes in the kitchen sends Reiss nearly under the table. Within seconds, a look of embarrassment crosses his face. "I, uh, need to leave."

A waitress walks toward their table.

Reiss panics as she gets closer. "I gotta go," he bolts out of the coffee shop.

"Reiss!" Sadie calls after him.

"Just let him," Gunner advises.

Sadie looks at Gunner, full of questions. "He has PTSD doesn't he? Or WARE…whatever we're calling it."

"Many of us do."

Sadie stares at Gunner. "He needs help."

"Many of us do."

"Then why didn't you try to stop him? Why didn't you try to help him?"

"He showed up…even talked a bit…that's a big step."

"I know, but I want…I want to fix him."

"What he saw overseas, Sadie…will take more than one conversation to process through."

"I can't do this anymore today, Gunner. I'm sorry. It's like the support is available and the help is needed…but the connection failed to take place…maybe this isn't going to work."

"It's not failure, Sadie…it's the first step. With everything and everyone, there's gotta be a first step."

Sadie frowns. "I know."

"We are meeting Monday?"

"Yeah," Sadie sighs. "Have a good weekend, Gunner."

"You too…and celebrate the victory of getting Reiss to walk through that door."

*

The speedometer climbs as Reiss's foot dominates the pedal.

A fellow driver lays on his horn as Reiss speeds past.

Reiss steps hard on the accelerator, adrenaline surging as his body clings to the black leather seat.

No particular place beckons him, just the thrill of open roads to quiet the noise in his mind.

*

Meg stares at the latest color strewn canvas, downing her usual meal of a cheese sandwich. "Hmmm...sticks of black intersect, balls upsetting the square format," she describes the painting out loud to land the perfect name. "A flash of color tossed from the end of each black stick...a mystery of which corner belongs to which square...or maybe each corner is part of every square."

Meg finishes her sandwich and writes on the back with black marker: *Flash of Genius.*

*

As Sadie sits on the park bench, she cannot stop the tears of disappointment from rolling down her face. While meandering back to her car, Sadie sees Laina with a puppy.

"Hey, Sadie! I got the puppy I was going to get my dad."

"Good for you," Sadie nods. "You look happy."

The puppy bounces awkwardly over to Sadie.

"What is his name?" Sadie asks.

"Pops," Laina beams.

Sadie smiles as Pops runs between her legs, falls on the ground, and begins nipping at her hand. "I'm starting a program with a focus of helping veterans struggling with PTSD. You're welcome to come to one of our meetings."

"You know, I'd love to come but I'm leaving for California in three days. Pops and I will live with my aunt for a while."

"Well, in that case, just know your story, and your dad, sparked this new project...we're hoping to help others."

"You know, that's cool. Really cool. I'm sure you will."

"Thanks...and I hope you and Pops have fun in California."

"Thank you. It means something, you know…to know my dad didn't die for nothing," tears start to form. "And I'm leaving before I start crying!" Laina smiles. "See you, Sadie!"

Sadie grins as she watches Pops bounce around Laina's feet as they walk away.

*

Jake grabs his coat as Sadie walks in the door. "I'm ready."

Sadie apologizes with her eyes. "I stopped at the park on my way home, babe."

"Without me?"

"Reiss freaked out today. I thought he and Gunner would hit it off, but Reiss left shortly after he arrived."

"What did Gunner say?"

"Time…that he needs time. I wish I could wave a magic wand over him and make him all better," a few tears escape.

Jake pulls her into his arms. "Reiss probably wishes the same thing, love."

*

Empty care package boxes sit stacked in Jake and Sadie's front hall, ready to be filled with items for the troops.

As D and Meg walk in the front door, Meg's purse catches the edge of a box and knocks the stack of boxes over. "I didn't break anything!" Meg announces.

"Still in those lucky seven years, huh?" Jake teases.

D inhales a lung-full of air. "I smell custom forms and pizza!" he hands Jake a six pack. "Dude, the one game you miss at my place…you so missed a good game last night. The guys were all over…it was crazy!"

"Crazy at your place, D? How unusual," Meg chimes in with sarcasm.

"I know, sista!" D adds playfully, "We're typically so diplomatic. It was a nice change to let loose; you may want to try it sometime…next game, you should come over."

"A platoon of your friends screaming at a television and talking with food in their mouths..." Meg grimaces.

D muses, "When you put it that way...you *have* to come now!"

*

Nina slides the crumpled paper with Gunner's phone number on the table in front of Drew.

His eyes narrow. "You pulled this out of the garbage?"

"You said you wanted something to change. Maybe this Gunner can help."

Drew slides the paper back to her. "If he doesn't sound like a know-it-all jackass, I'll meet him."

"Monday at 1 PM."

Drew shakes his head. "Damn, Nina, what if I said no?"

"You didn't. Monday at 1 PM at Sydney's...okay?"

"Then you're done nagging me?" Drew asks.

"Yep," Nina grins.

*

After dinner, Jake, Sadie, Meg, and D address labels and custom forms for care packages heading to troops overseas.

Meg nudges Sadie. "You okay?"

Sadie grins. "I'm okay."

Meg announces, "Girl break!"

D looks at Jake. "Snack time," he leaps up and starts dancing. "And Candy time. Show me your mistress, man."

Jake and D immediately start in on the car language.

As the guys leave, Meg removes her glasses, biting on the end. "I'm sorry I haven't been helping with the care packages...and that Jake had to miss D's party last night because he had to help you. I've just been so busy with the paintings and trying to finish the pieces before my show..."

"Meg, I'm glad you're finally painting. And Jake was okay with helping me last night...we had a good time," Sadie smiles, recalling the night before.

"Then what's wrong?"

Sadie adds a completed address label to the pile. "I'm bummed that I cannot fix Reiss's PTSD."

"Maybe Reiss needed to freak out with the dishes breaking and people staring...maybe that was the help he needed."

"Maybe."

"You do your thing, Sadie...though you might not be sure where it's going or why you're doing it...but you know it's right. That's called instrumental chaos."

"Instrumental chaos? I love that, Meg. That's my life."

D announces as he walks into the kitchen, "Custom forms are complete. Labels are addressed. You gals ready to watch the movie?"

Meg says innocently, "Are you guys finally ready? Done playing with the mistress?"

D laughs. "No way girlfriend, don't try and pull that on me. I know how girls talk and I just want to get home before tomorrow. I need my beauty sleep...can't maintain a body like this without beauty sleep," he flexes his arms like a bodybuilder as Meg rolls her eyes.

*

Drew looks at his caller ID. Wyla. He knows he shouldn't pick up but his hand betrays his mind.

"Drew?! I miss you," Wyla whines. "I want to see you." She continues as Drew remains silent. "I need a man, Drew...not a boy. Steve is a boy. I want my man back. Can I come and see you?"

Drew shakes his head. "Let's meet at our place...my place."

CHAPTER 16

If called upon to the burdens of the greater responsibility let us bear
them bravely at our best and let nothing rob us of simplicity,
sweetness, strength, sympathy and all that is sterling.
—William George Jordan

"Where are you going?" Wyla rolls over in bed.
Drew laces his old running shoes, ignoring her question.
"And why so early?"

"Were you talking to Asshole Steve last night?" Drew asks.

Wyla pulls the covers closer and turns away from him. "Drew, it's too early to fight."

"Damn, Wyla. Two months and now you're running back to Asshole Steve?"

"Drew, I'm not having this conversation! Besides, I can talk to Steve about things…he understands me…he listens."

Drew slams the front door and walks outside, hooking small silver music buds into his ears.

The sun peeks over the horizon.

As music begins playing, Drew begins running in the still-sleeping neighborhood…hoping the exercise calms his nerves and takes away the urge to destroy something.

*

A chime sounds as Meg pushes open the art gallery's heavy wooden door.

"Come in," a young voice yells from the back.

Meg walks in carrying her first painting.

"You're here for the show today, I presume?" a tall, skinny, bleach-blond hair kid asks with a boatload of arrogance.

"Yes, the other eight paintings are in my…"

"Name?" he dramatically tosses a silver banner to the ground and steps down a two-step ladder. "Sure, I'll help you right this second," he complains under his breath as he grabs a clipboard with a list of names.

"I can wait…"

"Name!"

"Meg Marx," her enthusiasm hangs on by a thread.

He taps his pen on the clipboard, reading a yellow note with her name on it. "Miss Marx, eight of your slots were given to another artist. You can show one painting," he suddenly perks up, enjoying every second of delivering this message.

"For real?"

"I'm not fond of repeating myself Miss Marx. So only ask a question if you require an answer. At 10 AM I'll show you where you can setup." He tosses the clipboard onto a white desk and picks up the silver banner, climbing the two steps of the ladder.

"On my invitation it said to be here at 8 AM to setup."

"8 AM is for the artists who have multiple pieces…and as we established one minute ago, you have one piece Miss Marx. One," he holds up a skinny long finger.

Meg walks outside, slides her painting back into the car, and pulls out her rescue pack of cigarettes. She puts a cigarette into her mouth, keeping it unlit, and envisions pushing bleach boy off his ladder, as the mere presence of the nicotine stick switches her focus from frustration to a solution to her new dilemma.

*

Sadie's mind is calm despite the fact that the Military Ball is today. As she walks outside to get the paper, a package on the front porch greets her.

Sadie, For the beginning of the rest of your life. Open after the Military Ball. -Meg

Sadie dials Meg's number. "You got me a present?"

"I thought you should have something to focus on…something beyond tonight to take some of the nerves away."

"Meg, that's so sweet! I'm pretty nervous. I was good when I woke up…now I'm kind of freaking out. But I wanted to wish you good luck at your art show."

"Yeah, it'll be great," Meg drones sarcastically.

"Are you already hating Chicago?" Sadie asks.

"Just another flip of the bird from the universe. But I'll tell you about it tomorrow…bleach boy is beckoning me to come inside and setup. Good luck tonight at the Ball!"

"Thanks! Good luck to you too! See you tomorrow, Meg."

*

Labor screams fill the room as Addison responds to the "One more push!" command from the nurse.

The second her baby enters the world a look of concern flashes across the doctor's face as she grabs the baby and whisks him away.

"Oh my gosh, why isn't he crying?" Addison begins to panic. "Oh my gosh, what's wrong?!"

*

"You look good in your dress blues," Nina attempts to lighten Drew's mood as they drive to the Military Ball.

"Thanks, you look good too," Drew manages a compliment. "You forgot something…"

"What?! What did I forget?"

"Chip clips for your hair," Drew cracks a smile.

Nina hits him on the arm. "Very funny."

"Sgt. Cooper might not recognize you without them."

"Your whole gang will be there, huh?" Nina asks.

"Not everyone, you'll at least know Reiss and Cooper…" Drew lets out a blast of curses. "I forgot about Jasper, and you being there tonight with the guys," he curses again.

"I'm glad you asked me to be your date. I'm sorry about Wyla leaving…"

"I haven't had a drink since her and I moved in together…and she left a note. I came home from running to find a fuckin' note. 'Drew, you haven't changed. I want a divorce.'" Drew's mind steams. "It doesn't matter."

As they pull up to the museum, Drew states his demand one more time. "I'm just here to show up, not to talk."

"We'll leave when you want to leave," Nina adjusts her left high heel and pulls out a blue moon-shaped marshmallow. She holds it up for Drew to see. "How messed up is my world? There is kid cereal in my heel!"

"It would only be messed up if you ate it," Drew grins.

Nina puts it into her mouth and bursts out laughing.

*

Sadie looks at herself in the mirror and takes a deep breath. *Here we go,* she silently coaches herself.

As she walks out of the bedroom, Jake whistles. "You're gorgeous."

"Thanks, babe. I feel like it's my birthday with all the people calling to wish me luck…and now we get to go to the Military Ball! This is so much fun!"

"Who all called?"

"Phoebe, Gigi, Gunner, D, and then I talked with Meg. And your sisters came over this morning to help me with my outfit for tonight. And Reiss called to find out what time I was coming. And now…I'm ready to roll."

"Then let's roll."

Sadie hooks her arm through Jake's as they stroll out the door.

*

White steel wings protrude from the side of the art museum like an eagle about to take flight over Lake Michigan.

Flags line a red carpet entrance.

Sadie imagines walking on Hollywood's red carpet when Jake becomes a top recording artist. She whispers to him, "This is our first red carpet walk. The next time will be when you are famous."

Jake smiles, a sweetness dancing in his eyes.

*

Curses flood Drew's mind as he sees Reiss's melted face across the room.

Nina takes a deep breath. "I'll meet you at our seats. I didn't think this would be so tough without Jasper." Nina waves her hand. "Go, Drew, I'm going to find some champagne."

"Okay," he regrets asking Nina to come.

"Sgt. Manning," Reiss approaches Drew. "Cooper made you come too, huh? Someone from our unit nominated Sadie and Meg. My bet is on you."

Drew avoids his question. "You clean up nice, Reiss."

"Nice blues and everyone's fuckin' staring at my face...might as well have come in my birthday suit...then they'd at least be staring at my..."

"No explanation needed," Drew grins.

Reiss sees Nina. "I heard we're having a moment of silence for Jasper tonight..." he pauses. "I'm uh...pissed off...all the time...because I can't remember what happened."

"Dang, Reiss," Drew shakes his head.

I'm pissed off all the time because I remember what happened, rings through Drew's mind.

Both guys look up to see Sadie and Jake arriving.

"Have you met Sadie yet?" Reiss asks. "I'm heading over to greet her. I'm their escort officer tonight."

"Not yet. I'll catch up with you later," Drew pats Reiss on the shoulder.

Iraq took my brother-in-law's life and Reiss's face, Drew's thoughts frustrate his attempts to appear calm.

CHAPTER 17

Be not afraid of greatness: some are born great, some achieve greatness, and some have greatness thrust upon them.
—William Shakespeare

"Miss Sadie," Reiss approaches Sadie and Jake. "Jake, good to see ya."

"Reiss!" Sadie hugs him.

Jake shakes Reiss's hand. "Good to see you too, Reiss. This is quite the venue."

"Well, I have the honor of escorting you two this evening..."

Sadie beams, "I know! I'm so glad. I'm really nervous so I'm glad to see a familiar face."

"With me, you've got no worries, Sadie. I'll give you a rundown of the night. Now is the social hour, a meet and greet with everyone arriving. I'll introduce you to a few people...so you both can follow me."

Inside the museum, the raised ceiling hosts red and white glass tubes dangling beside blue crystal stars.

A live band rolls out tunes that make it difficult for Sadie to keep her feet from dancing.

Floor to ceiling picture windows reveal a sliver of the moon casting its faint light upon the black lake.

A vanilla and rose fragrance floats through the air.

"It's like a dream," Sadie whispers.

Jake nods. "This is amazing."

Reiss pauses and turns toward them. "Sgt. Cooper is the host tonight. While he finishes his conversation I'll tell you about the formal receiving line. Before dinner, the host, Sgt. Cooper, and other dignitaries form a line. All guests give their title to the aide, and the aide introduces them to the host, who then presents them to the guest of honor. The guest proceeds down the line greeting each dignitary in the line as they enter the dining area. People seated at the head table are part of the receiving line…so that makes you and Jake part of the line."

Sadie puts her hand on Reiss's arm. "And you too?"

Reiss nods. "Yes, ma'am." Reiss looks over at Sgt. Cooper now taking a call. "In the line, people introduce themselves to the official party, shake hands, and move down the line. So if I'm going down the line, it would work something like this: I introduce myself and my pretend wife, who is super hot by the way, to the aide. The aide introduces us to the host. We shake hands, exchange pleasantries, and then he introduces my wife and me to the next person in the receiving line…essentially passing us off to the next dignitary in line until we're done. Rinse and repeat." Reiss looks over again at Sgt. Cooper. "I'll make a quick introduction before he gets pulled away."

Reiss leads them over to Sgt. Cooper. "Sgt. Cooper, this is Sadie Gallagher, and her husband Jake."

"It is a pleasure to finally meet you Mrs. Gallagher. And you as well, Mr. Gallagher."

"You can call me Sadie. And the pleasure is mine."

"Thank you, ma'am. I appreciate all you did for my guys. You were a bright light on many of our days out there." He touches the arm of the woman next to him. "This is my wife, Sophia. Sophia, this is our Guest of Honor, Sadie Gallagher."

"Sadie, darlin', thank you so much," Sophia's southern accent engulfs each word. "We just can't thank you enough for caring for our soldiers when they are away from home."

"It's my pleasure, ma'am," Sadie smiles. "Your dress is gorgeous."

"Thanks, darlin', I think the jaws of most of the men here dropped to the floor when you walked in tonight…" Sophia turns toward Jake. "You have a real sweetheart here, Jake."

"Thanks, ma'am. I agree."

Sgt. Cooper leans in to tell Reiss something, then frowns. "I apologize, I have to cut our greeting short. It was nice to meet you both and I look forward to talking with you more at dinner."

Sadie hooks her arm through Jake's. "It was a pleasure to meet you both as well."

Jake nods. "It was nice to meet you both."

As Sgt. Cooper and his wife leave, Reiss points the opposite direction. "Oh, I'll introduce you to Sgt. Manning and his sister, Nina, before dinner." Reiss whispers to Sadie and Jake, "Nina, is also the wife of Jasper...he was killed in action overseas."

"It has to be tough for her to be here..." Sadie's words drip with compassion.

Reiss quietly says, "Nina wasn't going to come but Drew's wife left him this morning, so Nina came with him...but you didn't hear that from me."

Jake shakes his head. "Some rough things to happen to one family."

"Roger that, Jake."

Drew sees them coming and greets Sadie with a hug. "It's nice to finally meet you, ma'am."

"You can call me Sadie. It's nice to finally deliver an actual hug instead of all my paper ones," Sadie laughs. "This is my husband, Jake."

"Jake, it's nice to meet you. I'm Sgt. Drew Manning," Drew shakes Jake's hand.

"Nice to meet you," Jake grins. "Thanks for your service."

Drew nods. "You bet. This is my sister, Nina."

Sadie gives her a hug. "Nina, you look beautiful."

Nina blushes. "Oh, I guess I'm not too much of a mess tonight," she laughs nervously.

As Reiss, Drew, and Jake talk, Nina pulls Sadie aside. "Thank you for sending them care packages when they were in Iraq. I didn't know Drew wasn't getting care packages from his wife and I wanted to send some over but with my two-year old and just life, I'd forget..." she sighs. "I really appreciate you thinking of them all."

"Of course," Sadie nods. "Thank you. We appreciate the families of troops as well...and know that you too make sacrifices with having your loved ones serve," she pauses. "And I'm sorry for your loss, Nina. I'm impressed and inspired that you are here tonight."

Tears form in Nina's eyes. "Oh gosh," she wipes her eyes quickly. "When Jasper was overseas, I missed him being next to me...I missed him every second, but I knew that it wouldn't be forever so I tried to be strong so that he could stay focused. Now," she sighs. "I just miss him. And it's that forever part that messes with me...but I've got my son and Drew...so Jasper didn't leave me alone." She takes a deep breath. "But let's talk about something else," she laughs anxiously.

Sadie whispers, "Have you ever been in a formal receiving line before?"

Nina waves her hand, "Oh, you'll do fine. Okay, repeat after me..." a huge smile spans her face. "Good evening!"

Sadie laughs and repeats, "Good evening!"

Nina nods. "One more." She smiles again, "Thank you."

Sadie repeats, "Thank you."

Nina laughs. "You got it. That's pretty much it."

Sadie grins. "I feel so much better!"

Reiss puts his hand on Sadie's shoulder. "Ladies...we have to make our way to the receiving line."

As they walk toward the dining area, Reiss looks at Sadie. "I'll be right next to you so you'll be fine. It's actually pretty fun."

"Thanks," Sadie nods, squeezing Jake's hand.

Jake whispers to Sadie, "Let's enjoy this, love. It's not everyday you're the guest of honor at the Military Ball."

*

Drew walks into the fresh evening air and lets out a deep breath.

"It was a nice dinner," Nina says, hooking her arm through Drew's as they walk toward the car.

"Yeah."

"And the tribute to Jasper…was nice. Really nice. Drew, I miss him. I really miss him. But I had to get out of there, before I turned into a mess. I'm sorry…for having to leave before the award ceremony and dance."

"Don't be, I was ready to go," Drew unlocks the passenger car door.

"I remember why I don't wear heels very often," Nina removes her high heels before getting into the car.

Drew walks to the driver's side and stares at the star studded sky before opening his door, trying to contain his emotions.

*

Reiss leans in toward Sadie and Jake. "I've got to catch my plane for Germany but I'll stay long enough to see you get your award."

"And my speech?" Sadie asks.

"And I'll stay for your speech," Reiss nods. "But you won't see me after. So I'll just tell you now how great you did. Sadie, you did great!"

Sadie laughs. "Thanks, Reiss!"

"Is this the speed vacation in Germany?" Jake asks.

"It is. A month of driving way too fast," Reiss grins. "I can't wait."

Sgt. Cooper walks to the front of the room and begins telling the attendees about the meaning of the Hometown Hero Award.

Reiss whispers, "Okay, I'll be in the back listening. Then I'm out. You kids enjoy the night."

"Thanks for being our escort, Reiss!" Sadie says.

Jake adds, "Give me a call when you get back in the States so you can come and check out Candy."

Reiss nods. "Will do."

Sgt. Cooper announces, "And now, ladies and gentleman, I'd like to introduce our Hometown Hero…Sadie Gallagher."

Sadie smiles as she walks on stage to a standing ovation, sensational energy streaming through the room.

Sadie graciously accepts the plaque from Sgt. Cooper.

Jake makes their heart signal with his hands.

Sadie grins, biting the edge of her lip. "I'm nervous...so if any words come out...that will be a success...and an even bigger success if they make sense."

Faint laughter lightens the air as the attendees sit down.

Sadie takes a deep breath. "Meg Marx and I accept this Hometown Heroes Award on behalf of our military men and women who have served and continue to serve our country. We do not undergo traumatic combat experiences that haunt our minds for life. We do not endure combat training that will forever affect our instincts. And we do not leave our families behind to preserve and protect freedom. We just send care packages.

"We do, however, have conversations with our warriors and find them to be some of the most incredible people around. And when the physical war is over, and they return home, many continue to fight a mental war.

"My question for the past few months has been, 'How can I help them when they come home?' After talking with a gal whose father, a veteran, committed suicide...I began a project called *Inspiration Behind the Warrior* with Gunner, a former marine. PTSD, what we've renamed Warrior Readjustment, or WARE, is a thief...but can become a murderer if veterans do not seek help.

"For those of you who are not veterans, step into their shoes for a moment. Fear and instinct have kept you alive, but now you're home. Your weapon is not by your side, yet the threats are still vivid in your mind. Only your fellow brothers and sisters in arms know where you were and the conditions you survived. But that's the thing—you survived. You came home. You still have a purpose or you would not have made it back. You're one of the lucky ones.

"We encourage our warriors to seek a path out of their darkness. We encourage them to share not what knocks them down, but what makes them get back up again.

"*Inspiration Behind the Warrior* is about spreading the awareness of WARE, and spreading the message that hope exists and healing is possible. This is how we plan to help more of *our* Hometown Heroes.

We hope you join us in the fight for peace...of mind. Thank you." Sadie smiles as she sees Reiss wave in the back of the room before he leaves.

With the crowd on their feet, Sadie's heart is ecstatic. "Thank you so much!" she walks back to her table, unable to fully grasp the appreciation directed toward her.

Jake hugs her. "Amazing, love!"

Sadie whispers, "Thanks. I'll be right back, babe."

Sadie passes a few new friends, thanking them with her eyes. The crowd of dress blues reminds her of her brother.

Sadie heads out the balcony doors to take in a moment of fresh air. A slight breeze drifts from the lake. She looks up at the stars as the band starts playing. *Time to dance!* she mentally celebrates.

Pain explodes in her head.

Sadie stumbles several feet to lean against one of the artistic beams on the balcony.

Her body collapses.

*

Addison curls up in bed, her pillow soaked with tears, her swollen eyes mere slits.

The doctor didn't even have to say anything; Addison knew by the look on her face.

A nurse attempted to comfort her with the words, "Sometimes that happens."

'*That*?' Addison's heart breaks. *My baby, my world, is gone.*

*

"You sure you don't want to stay the night here, Drew?" Nina asks for the fifth time before getting out of the car.

"Nah, I'm going to stay at my place for a while."

Nina analyzes him with her eyes.

"I've been fine at my place for the past few months, Nina."

"It's different tonight though, with the memorial thing at the Ball...I'm just worried about you, Drew."

"Don't." Drew's phone rings, phone number unknown.

"I'll talk to you tomorrow, Drew," Nina exits the car and closes the door. "Okay?"

Drew waves goodbye. "Sgt. Manning," he answers the call.

"Drew, it's Wyla. I'm using Steve's phone…I just…"

Drew hangs up. *Wyla doesn't get to 'just' anything anymore.* His phone rings four more times. *Asshole Steve's number.*

Drew unlocks his front door, tosses his phone onto the couch, and crumbles to the floor; moans of mental agony unite with tears from the guilt which plagues his memories.

*

Electric energy flows through the ballroom. Jake shakes hands with those around him, them thanking him and him thanking them. He looks down at his shirt and sees Sadie's signature in permanent marker.

"Jake?"

"Hey, Sgt. Cooper."

"I bet you're proud of your wife. That was quite a speech."

"It was, sir. And Sadie doesn't like giving speeches…"

"Well, she did a fine job, Jake."

A brief trumpet solo announces the first dance, 16 other orchestra members joining in song with their instruments.

"I'll tell her you said so, Sgt. Cooper," Jake nods. "I'm going to find her so we can catch the first dance."

"Sounds like a plan. I think I'll find my wife as well."

Jake checks the ballroom, halls, and restroom.

Something is wrong, eeriness creeps into his mind. Jake looks through the glass balcony doors toward the lake. He starts to walk away but then stops and turns back.

Damp night air rolls off the lake as Jake opens the balcony doors. *Something is terribly wrong,* terror seizes his heart.

Jake walks toward the large art beam and sees Sadie's motionless body. "Sade? O God! Please! No! Sadie!"

He cradles her in his arms and weeps.

CHAPTER 18

*Between stimulus and response lies a space. In that space is the power
to choose our response. In our response lies our
growth and our freedom.*
—Viktor Frankl

One week later...

Jake sits on the couch and stares at the wall—an activity that now
takes up most of his days.

"Hey," D knocks and walks inside with a stack of homemade
dinners and desserts. "Everyone's concerned. You didn't talk to
anyone at the funeral. Everyone wants to know how you're doing."

Jake shrugs. "I'm..."

Water fills the kitchen sink; dishes clank as they are washed, dried,
and put away. "I'm sorry, Jake. I'm really sorry. Okay, I'll see you
later," D quietly closes the door.

Silence surrounds Jake. "I'm...empty."

*

Drew hits the ignore button on his phone when he sees Wyla's
name. "Here we go again," he says to the ringing phone. "Five times
every day...that must be the cheating champion's number."

As his phone rings, he ignores the call again. "Wyla, thanks for
calling, can you read my message?" he holds up the *Fuck The World*
sign he made just for her.

"You inspired the creation of this sign, Wyla...you helpful whore.
And thanks to you, I've done some thinking. I no longer care what my
parents think...I'm a damn good soldier, whether they approve or not.

And I no longer care about you," he puts his again ringing phone on the special sign and leaves.

*

Carter wanders in the daylight to where Theo used to sit. "Theo?" he walks closer.

A stern voice, "Who askin'?"

"Sorry, mister, I was just looking for Theo."

"Got a dolla'? I'll tell ya where he is fa a dolla'."

A chocolate woman wearing four worn shirts, all too big for her small frame, hurries over to Carter and pulls him away from the man in Theo's spot. "Don't ya listen to him, sonny. Theo's gone. He dead."

"Okay."

"It's good. He wasn't doin' good. How ya know Theo?"

"He was my friend. He was my best friend."

"He was a good man, a real good man. He gave away all his money…gave away everything he had. Ya know that? Always was givin'. Ya all alone, sonny?"

"No." Theo told Carter many times the answer to this question is always no, no matter who asks.

"Well, ya better get movin' then back to where ya came from. Ol' grouchy der in the corner isn't fond of strangers." She whispers, smiling enough for Carter to see her brown and yellow stained teeth, "Specially little white ones."

Carter wanders the streets, careful to avoid police cars. Momma told all the kids this morning they were not to bring police or social workers around. Carter doesn't want to find out what the punishment is for doing such a thing.

*

Meg walks in the back door. "Shitalsha," she sighs.

Jake stares at her expressionless.

"Means hello in Juchitan, Mexico." Meg looks across the room. "She never opened it?"

Jake sees the painting she had given to Sadie.

115

Meg grabs a stack of care package boxes and custom forms from the guest room. Walking through the kitchen, she pauses. "I don't understand it, Jake. I'm still shocked."

Jake puts his head back on the couch.

Meg opens the door to leave.

Jake says, "I can't...feel anything."

Meg turns around in the doorway. "Then don't."

"What a waste, right?"

"What?" Meg asks.

"Everything."

"I'm sorry. I'm...so...sorry, Jake," Meg closes the door and carries the care package boxes to her car. The moment she sits in the driver's seat she starts crying.

Jake watches. He can't help her. Her tears are his. Jake walks over and unwraps the painting.

Seven instruments in a pile stare back at him. The piano keys are worn, like they have flirted with many fingers. A guitar rests on top of a few piano keys and musical notes float out of a French horn. On the bottom of the painting are the words, *Instrumental Chaos*.

The second word crushed his world.

He leans the painting against the wall, resumes his place on the couch, and stares at the picture...seeing nothing, feeling nothing.

CHAPTER 19

There is nothing like a dream to create the future.
Utopia today, flesh and blood tomorrow.
–Victor Hugo

Advertisements for the American Rockstar tryouts in Chicago irritate Jake as he pages through the newspaper. "Two months ago my answer was yes," he tosses the paper into the recycling bin and walks out the door.

Jake pulls into the school parking lot.

D holds up a flash drive as Jake gets out of his car. "Songs to choose from for our upcoming performance."

"What performance?" annoyance soaks Jake's words.

D ignores his mood. "She wanted you to tryout for American Rockstar, so I thought you and I would go down to Chicago…"

Jake tunes out the rest. *God bless America! My life is a disaster and you want me to sing!* his mind screams.

Jake grabs the flash drive. "It's not going to happen, D."

"You sure you're ready to teach, Jake? The school board understands if you want to resign or at least take a leave of absence for this last month of school before summer."

"I'm fine, D. At the least it's a distraction from misery."

"Okay. I'll call you later, Jake. Choose a song."

*

Nina looks up at the neon sign buzzing as she walks through the front door of Sydney's Café.

The aromas of coffee and cinnamon rolls greet her, making her mouth water. "Excuse me," Nina asks the gal behind the glass counter, where deliciously decorated desserts scream to be eaten. "Do you know where I can find Gunner?"

The gal points to the back of the shop. "Last table, near the exit sign."

Gunner looks up. "Nina? How are you, ma'am?"

"The cinnamon rolls are begging to keep my hips company…as if they need more company," Nina laughs nervously and slides onto the wooden chair across from him. "I asked for you and the gal gave me some sad look…like she pitied me or something. Do I look that messed up?"

"Nah, most of the people looking for me need help," Gunner brushes a white spec off the table.

"I need help," Nina leans back in the chair.

*

Jake tosses the flash drive onto the kitchen counter, knocking a piece of paper onto the floor. Sadie's handwriting on the paper stops him.

The phone rings. Jake sees D's name and lets it ring.

The phone rings again. Jake mutes it.

The phone rings again.

"Look D," Jake fumes, about to say something he'll regret.

"Jake, it's not about forgetting her, bro. It's about remembering her and going after a dream she put on your plate."

Jake rests his head in the palm of his hand.

"Just choose a song, Jake."

Jake hangs up without commenting.

*

Meg glares at her sixth painting. "What's wrong with it, Ruger? Something's missing."

Ruger opens his eyes and stretches, then curls back to sleep.

In the painted scene, rain pours upon a city. Shops frame a wide cobblestone road. Two trees, black sticks for trunks, embrace bouquets of yellow leaves, the space between the leaves exposing a sliver of silver sky. The slick street mirrors the city folk passing through with umbrellas in hand. Puddles befriend empty park benches.

Meg streaks white paint in the middle of the scene, starting where the tree trunks begin and continuing down the middle of the street to the edge of the canvas. In the foreground, a dignified man carries a magenta umbrella making his way up the street. In the middle of the splash of white, Meg paints a free soul: a girl with her arms outstretched, dancing with each raindrop.

"Now," Meg steps back to admire her work. "You fit your name, *Something to Say*."

*

Jake freezes when he sees Sadie's picture on the wall inside the On Purpose Journey office. Funds donated in Sadie's memory purchased the office building where she and Meg used to put together care packages.

Someone passes Jake in the hall with a greeting he misses.

He rips open cardboard boxes filled with donations and sorts the items, placing them into different colored bins so Meg can later pack them into care packages.

*

"Well, you're happy," grocery bags hang from Nina's arms as she walks inside.

"I guess so..." Drew tosses Edison a plush soccer ball.

"That's good, Drew. Oh, you'll never believe this..." Nina clips her hair back using chip clips. "I met with Gunner today. He's the guy I wanted you to talk with, but you didn't show up..."

"I forgot, Nina. I told you that."

"He's a solid guy...has this need for everything to be all straight and tidy which is a little messed up..."

"Why did *you* meet with him?" Drew interrogates. "Never mind, it doesn't..."

"So…" Nina cuts off Drew. "Gunner said that girl with the speech at the Military Ball…my brain is such a mess…can't remember her name…you know who I'm talking about."

"Sadie?"

"Yes! Sadie. She was such a sweet girl."

"What about her, Nina?"

"She died…there…that night! Her husband found her dead! Gunner told me…I was shocked, just shocked. She was so young!"

Drew leaves the room and grabs his running shoes.

"Isn't that awful? She was such a good speaker too…really sounded like she was going to make a difference…"

Drew closes the front door, popping silver buds into his ears and blasting music. He has intensely focused on patching his beaten mind, body, and soul, and in one second, his carefully stitched mental bandage rips off.

*

Expecting to see Sadie when he rounds a corner in their house, then remembering she's gone, sparks a special type of anger in Jake's world.

Jake grab D's flash drive and sees Sadie's note on the floor. He takes the note to her nightstand and opens the drawer.

Her leather journal stares at him.

"What a waste," he puts the piece of paper into the leather book. His name written in her handwriting catches his attention.

Song for Jake to become the next American Rockstar.

Phrases, words crossed out, and scribbles mark the page with song lyrics at the bottom.

"You wrote a song for me?" Jake turns to the first page in her journal and reads the entry.

Met Bill today at the Post Office. He did not receive much support overseas or when he came home. He could have complained or carried a lifetime of bitterness—but he chose to be thankful.

I'm trying to monitor my thoughts and change the way I look at things. Here is Bill, thanking me for the receiver of the care packages, and I am wondering "is it all worth my time"...I'm so selfish. Guess that just means I can learn from those around me. I won't say everyone, but the majority can teach me something if I am willing to listen. In every situation, EVERY situation, there is a thank you and there is a complaint. I get to choose which one I want to focus on. Complaints are always available and will wear me out. Thank you's are always available and will rock my world...so I'm going to shoot for the thank you.

"You took the wrong person, God." Jake lies on the bed and stares at the ceiling, dwelling in newfound misery.

*

Drew opens the brown bag containing his favorite Friday night Chinese dinner, Mongolian Beef with extra pea pods. His phone buzzes and beeps with a new voicemail.

Drew, it's your father. Your mother and I hope you are done...after, well, what happened to Nina's husband Ricardo."

Drew shakes his head. "Jasper would be pissed if he knew you used his first name."

Drew's father rolls out more foolish words.

I heard good news from the dean of the college today. He has agreed to let you back in and apply the credits from your past schooling. Son, we have doctors spanning back to your great-great-great-grandfather. It would be disappointing to say the least if you continue with this Army nonsense and end the family tradition...

Drew deletes the message and opens the kitchen drawer. Pulling out his *Fuck The World* sign, he places his phone by the sign. "More nonsense for you, father."

A full bottle of Jack stares at him. Drew curses at the thought of his Chinese dinner getting cold because of his father's idiotic anger-inducing message. Grabbing his shoes, Drew storms out for a steam-releasing run.

CHAPTER 20

Sometimes we become attached to things in this world
because they are meant to carry us to where we are supposed to be.
–Mollie Voigt

Traffic is heavy for a Sunday afternoon; the car ahead of Jake moves much slower than it should, aggravating his already tripped-out nerves.

In the bookstore parking lot, a father, mother, and child walk to the bagel shop; the child giggles as the parents swing him, his arms in their hands.

"It will only be ten minutes," Jake coaches himself in the car. "I can handle ten minutes in public."

He locks the door and heads inside the bookstore. Within minutes, he finds the journal that matches Sadie's. "Perfect!"

Customers crowd the checkout counter.

A petite blond laments, "I like the pink gift bag but the red is so…red…and pretty!"

Jake mumbles, "Just choose a stupid bag!"

A thin man with a face that has been severely neglected by a shaver holds a young child, the boy asking multiple questions, all beginning with the word "Why?"

The father commands, "No more questions! After this, we go home. Then you can ask your mother questions all day long!"

Jake shakes his head in disgust. He purchases his journal and walks out the door, searching his pocket for the keys.

He stares through the window at the keys on his front car seat. "You've got to be kidding me!" He kicks his tire and pounds his fist on the car window. "God…bless America!"

An older gal pokes her head around the corner of his car. "Oh, I've seen that look before," her shrill voice familiar to Jake. "Did you lock your keys in your car, son?"

Jake turns around.

"Oh for heavens sake, I didn't recognize you at first."

"Hey, Gigi."

"Well, it's your lucky day. My Bill is a locksmith. He'll have his kit in the car, so he can help you when he gets here."

"Great," Jake mumbles, unable to muster up any enthusiasm.

"Every Sunday I come to look around at the shops. Then Bill and I sit in the park for a while. We don't have too many Sunday's left...but let's go to the bench and sit down. These old feet wear out."

"Why don't you have many Sundays left?" Jake asks.

"Bill has cancer. Well, you knew that. The new treatment didn't work...golly, we were hoping it would. Each day is precious, dear. We may not see another one but that's no reason to cloud this one," she plunks down on the bench with a sigh.

"You look like you need some sunshine in your day, honey...hope you don't mind me saying. Bill says that I tend to say too much, but when you get old, you are allowed to say what you are thinking. Being old gives you the right to be forthright," Gigi laughs. "Enough about me, dear. Tell me what you are doing here on this fine day in town."

Jake's heart breaks. "Sadie...died."

"Oh, dear."

"So...existing is a challenge."

"Oh, dear. When did she pass away?"

"After her speech at the Military Ball."

"After she told the world her message."

Silence fills a few moments.

Gigi looks at Jake. "I'm going to tell you something that you may carry with you until you're ready for it, dear." Gigi puts her wrinkled hand on his. "Sometimes we become attached to things in this world because they are meant to carry us to where we are supposed to be. We can mourn the loss of those who have left us...or we can focus on the gift that such a special person shared moments in our life. You are being led to a place you never could have gone without Sadie."

A car pulls up next to the bench. Bill hobbles out with a cane. He tips his hat and says to Gigi with a great big smile, "Are you ready my darling? Your carriage awaits."

Gigi points to Jake. "Bill, you remember Sadie's husband, Jake."

"I sure do. How is…"

"Bill, my dear," Gigi interrupts. "Jake here locked his keys in his car so I told him you would help him."

Bill parks and begins to work on opening Jake's car door. After a few minutes, he reappears with Jake's keys. "I believe these will help you in getting home, son."

"Thanks," Jake nods.

Gigi writes something on a slip of paper and hands it to Jake. "Friends should stay in touch." She smiles and gets into the car with the assistance of Bill.

Jake shakes Bill's hand. "Gigi's quite the gal."

Bill beams, "She's my lucky star. Every moment with her is the best moment of my life."

As they drive off, Jake looks at the piece of paper Gigi gave him. Her name and number are on it, along with the phrase, *Catch me on Sundays at the park bench*, all in perfect cursive.

Back in his car, Jake opens his journal and writes.

Entry #1: My love, the journey begins.

*

Addison rolls white paint over blue stars and yellow moons. "I was ready for you," she whimpers. "I would have been a good mom." Erasing the nursery walls is one more check off her list of forgetting.

*

Carter crawls into his secure hideout—the bushes near the bench in the park.

His face burns and tingles all over. Momma's hits have been getting harder.

He grabs a leaf and eats it, spreading some of the chewed leaf over his cracked lips.

"I'll sleep here with you," he whispers to the bushes.

*

Jake picks up the box of cinnamon rolls on his porch step and walks inside. Sydney has dropped off cinnamon rolls every week since Sadie died...Jake doesn't know why. He puts the rolls on the counter and checks his two missed phone messages.

Message 1: *Hi honey, it's mom. Something is wrong with my computer so I'm hoping you can stop by after work...and maybe stay for dinner? Give me a call. Love you.*

Jake deletes the message. "Sorry, mom."

Message 2: *Jake! You haven't been to mom's place since Sadie...and it's not okay. You don't get to abandon the family. D has been stepping up to help mom...which is pitiful, Jake!*

"Thanks, Grace." Jake says aloud. "Have mom call D for help with her computer. There, counselor. Problem solved."

Jake walks to the bedroom and writes in his journal. *Entry #2: As far as thank you's go...I'm coming up empty, love.*

Setting his journal aside, he opens Sadie's journal.

Learning these concepts rocks my mental world. I am titling my notes...Journey with the Secret. After all, it is a secret to most people that they can achieve anything they want to achieve in life. The most successful men in history understood this message...and here I am, many years later, learning it. Maybe, just maybe, I can teach this secret to others. A whole new passion is starting to build inside me as I think about the future. I can feel my big leaves growing.

Tossing both books aside, Jake rubs his eyes. "This is depressing."

CHAPTER 21

We should not be merely an influence, we should be an inspiration. By our very presence we should be a tower of strength to the hungering human souls around us.
—William George Jordan

J ake places carnations by Sadie's grave. "I'd prefer to bring roses, love, but the petals quickly turn brown...and wilted flowers are a gloomy way to start our visit."

He lies down next to her gravestone and stares at the sky. *Note to self,* Jake thinks, *don't tell anyone I slept next to my wife this morning...they'll haul me off to the looney bin.*

After an hour, Jake walks back toward his car, seeing someone at the edge of the cemetery. As he gets closer he says, "Gunner?"

"Hey, Jake." He motions to his leg. "My first prosthetic."

"How's that going?"

"It's a process."

"Why the cemetery?" Jake asks.

Gunner hesitates. "My audience can't comment."

"Got it," Jake sighs.

"You haven't returned my calls."

"Sorry about that, Gunner."

"We were all shocked, Jake. I still have a hard time believing it. How are you holding up?"

"Fine, I guess. Is it hard...to learn to walk?"

"It's an adjustment...takes energy and effort and commitment. I was putting this off...uh, for a lot of reasons, but Sadie asked why others had prosthetics and I didn't. She was all ready to fight for me, like I was being mistreated or something," Gunner grins. "She knew just how to push people, didn't she? Not too forceful, but not too light where you didn't get the point."

"Agreed."

"It's a daily battle, Jake…trying to understand why certain things happen…trying to get over what was taken."

"What a waste, huh?"

"What's that?" Gunner asks.

"Her project…her passion."

"You don't know?"

"Know what?"

"Organizations across the country ask me to come and speak about *Inspiration Behind the Warrior*. I'm booked for speeches and meetings with support groups. And Meg and I are working on an international aspect of warrior support. What Sadie did that night was monumental. Her message didn't die with her…her message changed everything. As Meg puts it, 'It created a beautiful kind of chaos.' The way I see it is Sadie lit the fire, Jake…and we're here to carry the torches."

Jake tries to process Gunner's words.

"You should come by the café, Jake. In fact, you won't believe who is coming to our meeting today."

"Who?"

"Reiss. You remember Reiss?"

Jake nods.

"Reiss called me because Sadie was not returning his calls. I told him what happened. I don't know how long he'll stay at the meeting, but you should come."

"I'll think about it. Later, Gunner."

"Take it easy, Jake."

*

Carter wads up his flannel shirt and scrunches it into a yellow plastic bag.

Momma now works four hours on Sunday and four hours on Wednesday, which gives Carter time to go home, clean up, and take what he needs for the next few days in the park.

If he leaves before she gets home, he avoids her anger…but sometimes she tricks him and comes home early…stumbling and saying bad words. When this happens, Carter has a bad day…because Momma hates working…and she hates him.

Carter's heart drops as he hears her car pull into the driveway. She's early.

*

The bookstore parking lot bustles with eager shoppers.

Jake parks and grabs his keys before locking the door. "One time is enough."

Sitting down on the bench where he first met Gigi, Jake contemplates his miserable existence.

A high-pitched voice behind him squeaks, "How's my favorite Sunday friend?"

"Hey, Gigi," Jake slides over on the bench. "How are you?"

Gigi wearily sits down. "Oh, golly. My Bill is getting worse. I thought I'd be ready…guess our hearts are never ready to lose the good ones. Enough about me; tell me about you."

"People annoy me. Things annoy me. Life annoys me. But it's time, right? In time this all…goes away? Gets easier?"

"In time it can be sweeter, dear, recalling the memories."

A little girl struts past them gripping an ice cream cone with both hands, her mother one step behind.

Gigi continues. "Most people never grow out of their sadness to see the passion and purpose that awaits them. Sadie stayed with you until you were ready for this next phase of your life, dear."

Bill pulls up to the bench and parks.

Jake motions for Bill to stay in the car. "I'll help her today."

Gigi whispers, "Thank you, Jake."

"You bet, Gigi. I'll see you next Sunday."

"That sounds good, dear. See you Sunday."

*

Gunner closes his book and looks at his watch. Drew is forty-seven minutes late. Nina setup their first meeting for a second time...and for a second time, Drew didn't show up.

Gunner brings up Nina's number on his phone, then hangs up. He understands why Drew isn't showing up. He doesn't appreciate it, but he understands it.

*

Sadie's rainbow of pens stare at Jake from the bedside drawer as he grabs her journal and reads.

Is there beauty in death? Someone I sent cards to for years, died five months ago. What was I doing when she died? Was I busy making a difference? Or was I doing something meaningless, or worse, complaining about something insignificant? I have the choice each day to do something amazing...so what will I do when I wake up? At the end of each day, will I wish for more time or will I be satisfied with my contribution to the world? Will God be proud to call me His own or will He wish I took my days here more seriously? The complaint could be that I did not know about Gail dying five months ago. The thank you could be that she changed my world five months after she died. Gail may be gone, but I'm still here...because I still have a purpose.

Jake's chest tightens. "There is no beauty in your death, love," he sighs.

Jake writes in his journal. *Entry #3: I have the choice each day to do something amazing...I'll try.*

*

Ducks fight amongst each other in the cemetery pond.

Drew sits at the edge of the pond, flask in hand, and wonders if the dead are annoyed by nature's constant bickering.

A week ago Drew came to visit Jasper's grave and found the duck pond...where the ducks always seem pissed off about something...an oddly relaxing show.

129

After four months without Jack, Jack tastes good…even watered down Jack. "Talk, talk, talk. Everyone wants me to talk. Talking helps, Drew," Drew mimics in disgust.

A duck squawks and chases another duck across the pond. "You tell 'em buddy. Where's the respect, right?!" Drew talks to nature. "New rule!" Drew announces. "The day that meetings reverse shit that happened in the past, I'll gladly attend one."

*

Jake reluctantly walks into the café.

Sydney strolls over and shakes his hand. "Halo, Jake."

"Hey. Thanks for all the cinnamon rolls. Why…?"

"Sadie sent me Encourage Cards after my stroke…got me through some very rotten days. Encouragement was her department. Cinnamon rolls are mine," Sydney winks.

"Well, thanks. I've enjoyed every one."

"My pleasure, Jake."

Gunner waves Jake over to their table.

Reiss stands and shakes Jake's hand. "I'm sorry, man."

"Me too," Jake nods.

"Sadie's the reason I'm here, man."

"That's good," Jake's attempt to care fails. Memories of the last time he was here with Sadie flash through his mind. He keeps looking for her even though he knows she is not here.

Meg whispers as Jake sits next to her, "We all went through that when we first came back here."

Gunner begins explaining what *Inspiration Behind the Warrior* has become in the last few months.

Jake tunes out the conversation, noticing the glances and sad looks cast toward their table. Jake mentally smirks at the thought of their table…a 28-year-old widower, a soldier with half of his face melted off, and a marine who lost both legs. Meg is the only normal one at the table…a term she rarely rolls with.

Reiss nervously analyzes each person in the café.

Gunner turns toward Reiss. "You wanted to tell your story."

Reiss nods, clearly distracted by the stares.

Jake says, "Those stares are for me, Reiss."

"Bullshit," Reiss denies.

For Jake, reminders of Sadie are everywhere, and hanging around people who are "carrying the torches" makes him feel like hanging a rope around his neck.

Jake is about to leave when Reiss says, "I, uh, I can't do this." Reiss grabs his coat and leaves.

Meg asks Gunner, "Do we go after him?"

"Nah, he made it twice as long as last time. That's good."

Gunner is about to ask Jake something when Jake says, "I'm sorry, guys. I have to go too."

Meg says, "Go? Already?"

"Yeah, I'll see you later," Jake stands to leave.

Meg shoots Gunner a look of concern, but Jake doesn't have the energy or desire to share any more of his broken world.

Outside, Jake takes a breath of fresh air. As he walks down the sidewalk, he sees Reiss sitting in his car and swearing...loudly swearing. "You've got to be kidding me!" Jake mumbles, just wanting to go home.

Jake knocks on the passenger car window.

Reiss jumps at the noise before unlocking the door, his facial expression a blend of anger and frustration.

Jake opens the door and sits in the passenger seat.

"You need a ride home or somethin'?" Reiss inquires with obvious annoyance.

"No."

Reiss stares at Jake, then looks ahead. "The guy across the street has been sitting on that bench since I got into my car. He watched me get in. I think he did something to my car."

"Then we'll wait for him to leave," Jake reclines his seat.

"He's looked over at me a few times, man. It's suspicious."

Jake closes his eyes. "He'll have to leave sooner or later."

"Some bastard sits on a park bench and I can't drive away. I should go over there and..." curses freely fly.

"Reiss...why don't you just tell me the story you were going to tell inside the café?"

"Why?" Reiss asks.

"You're sitting here waiting for crazy terrorist bus guy to leave and I'm here with you. What else are we going to do?"

Silence.

Jake imagines Sadie furiously glaring from heaven at his lack of compassion. He slightly opens his eyes, wanting to see Reiss's response to his dire attempt at starting a conversation. "So...I hear it smells like shit over there."

Reiss's mouth curls. "Shit? Nah. Burning shit? Right on."

"So...you were a medic?" Jake asks.

Reiss sighs and looks out the window. "I saw so many dead and mangled bodies, man. I was sick to my stomach most days."

Reiss rubs the piece of metal hanging from his necklace as he stares ahead. "The people...smelled worse than the air. Go workout, sweat like crazy, take a dump in your pants, and lay around for three or four days...that is what ninety percent of those people smelled like...our homeless people are cleaner."

Jake shakes his head. "I don't know how you all do it."

"It was lonely, more often than not. In the end, you have the person next to you...that's it." Reiss's tone changes. "It's just nice when you get home...you feel like kissing the ground."

"I bet."

Reiss shifts positions, talking as if Jake isn't there. "I missed being in America, driving where I want to, drinking my favorite soda, and running outside where there aren't rocket attacks. But the deployment opened my eyes to how fortunate I have been in my life. Sometimes I wish all I'd have are the gun club mental movies—something people can't stare at. Other days, I wish the physical pain was all I had to deal with, because my face does not haunt me all day long. I still don't remember what happened that day...I just remember the rest of the shit I don't really care to remember."

"Are you done with surgeries?" Jake asks.

Reiss shakes his head. "Docs are still working on putting my face back together...and my brain is still looking for bombs and terrorists."

"So other than that…you're pretty much normal," Jake jokes.

Reiss laughs.

Terrorist guy boards the bus across the street. Jake and Reiss watch as the bus rolls away.

Jake brings his seat to its original position. "See you later, Reiss." Jake opens the door.

Reiss is about to say something when Jake holds up his hand. "It's all good. You just do what you gotta do, man. And we try to get by the best we can."

"See ya, Jake."

"Later, Reiss," Jake shuts the door.

*

At home, Jake pulls out Sadie's journal.

This is the beginning of the rest of my life as I start to write Journey with the Secret. I do not know the how of how it will all work out…I just know it will work out.

I want to make the most of my journey. It's no longer about being afraid that I might die. My focus now is making a difference and living my true purpose. No more fear; only love. I'm convinced that in the end, everything works out.

Jake rubs his eyes. "I'm not." Pulling out his journal, he adds an entry. *Entry #4: Make the most of my journey.*

CHAPTER 22

He who has a Why to live for can bear almost any How.
–Friedrich Nietzsche

Jake stares at the rain as he finishes the last drop of his morning fuel. Going anywhere now, especially to work, takes a dose of mental coaching and caffeine.

A flash of red pulls into his driveway. A tall, thin, blond woman runs to his porch carrying a brown cardboard box.

Jake opens the door as she is about to knock.

"Hi! Bye! Thanks!" she hands him the box. In a flash, she speeds away in her sporty little car.

Jake peels a damp white envelope off the top of the box. The scratchy handwriting reads, *He is exactly what you described! Healthy. Good companion. Already housebroken. Shot records and food are in the bag. Thank you for loving him! -Izzy*

As Jake reaches to open the box, a tiny head pops out. "You've got to be kidding me!" Jake picks up the tiny bundle of bones. "What am I supposed to do with a puppy?"

The solid black dog wags his short tail of curls.

Jake grabs a backpack and places the puppy inside along with the items from his box: food, a blue leash and collar, and a baby blue blanket.

Before going to the school, Jake makes a quick stop at the park to avoid any "puppy accidents" at school.

"Here we go," Jake says as they head into the school office.

The secretary eyes Jake's purple backpack. "Morning, Jake."

Jake offers a brief, "Good morning."

Jake closes his office door and breathes a sigh of relief. Next to his desk, he sets an empty paper box and transfers the puppy from the backpack to the box.

After staring at Jake for half an hour, the dog finally curls up in a ball with his blue blanket…giving Jake the peace of mind to leave and check on the puppy in-between classes.

At noon, Jake picks up a sandwich from the corner deli before walking to the park with the loaded backpack.

Sitting on the park bench with the puppy in his lap, Jake runs his finger over the symbol of love carved on the bench. *I lost everything when I lost her,* his mind starts a downward spiral.

A cold nose presses against his chin.

"You're interrupting me feeling sorry for myself," Jake puts the puppy on the ground, dumping brown pebbles of food into a plastic bowl.

After lunch, Jake looks again at the carved heart on the bench. "What about Hart? The heart is the strongest organ, amazing in its capabilities, and unpredictable," he speaks the last word with a bitter edge. "Come here, Hart!"

Hart bounces over and rolls on the ground by Jake's feet.

*

"Meg!" Gunner calls out when Meg walks into the café.

Meg walks over after placing her order. "Do you ever go home, Gunner? You have a bed in the back, don't you?"

Gunner grins. "That's confidential information, Meg."

"Confidential, huh?"

"You're just the gal I wanted to see."

Meg wipes the café seat with a napkin before sitting down. "Code words for you need something."

"You and Sadie sent packages to Drew Manning, right?"

"Roger that, sir."

Gunner narrows his eyes in amusement. "Did you ever meet Drew's sister, Nina?"

"Negative. Never met Drew either. Sadie was the talker. She loved troops and troops loved her. I'm not…a people person."

"Nina, Drew's sister, lost her husband overseas. His name was Ricardo but everyone called him by his last name, Jasper."

"We sent Jasper care packages. He had a mouse trap invention that he was working on…and he always replied back when he received packages…a stellar guy. It was a miserable day when we found out that he was KIA and Reiss was wounded."

"Nina said Jasper and Drew were best friends. She came to me for help…only thing is that I can't help her help Drew…"

"Because only Drew can help Drew," Meg nods. "So, you want me to do what?"

"Nina doesn't have any friends, Meg. None. She takes care of her son and her house and worries about her brother."

"Aren't there support groups for women like her?" Meg asks.

"Yes."

"Gunner, when I say I'm not good with people…I mean I'm not good with people. I find people dull, fickle, inconsistent, irritating, full of false entitlement, and ignorant when it comes to spreading germs. I'm not a fan of humans and I'm not a good source for helping someone who needs support."

"Meg, Nina needs a friend…a female friend. I'll ask her to wash her hands before meeting you."

Meg laughs. "You're stubborn."

"You bet," Gunner turns the salt shaker so the label is facing toward them.

"Things don't work out well for me, Gunner…the universe tends to flip me the cosmic bird."

"I'm aware of the bird," Gunner points to his wheels.

"Fine," Meg sighs. "But I don't candy coat, I don't shop, I don't do makeup, and I don't talk girly talk."

"Here's her number," Gunner writes down Nina's information. "Thanks, Meg."

"No promises," Meg stands to leave. "Adios, Gunner."

*

136

Jake's phone rings as he walks in the front door with Hart.

"Hi honey, how are you?" concern evident in Phoebe's voice.

"I'm fine, mom," Jake bends down and unhooks Hart's leash.

"Your sisters are coming over for dinner on Friday…if you want to come."

"Maybe next time."

"Okay, honey. If you change your mind, just come over."

"I'm sorry, mom."

"Jake, you just come when you're ready."

"Thanks," a wave of gloom begins to tip Jake's mood as he hangs up.

A little black face stares up at him.

"Just so you know, I feel as confused as you look."

Hart tips his head and wags his tail.

"Well, okay, then."

*

Meg looks out the spy hole on her door. "D?"

"Hey, sista!"

"You never come here," Meg opens the door.

"You weren't answering your phone."

"It dropped into a puddle yesterday and is now caput. I need a new one. Why were you phoning me?"

"Can I come in?"

"Fine," Meg playfully rolls her eyes. She narrows her eyes. "Let me guess…something with Jake."

"He's been ignoring my calls and I know he didn't drop his phone into a puddle. He doesn't go over to his mom's place to help her out. Grace has been calling me to help Phoebe with stuff…not that I mind, but Jake is here, and it's not like he's busy. Even at school…he's…" D plops down on Meg's couch.

"He's only been teaching for a week, D…and Sadie's only been gone for two months. Can I get you anything? Water, a cheese sandwich…"

"Nah." D's eyebrows scrunch together as he looks at the paintings. "Dang, girl, who painted these walls?"

"Yours truly."

D stands. "Right on, sista! Is this a particular location?" he points to the living room wall.

"Colorado. I painted the scene from a picture my grandpa gave me. He called Colorado 'God's best work.'"

"And the hall?" D walks down the hall admiring the stage.

"My grandpa played swing tunes with a group called The Jitterbug Boys when he was in his twenties…those are the guys he played with. After painting the hall, he insisted I start painting on canvas, so I could sell my art. He bought my first painting."

"Meg, these are almost as…fine as me."

"It's too bad you have such low confidence," Meg jokes.

"It's called humility, Meg," D teases. "How many paintings have you done?"

"A few. I made nine to display at an art show…and when I got down to Chicago, the kid there said I could show one…so every hour I rotated my displayed painting. You should have seen the look on the kid's face…it was priceless. Anyway, I sold four, and gave one away…so four are hanging out with me."

"Can I see them?"

"Sure. Follow me," Meg walks to the bedroom.

"Your dog didn't even get up when I came in."

"He only greets people he likes," Meg grins. "Actually, Ruger's sick. The vet said we should know in a few weeks if the meds are working." She removes the sheet covering four paintings. "Here they are. This first one is called *Rhythmic Spark*."

"It reminds me of a cultural dance with the feathers flying to music."

"Because you've attended so many cultural dances, D?"

"You have a lot of sass, girl…I like it. Okay, what's the title of the next one…looks like a sunset on a beach?"

"*Secret Admirer*."

"Cool but calming…I dig that one."

"It's the pink that attracts you, yes?"

"Actually, yes," D grins. "Real men aren't afraid of pink."

"I'll keep that in mind. Next one is *Flash of Genius*."

"Shapes, lines, scribbles…perhaps found in an engineer's office?"

"Perhaps," Meg grabs the next painting. "And this is titled *Something to Say*," a hint of emotion tints her words.

D steps closer to look at the rainy city scene.

Meg points to the white strip down the middle. "It was missing something so I added this strip…it just reminds me of Sadie," she pauses. "You want something to eat or drink?"

"No water or cheese sandwich, thanks." D points to the walls of her bedroom. "Where is this location?"

"A San Diego sunset at Coronado Beach. The sand there turns your feet gold."

"Oh, that's why you have gold footprints on the floor. You think he's okay?"

"Back to Jake? Yeah, I think he'll be fine. Probably different, but fine."

"A few months ago we were all hanging out."

"Unexpected and tragic," Meg covers the paintings with the sheet and walks into the kitchen.

"Where is this?" D points to the kitchen walls.

"Italian Eis Café in Bitburg, Germany." Meg points to a blue and yellow plate painted on a red café table, with a dessert in the middle of the plate. "This is called spaghetti eis…it tastes better than ice cream here in the States."

"Are there really marble columns…in an ice cream shop?"

Meg nods. "Over there, you almost feel like dressing up just to go get dessert. Under each creation is a blob of cream, real cream. Then the owner takes this contraption and puts the eis in there, then squeezes out eis noodles. The noodles are topped with fruit or chocolate…and a cookie wafer. If I was stranded on an island and had to choose one thing to eat for the rest of my days, it would be spaghetti eis."

"That's quite an intense love for ice cream."

"Once you go eis, you never go back. What about you? Food you'd choose to live on forever?"

"Maybe ravioli."

"Ravioli?" Meg shakes her head. "I'll give you time so you can come up with a better answer."

"Isn't this my food to live on forever?"

"D, I'm saving you by not letting you choose ravioli."

"I'll think about a better, more Meg approved food." D opens the door to leave. "Thanks for the painting tour."

"Adios, D."

*

Jake pulls out Sadie's journal.

Hart jumps on the bed and curls up next to him as he reads.

Met Reiss today! To meet a visual stranger I have been emailing for years was amazing. I felt sad that he had to go through such a horrible thing with being burned...and I felt a bit angry someone hurt my friend. But being sad and angry won't help him...so I try to be supportive. He has a passion deep inside. I wonder what amazing things he will do.

And we met Gunner. What an inspiration! I guess we all have our challenges and we just do the best we can. Having faith to follow a path we are not necessarily familiar with, going in a direction that was chosen for us, not by us. I like that Gunner does not seem to be wasting his present moments by reliving his hardship. God bless his soul for being so strong.

Jake makes a note in his journal. *Entry #5: Don't waste present moments by reliving your hardship.*

Jake sets aside his journal and finishes reading the entry.

And there's Laina. Her father was a hero of our country who paid the ultimate price: his life. I'm intrigued by the connection of PTSD to the suicide rate. There has to be a way for troops coming home from combat to somehow untrain their brain, respecting the madness of the mind. Hope must exist for my military friends...even the ones I don't yet know.

No matter how many people tell me how amazing I am, I don't see that person in the mirror. I see someone struggling to make a big enough difference so one day I can say with confidence, "I made this place better while I was here." I'm determined to learn how to let go of my fear and lovingly embrace myself. I'm going to believe that what

I'm meant to do while here, I will do. It's easy to love others with their flaws. It's hardest to love good ol' me...go figure.

"You believed in me and I believed in you, love. Maybe that was our magic," Jake closes her journal, shaking his head. "God, it was a mistake to take her."

*

The sun hovers above the horizon, bidding the day farewell.

Carter slides his finger over the medal Theo gave him. He wishes Theo was in the park with him, watching the happy people.

At the far end of the park, a dog chases a ball. The dog returns with the toy, jumping and hopping around the owner, howling as he awaits the next throw.

Carter grins, the cracks in his lips burning in response to the stretching action. *One day*, he thinks, *I will be happy too.*

CHAPTER 23

The Vision that you glorify in your mind, the Ideal that you enthrone in your heart—this you will build your life by, this you will become.
–James Allen

"It's open," Jake yells.

As D walks in the back door, Hart runs behind the couch and peeks around the corner.

"A dog? You got a dog, Jake?"

"Yeah. D, what do you know about a red car, a tall blond, and a black little dog?"

"Is this a joke or a riddle?" D asks. "I'm good at both."

"Neither. I'm serious."

"Bro, I've seen red cars, tall blonds, and black dogs...but I don't know anything that would tie them together in your world. What's the link? Let's start with the blond. Was she wearing a ring? Taller than me? I might be able to make that work..."

Jake tells him the story about Hart showing up.

"Jake, next time a blond driving a red car pulls into your driveway, call me and I will walk you though the greeting process. In fact, I'll come over and talk with her for you..."

"Always so helpful," Jake rolls his eyes.

"That's my middle name," D walks toward Hart. "Hey, buddy."

Hart madly spins in a circle then runs into the bedroom.

D laughs. "A true watchdog. Did you pick a song, Jake?"

"No, but I've errands to run...so I gotta get going, D."

"Okay," D shoots a look of concern toward Jake. "I'll see you later."

"Later, D."

Hart peeks out of the bedroom as the door shuts.

"What's that all about?" Jake asks the dog.

Hart runs to him, wagging his barely-there tail.

"Whatever. You have issues; I have issues. It's all good."

*

Drew opens his front door to a flying Edison. "Hey, buddy. It's you and me today." Giggles erupt from Edison as Drew picks him up and tosses him over his shoulder.

Nina hands Drew a bag of supplies.

"Are you going out for a week?" Drew teases.

Nina scolds him with her eyes. "I'm making sure you're prepared. There's an extra change of clothes in case…well, in case he makes a mess of the ones he's wearing."

"This opens up a whole new line of possible activities…"

"Drew, when you have an almost three-year old, you'll pack all possibilities too."

"Let's hope that doesn't happen for a while."

"You don't want kids, Drew? You're so good with Edison."

"Wish we could talk about my dreams, Nina," Drew spews sarcasm as he points toward the street. "But I believe that's Meg pulling up." Drew answers before Nina asks, "Yes, we're fine. Enjoy the movie."

*

At the cemetery, Hart pounces on a stick, picks it up, and runs in circles around Jake, tangling Jake's legs with the leash.

Jake pauses and stares at Hart.

Hart looks at Jake, then zigs and zags with the stick, pulling the leash tighter around Jake's legs.

Jake shakes his head, untangles the leash, and continues toward Sadie's grave.

After lying next to Sadie's grave for an hour, Hart's head on his lap, Jake sits up.

Hart sits up and begins wagging his tail.

"Everything's always about you, huh?" Jake asks. "Let's go meet Gunner."

As they get close to Gunner, Hart tries to bolt, the leash restricting his escape.

"Come on, Hart," Jake gives the leash a tug.

Hart digs his paws into the ground in resistance.

"You'll be fine, buddy," Jake encourages.

Gunner's perfect pearly whites make an appearance.

Hart runs behind Jake, looking at Gunner through the space between Jake's legs.

Jake shares the dog drop off story with Gunner. "So I have no idea where Hart came from. How's the leg therapy going?"

"It's intense but there's progress."

"Good. That's good." Jake looks at Hart now lying between his legs. "Well, we're off to run errands."

"Take it easy, Jake."

"Later, Gunner."

As Jake leaves, Gunner looks at the four grave markers in front of him and sighs. "Maybe I'll introduce you all some day."

*

"A little dog?" Gigi's face lights up with a big smile.

Jake drags Hart on the leash enough to sit down next to Gigi. "He has some social issues."

Jake dives into the mystery of where Hart came from.

Gigi grins. "It's nice you have a distraction, dear."

Hart creeps slowly toward Jake's feet, eyeing Gigi.

Jake shakes his head as he watches Hart. "I want to remember everything about Sadie…but I want to forget the pain."

"Take hold of the truth that you still have something to give to this world, dear, whether it's to one old lady," Gigi says, "or thousands of people. If this was your last day…are you happy with how it turned out? If so, good. If not, change tomorrow. Focus not on why Sadie left, but why she was a part of your life."

"I don't know if I can…get past her leaving," Jake laments.

"We can't control death, Jake. We only can control what we do until it happens to us."

Jake looks at Gigi then puts his arm around her shoulders.

"You will, dear. You will," Gigi smiles.

*

Edison rambles in his own language as he and Drew walk hand in hand down the street back to Drew's house.

A car speeds past them.

"Slow down!" Drew yells.

Edison looks up at Drew and mimics him. "Low Dow!"

Drew kneels next to him. "When you get your license, make sure you drive slowly in neighborhoods with kids, okay?"

"Okay," Edison nods, as if he understands Drew's words.

"Okay," Drew stands. "Good man."

A screen door slams, the bang followed by popping noises.

Drew's pulse accelerates.

He searches the area with his eyes and identifies two boys firing yellow popping guns at each other on a front lawn. A little girl sits on the porch holding a red ball; she smiles and waves at Drew.

Drew's chest tightens.

"Whee!" Edison giggles as Drew sweeps him up and sprints toward home.

Drew knocks on Gigi's door.

"Why, what a…" Gigi greets in her energy spiked manner.

"Keep him safe!" Drew commands, placing Edison next to Gigi.

"What's wrong, dear?" Gigi asks.

Halfway down her driveway, Drew turns to yell back. "Keep him safe!"

Gigi looks at a wide-eyed Edison. "Hi, dear. Do you like apple pie? Let's go have some apple pie," she reaches out her hand toward Edison.

"Momma," Edison whines.

"I'm sure your momma will be home real soon. Right after we eat some pie, dear. With ice cream. Do you like ice cream?"

"I cream!" Edison cheers, throwing his arms in the air.

"Ice cream it is," Gigi takes his hand as they walk into the kitchen. "You can sit right here," Gigi pulls out a chair.

Edison climbs on the chair and cheers again. "I cream!"

"Yes, dear, we'll get that for you right away. Bill!" Gigi calls down the hall, urgency in her voice. "Bill!"

"Hey there," Bill greets Edison, his pale face adorned with a friendly smile.

"Drew needs your help, Bill. He needs your help right now."

Bill points at Edison. "Save me a piece of pie."

Drew swings open the door as Bill reaches to knock.

"Where you headed, son?"

"Step aside, sir," Drew commands.

"Oh, I think we both know that wouldn't be a smart idea."

"Sir, I don't want to hurt you."

"Unfortunately I know that look, son," Bill blocks his way.

"Move old man!" Drew threatens.

Bill calmly stands in front of him.

"Fuck!" Drew leans against the door frame.

"Let's go inside, son," Bill nudges him and walks inside.

"Fuck!" Drew regrets. "Is Edison okay?!"

"He's eating pie and ice cream...I suspect he's doing well."

"Fuck," Drew sighs.

"Use your words, son."

"Fuckin'..." Drew shakes his head. "We were on patrol, and this little girl waves to me, nothing big deal...the kids loved us...especially Jasper...so this girl waves to me, and she was holding a red ball...and uh, I waved back to her and then heard the blast of the IED." He swallows in agony with memories. "He let out this scream...and uh, I was too late. I pulled out Doc Reiss, his face, was...he was in pain...I did basic medic tasks until the bird landed. I don't know how the fire started. Jasper and Reiss were being fuckin' heroes though...so the rest of my guys were fine. I wonder...if the girl with the ball knew...or fuckin' helped...in blowing up my best friend." Drew blows out a lung-full of air, his eyes reflecting soul-torturing pain.

"That's a lot to carry, son."

Drew nods. "Nina's going to be pissed."

"What's your plan?"

"My plan, sir?"

"I'm glad I'm back to sir and not old man," Bill grins.

"I apologize. Not my best moment."

"I've had a few of those. Let's bring Edison back here now that my Gigi has loaded him with pie and ice cream."

"Okay."

Bill continues. "And you'll come to a meeting with me. Only veterans. We've all got skeletons. We've all got stories."

"I appreciate the offer, Bill, but I'm fine."

"You're going see a red ball again, son. Or you're going to smell something that reminds you. Or you're going to hear something that reminds you of what happened over there."

"Meetings aren't my thing."

"Golly, you're a tough nut to crack. You don't have to meet anyone or say anything…but you're coming with me once. Good grief, you're a grenade with the pin missing, son."

"One meeting," Drew nods. "Nina's going to be home soon."

"Then we best be getting little Edison over here," Bill opens the door and Drew follows him out.

"You need help fixing your mailbox…it seems to be leaning quite a bit," Drew comments.

"Soon the box will dump the mail right back into the mailman's hand," Bill chuckles.

Drew grins. "I'll fix it."

*

At home, Jake falls onto the bed to read Sadie's words before drifting off to sleep.

I'm going to the Military Ball to receive the Hometown Heroes Award! I'm honored, but Meg and I are not heroes. We support heroes. I guess I'll accept it on their behalf.

I wrote on Jake's shirt in a spontaneous moment and almost died laughing. It was so funny...he didn't think so...but he'll soon love that shirt.

Jake glances toward the closet then continues to read.

I'm learning that most of our stress comes from thinking or worrying about things we are concerned about, not things we can influence or control. The things we can control are our actions, thoughts, and dreams. Things related to others—their actions, their thoughts, their dreams or lack of them—we cannot control. I want to focus on things I can control and let the uncontrollables to God.

I'm excited to work with Gunner on our project. Our warriors should not come home and want to kill themselves. They should come home and know they are loved and that a spot is waiting for them. After all, we all want to believe that a spot in this world was made just for us.

Jake writes in his journal. *Entry #6: Focus on what you can control.*

*

Addison opens the last drawer in the nursery dresser. "Ooh," she holds up a pair of blue socks the size of her thumb.

Pulling out the drawer, Addison sits down in the middle of the empty white-walled room and transfers socks from the drawer to a plastic bag. "I didn't want to be a mom...then I was one. Then I wanted to be a mom...and I no longer was one."

"Bye, baby," she sets the last pair of football brown socks into the plastic bag then ties the red handles into a knot.

Addison picks up the bag and scans the room before closing the door. "Were you ever here or was it all just a bad dream?"

CHAPTER 24

You are not just a drop in the ocean, you are
the mighty ocean in the drop.
–Rumi

Hart stands in the middle of the hallway, between the kitchen and the living room, staring at Jake.

"Come on!" Jake whines when he sees his work pants in Hart's mouth.

Hart runs in a circle and darts around the couch, tripping once on the pants, and ending back in his original location.

"Hart!" Jake lunges after him.

Meg knocks on the back door then slowly opens it. "Hello?"

"Come in, Meg," Jake calls out. "Hart, get over here!"

Hart races around the couch again. Seeing Meg, Hart spins in a circle, drops the pants, and runs into the bedroom.

Meg looks at Jake.

"He's into this clothes thing...socks, underwear, shirts, pants...he finds them and runs around the house, dragging them all over. I should teach him to do the wash."

"Or you could put your clothes away...and not live organizingly challenged."

"Organizingly? The latest Meg word I presume?"

"You're the one with pants in your living room," Meg picks up the pants then abruptly drops them. "Correction, wet pants in your living room."

"Are you here for a reason or just to touch my wet pants?"

"Ooh, sassy. I heard you had a dog. And that you don't answer your phone. And you don't go see your mother."

"And?"

"I wanted to see the dog. Why is the puppy hiding?"

"I don't know, Hart does that."

Meg pulls a hamburger toy out of her purse and begins squeaking the middle of the rubber toy.

Hart slowly creeps toward the squeaking noise.

Meg bends down when Hart is a few feet from her.

Hart scurries behind the couch.

Meg places the burger on the ground. "Okay, this was fun."

"He'll be playing with it the second you leave."

"Good. You okay?" Meg asks.

"I'm fine."

Meg nods. "Bueno. Adios, Jake."

"Later, Meg. Thanks for the hamburger."

Meg opens the door to leave. "Thanks for letting me touch your wet pants."

A brief laugh escapes Jake.

Meg closes the door and Hart rushes over to the hamburger. After squeaking the middle with his paw, he brings the burger over to Jake.

"Are you telling me that if I buy you toys…you won't run around the house stealing and slobbering on my clothes?"

Hart squeaks his burger and drops it again by Jake's feet.

"Fine," Jake says, tossing Hart's burger down the hall. "We'll make a trip to the toy store, then to the park," Jake picks up his pants. "After I finish the laundry."

*

"Thanks for watching Edison, Drew." Nina tosses Edison's toys into a blue bag.

"No problem. How is Meg?"

"Good. Fun. Funny. It's just nice to talk with a woman instead of a toddler. Meg doesn't say much…I tend to talk more, but it's still nice. She probably thinks I'm a mess. You should meet her…I think you'd like her. But I'm glad you're going to a meeting. I'm surprised you're going with Bill though…how'd that happen?"

"Doesn't matter," Drew shrugs.

The doorbell rings.

"I'm just glad you're going." Nina zips up Edison's jacket.

"You ready?" Bill grins as Drew opens the door. "Evening, Nina. Hello, Edison."

"Hey, Bill!" Nina smiles, grabbing Edison's hand to walk outside.

Drew grabs his car keys and follows them out.

As Drew and Bill pull out of the driveway, Nina runs to the car with a container. "Here are cookies you can take!"

Drew shakes his head. "I don't think…"

"Sure!" Bill exclaims. "The boys would love homemade treats! Thank you, Nina!"

Drew sighs and grabs the cookies.

Nina waves as Drew and Bill leave.

Gigi opens her front door and calls out in her typical high-pitched voice. "Hi, dear! Do you like tea? I was going to put on tea for us."

Nina grins. "I love tea! I'm just going to toss Edison's toys into the car…so I'll see you in a few minutes!"

*

Jake rolls Hart's new tennis ball like a bowling ball on the green grass of the park. "Go get it, Hart!"

Hart darts toward the ball, his little legs a blur.

Jake walks over to his normal bench and is about to sit down when he notices a bright yellow bag in the bushes. Kneeling on the bench, he reaches to grab the bag.

A kid in the bushes cringes as if Jake is about to hit him.

"Oh," Jake leans away from the bushes. "Hey."

Carter sheepishly looks up. "Hi."

"I'm Jake. What's your name?"

"Carter."

Hart returns and drops his ball next to Jake's feet.

"Carter," Jake points to Hart. "This is Hart. And Hart runs away from people he doesn't…"

Hart walks over to Carter and sniffs him.

"Okay," a puzzled look crosses Jake's face. "Usually Hart runs away from everyone I introduce him to...except you."

"Oh," Carter extends his hand for Hart to sniff.

Jake looks around. "Are you here alone, Carter?"

"No." Carter crawls out of the bushes. "I don't mean to bother you, mister," he starts walking away.

"You're not bothering me. In fact, I think Hart might like to have another friend." Jake holds out the ball when Carter turns around.

"Okay," Carter grabs the ball and rolls it just like Jake did.

Hart takes off after the ball.

After a few minutes of silence, Carter says, "Are you a social worker?"

"Nope," Jake shakes his head.

"Are you a cop?"

"Nope."

Carter studies him intensely.

"I teach music to grade school kids."

"Oh. I love music."

Hart drops his ball by Jake's feet. Jake hands the ball to Carter. "Do you go to school, Carter?"

"No," Carter rolls Hart's ball then sits back on the bench. "I have a foster mom. I don't fit in with the other kids. I can't bring cops or social workers around or I'll get in real trouble. My real mom died from drugs. And my friend Theo died too. He was my best friend. I never had a dad. I live over there," Carter points. "But I love watching happy people here."

Hart returns with his ball and drops it at Carter's feet.

Carter grins and throws the ball.

Jake unwraps his deli sandwich. "Do you want half?"

"Okay," Carter nods.

"How old are you?"

Carter takes a tiny bite of the sandwich. "Six."

Six, starving, dirty, and alone, Jake mentally comments.

"This is so good!" Carter takes another bite before throwing Hart's ball.

"Can Hart and I walk you home? It's getting dark."

"No, I'm okay," Carter stands. "Thanks for letting me play with Hart."

"Anytime."

"Bye, Jake," Carter pets Hart one last time. "Bye, Hart."

"Later, Carter," Jake clips on Hart's leash, and watches until Carter is out of his view. Jake pets Hart, "He seems like a good kid."

*

Carter waits until Jake and Hart leave, then walks back toward the bushes. The sandwich he ate was the best meal he's ever had…but with food now in his stomach…he can't go home.

*

Drew sits in the driver's seat after they park.

Bill opens his car door. "Come inside, son. Waiting in the car wasn't part of our deal. And bring Nina's cookies."

Anger builds and curses fly in Drew's mind as he locks the car and follows Bill down a sidewalk, through an iron gate, and into a duplex.

The aroma of freshly ground coffee beans greets them.

"Faye!" Bill hoots. "How are you, dear?"

Faye waddles around the counter to give Bill a hug.

"Golly!"

"He's getting big, Bill. Big and feisty," Faye drones, patting her huge baby belly. "This boy kicked me a good one yesterday, right in the bladder, almost had me going right on the floor."

"He sounds strong like his momma." Bill turns toward Drew. "Faye, this is Drew. Drew, Faye."

"Evening, ma'am."

"You a veteran?"

"Active sergeant in the Army, ma'am."

"Welcome."

Bill puts his hand on Drew's shoulder. "I'll be upstairs. You can stay here, get yourself some coffee, or come up to meet the rest of the boys. It's up to you," Bill winks at Faye.

"Can I get you some coffee, soldier?" Faye asks.

153

"No thanks, ma'am."

"What's in the container? Did you bring me something good?" Faye belts out a laugh.

"My sister made cookies." Drew opens the tin. "You want a cookie?"

"Yes!" Faye reaches in and grabs a cookie. "Mind if we sit down if you're not having coffee...my feet are screaming at me."

Drew shakes his head and pulls out a chair for Faye.

"Thank you," she sits down. "So, how do you know Bill?"

"He's my neighbor."

Faye motions for Drew to sit. "Please, sit. Oh my gosh...this cookie is delicious! If my baby wasn't kicking me right now, I'd think I was in heaven. You married?"

"Was. How about you?"

"My hubby's..." dark curls frame her puppy dog eyes as she purses her lips, "somewhere in uniform. I was able to talk with him yesterday." She pats her belly. "He was kicking while daddy was on the phone. It was cute...but it's tough without him here...when I'm doubling in size every day," Faye laughs.

"It's nice you get to talk with him."

"Mostly it's letters. Lots of letters. So, what brings you here?" Faye slides a chair next to her and puts her feet up.

"Bill wanted me to come."

"Iraq or Afghanistan?"

"Last deployment was Iraq."

"You headed back overseas?" Faye asks.

"Probably."

Faye stares at the cookie tin.

Drew holds out the tin.

Faye smiles and takes another cookie. "Why did your sister make cookies?"

"Nina bakes a lot of cookies; she's always making cookies."

"Is Nina's husband overseas?"

"He was," Drew nods.

"He's home now and she's still baking cookies...for you?"

"Nah, he, uh...died overseas...in combat."

"My worst nightmare!" Faye shakes her head. "Your poor sister. Then the cookie baking makes sense."

"Oh yeah?" Drew asks.

"I was talking to another military wife the other day saying how I really missed my husband…like, all the time. Plus with keeping everything running at home while trying to work as far into my pregnancy as I can…can get overwhelming. Anyway, this gal, who was likely very well meaning, told me how she baked cookies every week when her husband was deployed and it helped her cope with him being gone. I guess we all have our methods of coping, right?"

"Did you start baking cookies?" Drew asks.

Faye laughs. "I practically crawl into bed with exhaustion every night…so a boatload of dirty cookie dishes wouldn't help me. That's my way of coping…working until my mind shuts down."

Drew holds out the tin of cookies.

Faye grins. "One more…but just because the baby wants one."

Drew nods. "Right on. The little man needs food to grow."

"I'm sorry, I just keep talking. You're missing the meeting!"

Drew shrugs. "Doesn't matter."

"You came…but you didn't actually want to come?"

"Something like that," Drew grabs a cookie.

"Well, if you're not going to the meeting…can I ask you something?"

"Sure."

"You've heard of PTSD, right?"

Drew nods.

"I read that at twenty-four years of age, the average soldier has moved away from home, been deployed, been promoted several times, bought a car and crashed it, has had a relationship and financial problems, has seen death, is responsible for other soldiers, and maintains millions of dollars of equipment, but gets paid…well, not that much."

"Sounds about right."

"I'm afraid my husband is going to come home and…be different. I've heard so many stories."

"He might. War changes…everything."

"Even who you love?"

"I don't know. With my marriage…I still love her but she fell in love with someone else when I was gone. I'm over there getting shot at and she's here fu…falling for someone else."

"It can be lonely here," Faye moves her feet from the chair to the ground.

"It can be lonely overseas. I'm not sure if war changes who you love…maybe how you love them or how you show it. For me, when I'm not on base, mental noise and flashbacks make it hard to hang around people like I used to…if that makes sense."

"That makes sense."

"I think instead of worrying about him changing, you just figure it out when he gets home. Plus, you're talking with each other and writing…so you both may be changing but changing together. It's hard to describe what happens over there…and I think it changes everyone…but I've seen guys fall deeper in love with their wives when gone because they have an admiration and more of a respect for her running things while they are gone. I think the important thing is communicating and being open to how you both change."

A forty-something balding man walks into the shop. "Evening, Faye!"

Faye stands for a second mouthing "Pregnant dizziness" to Drew, before walking behind the counter. "Black with sugar?"

"You got it!" the bald man replies, taking a seat at what looks to be his normal table.

Bill walks down the stairs and nods to Drew. "Ready, son?"

Drew eyes him curiously, wondering if Bill is going to have an issue with Drew not attending the meeting. "Yes, sir."

Bill tips his hat to Faye. "Have a good evening, dear."

Faye nods, shooting Bill a look of confirmation. "You too, Bill." She looks at Drew. "Good night."

"Good night, ma'am," Drew hands her the tin of cookies before leaving.

Bill slowly walks down the sidewalk. "Did you enjoy it?"

"I did."

Bill stops and looks at Drew. "Good," he continues walking.

*

Jake turns on the bedside light and pulls out Sadie's journal before going to sleep.

If the words in a conversation are only ten percent of what someone is saying, how many times are we completely missing the message? How many times do people want a response? Or do they merely want to share their story with someone and just need someone to listen? Most people can figure out their own challenges without the advice of others. They may just need someone to act as a sounding board so they can hear their choices out loud. I've tried to be a sounding board, but I've always thought I needed to respond. Now I know I don't. I want to be an understander, not a responder.

Gunner and I talked about having to be strong and confident to share a story of weakness. And most times when sharing a story of weakness, people are not looking for direction from others, but direction from within themselves.

Gunner is an incredible person...he has a fire inside his soul. He tries every day to let go of the negativity in his life...his past and self-sabotaging thoughts...the same thing I'm trying to do...because when the mental junk is gone...only passion and love remain.

Every day, we choose to either find drama in everything and hate life or rise above the negativity and choose greatness for our moments. We may slip, every other second, but the choice is ours right now...and right now...and right now. Peace is a hassle...but with every trial and tragedy, we have the opportunity and ability to rise out of our darkness, whatever our darkness may be, and choose greatness.

Jake's stomach drops. He pulls out his journal and adds an entry. *Entry #7: Be strong in sharing your story of weakness. We have the opportunity and ability to rise out of our darkness and choose greatness.*

"I don't know how to rise out of losing you, love," Jake says, as he places the journals back into the drawer.

*

Drew sits on his couch, staring at the envelope that greeted him when he came home from the veteran meeting he didn't actually attend. A note from Wyla is taped on the front.

Sign the papers as soon as you can, Drew. Steve and I are engaged. –Wyla

He couldn't save his best friend.

He couldn't save his marriage.

Both are gone...and he doesn't know how to let go of either.

Drew places his *Fuck The World* sign on the divorce envelope and heads out for a run.

CHAPTER 25

Be still my soul, and know that peace is thine. Be steadfast, heart, and know that strength divine belongs to thee. Cease from thy turmoil, mind, and thou the Everlasting Rest shall find.
If a man would have peace, let him exercise the spirit of peace; if he would find Love, let him dwell in the spirit of Love; if he would escape suffering, let him cease to inflict it; if he would do noble things for humanity, let him cease to do ignoble things for himself.
If he will but quarry the mine of his own soul, he shall find there all the materials for building whatsoever he will, and he shall find there also the Central Rock on which to build in safety.
–James Allen

To an early Sunday morning knock, Drew opens the front door sporting workout pants and an old t-shirt. "Can I help you?"

Meg's eyebrows rise. "You're not Gigi…"

"Gigi's my neighbor."

Meg looks at the piece of paper. "Nina wrote down the wrong address…hmmm…well, can you point out which neighbor Gigi is?"

"Are you Meg?"

"I am. You…oh, you must be Drew."

"That's me."

"Well, it's nice to finally meet you Drew."

"Thanks for the care packages. The guys overseas really appreciated them. You still doing that?"

Meg nods. "Yep, with Sadie gone it's a bit more work…but what you guys go through is much…worse. Anyway, I just came to drop off some information for Gigi's husband…I guess he's going through some nasty cancer or something?"

"Bill?" shock evident in Drew's voice.

159

"And I just shared someone's personal information with you..." Meg grimaces. "So far so bad...I should leave...soon."

Drew grins. "Do you want to come in? I made a huge breakfast and...it's getting cold."

"Okay, sure," Meg walks inside. "Bacon, pancakes, coffee, fruit...you expecting company?"

"No, just...hungry."

"Shazam! You're very very hungry."

Drew hands her a plate and begins piling food on his.

"You always make such a big breakfast for...yourself?"

"I'm getting divorced."

"Oh," Meg pauses. "You always make a big breakfast when getting divorced?"

"Hopefully it will just be a one time thing."

"The big breakfast or the divorce?"

Drew shovels a forkful of food into his mouth. "The divorce."

"Got it," Meg nods. "Well, thanks for making breakfast."

Drew's phone rings. Seeing the name, he ignores the call.

"I don't mind if you take the call," Meg savors the homemade pancakes.

"I try to avoid talking to ignorant humans...aka my parents."

"Oh yeah, Nina said they were coming into town."

"Oh yeah?"

Meg shakes her head. "I did it again. I'm not going to talk anymore."

"It doesn't matter. I don't talk to them. Nina does."

"Why don't you talk to them?" Meg asks.

"I made a sign for when they call and I ignore their calls."

"What kind of a sign?" Meg sips the strong coffee.

Drew walks to the counter and holds up his *Fuck The World* sign.

Meg almost spits coffee across the table, half choking as shocking laughter erupts from her.

Drew puts the sign into the drawer and sits back down to eat. "You okay? I do have basic medic skills if you're in need."

Meg coughs the coffee she inhaled out of her lungs, taking a moment to recover. "So you don't get along with your parents."

Drew nods. "We have a…difference of opinion."

"Do share your story." Meg adds, "And I love crispy bacon."

"I love crispy bacon, too. My story? I dropped out of medical school and joined the Army. My parents were pissed I gave up a full ride scholarship, thought I was an idiot for joining the Army during a time of war, and I am currently ruining the family tradition of generations of doctors." He rolls his eyes. "I was a disappointment when I joined and I'm a disappointment still being in the Army. If I become a doctor, they'll somehow find me to be a disappointment there too."

Meg says with straight face, "But other than that, your family is pretty tight?"

Drew grins. "Your turn."

"My story isn't as interesting."

"I'm easily amused."

"You asked," Meg warns. "My brother died in high school lifting weights by himself. Well, a friend was there…but he left for a few minutes and my brother dropped a weight on his chest and died."

"Damn!" Drew comments.

"After that, my parents split up, and I moved in with my grandpa. And a few years ago, my grandpa died. In the course of time, my folks both remarried, both divorced, and now both live in Florida. And when they call me, they ask when I'm getting married and when I'll finally give them grandchildren."

"So they are back together?"

"Yep. But I'm not a disappointment to them. I just confuse them with not allowing a man to slip a ring on my finger or put a bun in my oven."

"And?" Drew washes down pancakes with coffee.

Meg calmly replies, "People in general annoy me."

"Roger that. Everyone's got an opinion…usually a misguided unimportant one at that."

Meg looks at her watch. "I should be leaving…but this breakfast was stupendously amazing. Thanks for inviting me in."

"Thanks for sending us packages…"

"Thanks for going through a whole bunch of awfulness to keep our country safe," Meg opens the door to leave. "I don't think what you guys do or go through is well-known, but it is appreciated. I hope you at least know that."

"Thanks," Drew points to Gigi's house. "That's the neighbor you are looking for."

Meg grins. "Thanks. Adios, Drew."

"See you, Meg."

*

Jake stops by the deli and picks up two sandwiches before going to the park.

Hart bounces along as Jake walks beside the river admiring the twisted trees framing the scraggily stream.

"Hey, Jake!"

"Hey, Carter," Jake turns around, holding up the sandwiches. "I brought one for you. Hungry?"

"Thanks!" Carter grabs the sandwich as if he was just handed a trophy.

After greeting Carter, Hart sniffs the air then picks up a stick, proudly carrying his wooden treasure as Jake and Carter silently walk along the river.

"Do you ever read books?" Jake asks.

"I know how to read."

"Who taught you to read?"

"Theo. He was my best friend. He died," Carter finishes the last of his sandwich. Carter's shirt sleeve slides up when he reaches toward a tree branch above him.

Jake points to bruises on his arm. "How did you get those?"

"It don't matter," Carter quickly pulls his sleeve down. "Thanks for the sandwich, Jake. See you when we see you!" After petting Hart, Carter quickly walks away.

"Carter!"

Carter turns around.

"Are you okay?" Jake asks.

"I'm okay," Carter waves and continues walking away.

Jake looks at Hart. "Nothing. Again, we can do nothing."

*

At home, Jake pulls out Sadie's journal for his dose of nightly intellectual medicine.

PTSD is a thief. We can try to stop it from continuing to be a murderer. I'm not sure how much I can help, but maybe I can be a ripple or a drop of hope in the PTSD pool.

Gunner says the secret we share with others is not our horror story, but how we make it through that certain point in time. He calls it "Inspiration Behind the Warrior." He should be an inspirational speaker. His passion is viral. You can't help but hang onto hope when talking with him.

Hart dives into Jake's lap on the bed with his hamburger toy from Meg.

"It's a little late to play, man."

Hart stares at Jake wagging his tail.

Jake throws the toy down the hall then writes in his journal. *Entry #8: Maybe I can be a ripple or a drop of hope.*

*

In the bushes for the night, Carter pulls his sleeves over his hands and curls into a ball.

CHAPTER 26

I know of no more encouraging fact than the unquestionable ability of man to elevate his life by a conscious endeavor.
–Henry David Thoreau

D taps the doorframe of Jake's office. "You going with Meg to the Memorial Day thing this afternoon?"

"Yeah, Gunner and Reiss are supposed to be going too. You?"

"Heck no, bro! I told you about my cookout…got the guys coming over…you're still welcome to ditch them and come to my place. I can write you a coach's excuse note to give to Meg."

"I don't think Meg would approve…and I'm pretty sure she'd remind me of my bad decision for years to come."

"What about me, bro? You ditched my party to go with them. How's the guard dog?"

"Good," Jake looks under his desk at Hart sitting in his paper box. "Hey, I met a foster kid in the park a few days ago."

"Oh, yeah?" D's facial expression changes.

"I noticed bruises on his arm and when I asked him about it, he took off. And from what you've said about growing up in the system…I'm kind of worried about this kid, D."

D shakes his head. "There are some really great foster parents and some not so great foster parents. A friend of mine is a social worker. I'll see what she suggests. It can be a touchy situation though. What's his name?"

"Carter. You know how easy it is for the young ones to get into trouble, D. Carter's got a spark that could really take him far…in the right environment."

"I'll call my friend, bro. What are your final thoughts on the singing competition? You know you want to. I know you want to. Are we going to?"

Jake sighs with extra effort. "I knew you would bring that up. Sadie wrote a song for me…thought I'd try to put some music to her lyrics and use the song for the audition."

"Sadie wrote a song for you?" shock flashes across D's face. "Is it about my smokin' hot abs?" D pats his gut.

"Yeah, it's all about you," Jake remarks with sarcasm.

"So…it's a yes for the competition?"

"I guess so."

"Good. I'll call my friend and see what she says about the foster kid."

"Thanks. Later, D."

"See you later!" D hoots, flashing the peace sign.

*

At the park, Carter is on the bench studying an apple.

"Where did the apple come from?" Jake hands Carter a sandwich.

Carter excitedly takes the sandwich and sets the apple aside. "I found it. Another boy said it could have a knife in it, but I don't see no knife. This sandwich is so good!"

"Here," Jake hands Carter a book.

Carter holds the book like a breakable vase. "Should I read it now?"

Jake shakes his head. "The book is yours to keep. I read it when I was your age."

"I'll take real good care of it, Jake. Thank you."

"You bet. I hope you like the story."

"I'm going to start reading it!" a bounce accompanies Carter's step as he walks away carrying his sandwich and book.

*

The veterinarian walks into the small room, puffs of pet hair rolling across the floor with her entrance. Her face tells Meg what she doesn't want to hear.

165

Meg pets Ruger as he lies on the blanket covering the steel exam table. Meg sighs. "The pills didn't work. So now what?"

"Surgery is a possibility…but we don't know. Ruger needs to see the heart specialist. He'll run more specific tests."

"Is Ruger in pain?" Meg asks.

"I think he's just tired, Meg. Exhausted. But not in pain."

"Okay," Meg picks up Ruger. "Then I'll take him to the specialist." She says to the dog, "We'll get you fixed up."

*

Drew taps on Nina's door and walks inside. "That was clever what you did yesterday…having Meg stop at the wrong address…"

Edison races to greet Drew, flour on his hands and arms.

"Hey, buddy! Are you helping mom make cookies for dinner?"

Edison nods with glee and walks toward the kitchen.

"Where is your mom?" Drew follows Edison to the kitchen where flour covers the kitchen floor. "That's not good. Nina?!"

*

A dark green canopy hides 10,000 black balloons stamped with a white *POW/MIA Never Forgotten* message. Multiple people act as anchors holding the edge of the canopy so the wind doesn't release the balloons before the slotted time.

"Gunner!" Jake calls out as Meg waves at Gunner.

Gunner spots them in the crowd and wheels toward them. "I'm glad you both could make it."

Meg looks at her watch. "Reiss is meeting us here, right?"

"I called Reiss yesterday and today but couldn't reach him. He said a few days ago he'd meet us here," Gunner says.

Meg pulls her phone out of her camouflage cargo pocket. "I'm on it," she walks a few feet away to call Reiss.

Jake asks Gunner, "You've been here before?"

"Nah, first time I've been to this ceremony. I know the person who set this all up…she asked me to place a wreath at the POW chair during the ceremony."

166

"Sweet," Jake nods. "What's the POW chair?"

Gunner points to a covered chair. "They unveil it for the ceremony. It has the branches of the Armed Forces on it with an eagle and the words 'In Memory Of Our Troops, Defenders Of Our Freedom,' for all those who didn't make it home from war."

Jake shakes his head. "That has to be rough for families, never knowing what happened to their loved ones."

Meg returns. "Reiss can't come. He said today was not a good day for him. What does that mean?" she asks Gunner.

"Military holidays can be tough with the memories they drum up. What's done in war...you come home feeling thankful that you're alive...but sometimes the guilt catches up with you. We're not just eating a hot dog and listening to music...we're recalling those we fought with, those who died, what we did, what we didn't do, what we couldn't do, and why we're still here...and for some of us, that the guy standing next to us would be wearing body armor if he knew what we were capable of. A lot of different emotions can be stirred by a day like today...just depends on experiences and the healing process."

Military combat patches mark the black leather vest of a veteran who taps Gunner on the shoulder. "Sorry to interrupt, but I've got to steal you for the ceremony."

"Good luck, Gunner!" Meg beams.

Gunner's crooked smile flashes. "Thanks."

*

Nina curls up in the corner of the bathroom. "I couldn't breathe, Drew," she shakes her head. "I'm such a mess. I can't go to the Memorial Day Ceremony."

"We don't have to go."

Nina wipes her eyes. "I'm supposed to be thankful today for all those who gave their lives so we can live in freedom...but I'm not thankful," tears fall down her cheeks. "My husband, my son's father...is dead. He is never coming home," she sobs.

"We don't have to go, Nina," Drew repeats.

"It's selfish of me to not stand with those whose loved ones have never come home...but I can't handle more tragedy."

"We won't go, Nina."

"They are going to read the names of those who have died...and when they call off Jasper's name...I," she bites her lip to stop from crying. "I don't want his name to float into the air without a heart to say 'I knew you'...and I'm too weak to be that heart. I'm mad I'm not strong enough to be that heart."

Drew stands in silence.

"I was never cut out for this, Drew."

"I don't think anyone is, Nina."

"Will you go?"

Drew nods, everything inside of him protesting.

"Is my kitchen a mess?" Nina asks.

"Flour is all over...the kitchen and Edison."

Laughter bubbles out of Nina.

*

As Jake and Meg walk toward the flag lined terrace where the memorial ceremony will be held, Meg says, "Sadie knew how to do all of this, Jake...how to talk to all of them. No promises on me not messing up her whole project...I don't have what she had."

"Reiss wouldn't take Gunner's calls, Meg...but he took yours. That's something," Jake says.

A woman wearing a brilliant blue dress pierces the air with a flawless rendition of the National Anthem.

A veteran approaches the podium and invites the crowd to join in reciting the Pledge of Allegiance. All right hands rise to either salute or find a position over a heart.

Two planes fly overhead, so close to the ground they almost tap the wires of the telephone poles.

Meg turns and sees Drew several yards away. She waves.

Drew grins and walks toward Meg. He whispers to her, "Nina and Edison stayed home."

Meg quietly says, "I'm glad you came."

Jake reaches around Meg and shakes Drew's hand.

A veteran shuffles to the podium and delivers a flurry of commands that unveil the POW chair as well as surround the chair with red, white, and blue flower wreaths, with Gunner placing the last wreath.

A soldier stands next to the podium. As the veteran calls out the names of fallen warriors, the soldier exclaims "Absent!"

"Ricardo Jasper!" is yelled out by the veteran, followed with a sharp "Absent!"

"Oh my gosh," Meg's hand covers her mouth.

Drew closes his eyes for a good three seconds. He curses under his breath and walks away.

Drew reaches the edge of the terrace then stops short.

Tears fill Nina's eyes as she looks at Drew, Edison's arms wrapped around her leg.

Without words, they embrace.

After Taps, a veteran walks up to the podium. "Thank you for attending this memorial ceremony and paying tribute to America's heroes that never came home. I wrote a prayer poem that I'd like to recite before we release the balloons..." he continues with the prayer.

At the conclusion of the prayer, 10,000 black balloons release into the sky. The wind carries them past the flag of the United States, the POW/MIA flag, and the five flags of America's Armed Forces.

"It's like watching my black cloud leave...I'm just not sure I want my black cloud to leave," Nina thinks aloud.

With Edison in Drew's arms gleefully pointing at the sky, Drew watches the last of the balloons bounce into the air. "I think we should go and make cookies."

Nina grins. "Let's go home and make cookies."

CHAPTER 27

Don't wait for a light to appear at the end of the tunnel,
stride down there and light the bloody thing yourself.
–Vincent van Gogh

A fter his morning classes, Jake walks with Hart, sandwiches in
hand, to the park.

Carter is in the bushes next to their bench.

"Hey, Carter!" Jake puts the bag of sandwiches on the bench.

Hart runs over to Carter with his ball.

Carter ignores Hart's attempts to play.

Jake walks over to the bushes. "Why are we hiding…"

Bruises. Blood. Ripped clothes.

"Carter, what happened?!" adrenaline pumps through Jake's body.
He calmly asks, "What happened?"

Carter's hands come away from his face to reveal more bruises and
cuts. "They…took…my…book. I'm sorry," he avoids looking at Jake.

"Who took your book? Who hurt you?"

"It don't matter."

"Carter, who did this to you?" Jake's blood boils.

"The pretty foster boy found me with the book. He took it and ran to
Momma. Momma was drinking again. I don't bother her none, but I
wanted your book back. She ripped the pages out. And then I cried. She
threw your book away. I'm sorry." He starts crying and covers his face.

"Oh Carter," Jake sighs. "I don't care about the book. There are
millions of books."

"Millions of books?" Carter looks at Jake.

"But only one Carter. Why don't you come and sit on the bench so
I can take a look at your face."

170

Carter crawls out from the bushes carrying his yellow bag and sits on the bench.

"That's where I work," Jake points toward the school. "And my best friend works there too. He has ice packs and ointment that will help your bruises and cuts. His name is D. Let's go and get you all put back together, okay?"

"Is he the police?"

Jake shakes his head.

"Is he a social worker?" Carter asks.

"No. What that lady you call Momma did to you…is wrong."

"It don't matter."

"How often does she hurt you?"

"I try to be real good…but I make her mad a lot."

Jake grabs the sandwiches and puts Hart into his backpack. He holds out his hand.

Carter grabs his hand. "Is one of those sandwiches for me?"

Jake grins. "You bet." He pulls out a sandwich and hands it to Carter as they walk to the school.

*

D ends his lunchtime conversation with another teacher when he sees Jake walk in with Carter. He leads them to the sports office and closes the door behind them.

Carter holds tightly to his yellow bag and stares at D.

"You must be Carter," D smiles. "My name is Devin. You can call me D."

"Are you the police?" Carter asks.

"No."

"Are you a social worker?"

"Nope. I'm a soccer coach, so I am an expert with bruises. Mind if I take a closer look at your face?"

Carter looks at Jake and then back at D. "Okay. My best friend was chocolate too."

"Chocolate? Oh, dark skin? Right on! Where is your best friend now?" D applies ointment to Carter's face.

"Theo died."

"Oh, sorry, kid," D wraps gauze pads over cuts on Carter's arms. He hands him an ice pack. "Put this on the bruise on your face, okay? I'm going to talk with Jake for a minute."

"Okay," Carter holds the ice pack to his face.

Jake shakes his head. "He can't go back, D. I gave him a book…the mom ripped it up, then hurt him."

"I'm going to call my friend, Jake. She'll want to see Carter. They will place him somewhere until they can find a permanent place for him to live. I know you, Jake, and just think about this, bro."

"D, with me, he will at least be safe."

"I know, bro," D holds up his phone. "I'll make the call."

*

A laptop hums on a silver and black desk in the loft. Next to the desk, the top of a black file cabinet hosts an assortment of Reiss's electronics connected to a hybrid silver solar charger, a possession often borrowed from Reiss when in Iraq.

To the right of the desk, an aluminum four-pod stand floats a circular bed, steel framing the hammock-type mattress. A pillow, memory foam, and a worn green blanket invite the weary to drift into dreamland.

Reiss installs the last of six drum pendant lights which drop from the ceiling, the black and silver fixtures adding to the modern design of the room. "And now, for the ultimate test of my electrical skills…" he flicks the light switch and nods as the lights illuminate the loft.

"No more IED lights," Reiss sets the former ceiling lights, remarkably similar to IED's in Iraq, into a black plastic bag and ties the bag shut.

He carries electrical tools and the bag down a black spiral staircase into his living room, and places the bag by the front door. "What's next?" he asks himself, crossing the light fixture task off his checklist.

Prescription bottles gawk at him from his kitchen counter. He reads the reasons for the remedies. "Spasms, pain, headaches, anxiety, more pain, trouble sleeping, antidepressant. Drugs to combat the side effects of the other drugs…drug, drug, drug…fuckin' drug us til we drop," he declares to an empty room.

Reiss shoots hoops with the bottles, tossing each one into the garbage can.

*

Angela walks into D's office wearing a white shirt with white slacks. Gold globes dangle from her ears, the globes partially hidden by her long, caramel brown hair. Concern fills her compassionate deep brown eyes.

Carter's eyes sparkle with the sight of Angela's light chocolate skin.

"Jake and Carter," D motions toward Angela. "This is my friend, Angela."

"Hi Angel," Carter mispronounces her name.

D adds, "Angela is a social worker."

Carter frowns. "I don't talk to social workers."

"Angela is here to help you, Carter," Jake says.

Carter shakes his head.

Angela bends down to Carter's level. "What if I ask you questions…and you just nod yes or shake your head no. Then you don't have to talk to me. Would that be okay?"

Carter stares at her. "Yes, Angel."

"Okay, honey," Angela begins asking him questions.

Jake and D step aside as Angela makes notes while she listens to Carter's answers.

"You did very good, Carter. I'll be right back," Angela walks over to Jake and D. "We'll find him a legal guardian until we find him a new home."

With confidence Jake says, "I'll be his foster parent."

Angela looks at Jake's wedding ring. "Oh, you're married?"

"I…was married. My wife…died." Jake pauses, adjusting to Angela's seemingly harmless observation which is more of a gut-wrenching mind-shattering remark. "Carter and I get along. I have a home with an extra bedroom. I work at this school. He even gets along with my dog. He needs a safe place to live and someone who will not starve or hit him. I'm that guy. And I can't stand the thought of him being somewhere equally as bad as where he is now."

D adds, "The kid can watch soccer films and hang out with me during Jake's classes."

Surprise marks Angela's face. "I'm sorry about your wife, Jake. And with Carter, we do our best to place the kids in safe homes. With the current system, some fall between the cracks until they are brought to our attention with unfortunate events like this." She taps a pen on her pad of paper. "I'll make a few calls and see what we can do. Jake, are you sure you can take care of Carter with your current emotional situation?"

"I'm sure," Jake nods.

Angela puts her hand on Jake's shoulder as she passes him on her way into the hall. "What you're doing is really kind. I'll get the paperwork."

Angela returns with a stack of documents. "Should we jump right in?"

"Let's do it," Jake says.

Angela explains the process with impressive simplicity.

As Jake signs the last document, he takes a deep breath. *I'm probably not ready to be a dad, but I know I can be a better dad than Carter has now*, the thought rolls through his mind.

Angela is about to make a call when her phone rings. "He just signed them," she answers. "The officer is about to talk with Carter. Okay, I'll tell him. Thanks." Angela taps her fingers on the desk for a minute. "Was your wife's name Sadie?"

"Yeah. Why?"

"A former military gal and guy from our office received care packages from Sadie when they were overseas. Kind of funny how things are connected. Anyway, you're set to take Carter home tonight. I have a police officer waiting in the hall. He's going to ask Carter a few questions."

"Does the officer know he'll have to ask yes and no questions? Carter can't talk to police officers either."

Angela's eyebrows rise. "You talk with Carter and I'll let the officer know."

"Deal." Jake walks over to Carter. "Looks like you'll be coming home with Hart and me tonight."

Carter shakes his head. "I can't."

"You don't want to come and live with me?"

"It don't matter."

"Carter, I want to take you away from her. You'll be safe living with me. I promise."

"I'll live with you instead of her?" Carter asks.

"Yep. You'll have your own room and your own bed."

Carter's face lights up as he wraps his arms around Jake. "I'll be real good. Please don't make me go back."

"You're safe now," Jake says, hoping his words are true.

*

Gunner sits on a bench in the cemetery, staring at four grave markers which all share his last name. "Yesterday was tough with all the people," he tells the dead. "I've been traveling a lot with the *Inspiration Behind the Warrior* program. For some reason, people want me to share my story...though I only share the story they can see...I haven't told anyone but my closest guys about you guys...and those guys are now where you guys are...hope the party in heaven is not too fun without me," Gunner grins.

He grabs his crutches and stands on his prosthetic leg. "The therapist doesn't think it's odd I'm having trouble walking with one leg...something about retraining the brain after injury." He adds with sarcasm, "My curse of surviving, right?"

*

In makeshift pajamas, a t-shirt and shorts from Jake's closet, Carter smells his clean bed sheets.

"You brush your teeth, right?" Jake calls out.

"I had a toothbrush once!" Carter answers.

Jake pulls out a new toothbrush and hands it to Carter.

Carter slowly pulls the brush out of the plastic container. "This is like Christmas!"

175

Jake squeezes toothpaste on the brush and shows Carter how to brush his teeth, handing Carter the brush to finish the job.

After five minutes Jake pops his head into the bathroom to see Carter still brushing his teeth. "They're definitely clean now."

Carter says with a mouth full of foam, "It tickles!"

As Jake walks to his own room, Carter follows him. "Oh, right. Let's get you into your own bed."

Carter slides to the ground and cries.

"What's wrong?"

"It don't matter."

Hart drops his hamburger next to Carter's feet.

Carter rolls the hamburger down the hall.

"Okay," Jake says. "Time for bed."

Carter walks to his room and crawls under the covers, his yellow bag on the floor next to the head of his bed.

Jake plugs in a nightlight and turns off the lights. "I'm just down the hall. Sweet dreams, Carter."

"Good night, Jake."

Hart walks into Carter's room and lies down.

Jake smiles. "Looks like you have a guard dog tonight."

Carter tickles Hart on the head. "Good boy."

Jake walks to his room and falls onto the bed. "Love, I have a dog and a son...just missing you."

CHAPTER 28

*What man actually needs is not a tensionless state but rather the
striving and struggling for a worthwhile goal, a freely chosen task.
What he needs is not the discharge of tension at any cost but the call of
a potential meaning waiting to be fulfilled by him.*
–Viktor Frankl

T he clock alarm awakes Jake. He looks toward Sadie's side of the
bed where a dog and a kid stare at him.

Carter smiles. "Can I brush my teeth again?"

Jake grins. "Every day, two times a day."

*

"Beautiful with endless potential," Meg sets up a blank canvas in
her living room. She studies a picture of the bronze memorial stand
she photographed at the Memorial Day Ceremony.

Setting the photograph aside, she chooses paint colors and a few
brushes.

*

Jake, Carter, and Hart arrive at D's office.

Carter takes Hart out of the backpack and walks to D's desk, his
yellow bag secure in his hand.

"What's with the yellow bag?" D asks Jake.

Jake shrugs. "I don't know."

"How did the night go?"

"I want to adopt him."

"A kid, Jake? Oh, bro," D puts his hands on his head then rubs his
eyes. He sighs. "I'll call Angela."

177

"I know nothing about raising a kid but I can do better than whoever was doing it before. You okay with Carter until lunch?"

D motions with his hand. "Leave the dog, too. We have films to check out and equipment to prep. We'll be busy."

"Thanks, D." Jake walks over to Carter. "I'm going to teach classes and then I'll meet you for lunch, okay?"

"You'll come back, right?" Carter asks.

"You bet I'll be back."

Carter watches as Jake leaves, peering around the corner of D's office as Jake waves from down the hall.

Carter walks over to his yellow bag, and pulls out half a loaf of bread. He hands it to D.

D remains expressionless as he looks at the bread. "Bread? You want me to…make you a sandwich?"

"I brought it for you," Carter beams. "It's still soft."

"Thanks, kid. Thanks for thinking of me…but you don't have to bring me food. In fact, you don't have to take care of others anymore. Jake will take good care of you."

"Will you be my dad?" Carter asks.

"No, kid."

"Okay," Carter's expression sullen.

"Uncle. What about if I'm your uncle?" D asks.

"Okay!" Carter grins.

*

Moody blue paint with three white puffs form the background of the canvas scene.

Meg dips a brush into charcoal black and begins painting the boots of the memorial stand in the lowest white cloud which hovers at the bottom of the canvas.

*

Hart frantically runs after his ball in the park.

Jake turns to Carter. "I need to talk to you."

"I'm sorry."

"Why are you sorry?"

Carter tightly holds his yellow bag. "I stole your bread."

"You stole my bread? Were you hungry?"

Carter shakes his head. "I gave it to Uncle D."

"Was Uncle D hungry?"

"I don't know. He's nice."

"He is nice. But if you want to give Uncle D something, or anyone else, just ask me instead of stealing it. Okay?"

Carter braces for punishment. "Are you going to send me back?"

"Of course not! I spoke with Angela today and..." Jake takes a deep breath. "I want to adopt you, Carter."

Carter stares at Jake in silence.

"I am new at being a dad, but you will never go hungry and I will never hit you."

Carter says in a quiet voice, "I want you to be my dad."

"Me too," Jake grins. "You may have to testify, that means tell the judge in a courtroom, that your last foster mom hurt you. Can you do that?"

Carter shakes his head.

Jake kneels in front of Carter. "Sometimes we think about the outcome to get through the process. What that means is we might have to do some things we don't want to do...because we want the result. You have to testify to save other kids from being hurt like you were. And you won't be hurt anymore because you will be with me. I have an idea to take your fear away. Are you ready?"

Carter nods.

"When you are in the front of the courtroom, you and I will not be able to talk but I want to teach you a signal that Sadie and I used to use."

"Who is Sadie?"

"She was my wife...she died. She was my best friend like Theo was your best friend."

"I miss Theo. Do you miss Sadie?"

"Every day, buddy." Jake continues. "The signal goes like this. You put your fingers of both your hands together to form the top of a heart. Then you put your thumbs together to form the bottom pointy part of the heart. If you get scared, just look at me and I'll give you the signal." Jake makes the heart shape with his hands.

Carter makes the heart signal. "Like this?"

"Just like that," Jake grins.

*

"Hi, soldier!" Faye greets as Drew walks through the door of the coffee house.

Drew grins. "Ma'am."

"Did you bring us cookies?"

Drew holds up a tin.

"What kind?" Faye waddles around the counter.

"Chocolate chip."

"Yum!" she grabs a cookie. "How's your sister doing?"

"Nina's okay. How's your husband doing?"

"Journey's good. I told him about you."

"His name is Journey?"

"Yep, that's my hubby. At first he was glad our conversations made me feel better...and then he was jealous like you and me were doing something we weren't supposed to do." Faye grins, "Obviously he underestimates how big I am when I say I am a huge momma! I told him, 'Baby, you're the only man that will appreciate me carrying a fifty pound water balloon!' He was like 'Baby, I know, I'm just on edge, that's all.' But it's like you said about communication. I think we've both changed...me with a big ol' belly and raging hormones...and him with whatever he's doing wherever he is. I heard shots in the background when I talked with him. Maybe that's why you were kicking," she says to her belly. "What did you do for Memorial Day?"

"The POW/MIA Ceremony with the balloons."

"The ten-thousand black balloons? That sounds fun!"

"They called off my best friend's name. He was killed in Iraq."

"That sucks," Faye shakes her head.

"Yeah," Drew nods. "Then we made cookies. What did you do?"

"This big momma sat around and ate a lot of food! I read an article about IED's and concussions. I got all worried about Journey so when he called, that's what I was asking about. He downplays it all so I don't worry...but I'm a smart girl." She looks at Drew with frustration. "With millions of dollars of equipment to find IED's...our guys are still hitting them?!"

"Sometimes you feel like a pawn over there. When we use metal detectors, they make IED's with pressure plates with no metal. When we use ground penetrating radars to see under ground, they learn what type of soil we can't see through. When we use rollers, they offset the charge from the pressure plate to take away our advantage. It's a chess game. Did you know Bill is sick?"

Faye nods. "It's a shame. He's so nice and he does so much for veterans." Concern enters her eyes. "Is he getting worse?"

"Yeah," Drew puts the tin of cookies on the counter. "I have to get going."

"You coming back for a veteran meeting sometime?"

"Maybe."

"Please thank your sister. The veterans loved the last batch of cookies she made," she reaches beneath the counter then hands Drew the previous tin he left.

"I'll tell her," Drew says.

Muggy evening air greets Drew as he leaves the coffee house. His phone beeps with a message from Wyla.

Drew, call me. I need to talk to you. It's important.

Drew deletes the message. "I'm sure it is."

CHAPTER 29

Be yourself. Everyone else is already taken.
−Oscar Wilde

"Which one do you like?" Jake holds up two backpacks.
"The green one," Carter whispers.

"Done," Jake tosses the backpack into the cart. "Clothes, shoes, backpack...do we really need to get dog toothpaste?"

Carter grins and nods.

"Okay," Jake sighs. "Toothpaste, then we're done."

Jake rolls the cart into the checkout aisle.

Carter watches the checkout gal slide items through the laser then place them into plastic bags. "A lot of this is just for me...it's like Christmas!"

The checkout gal smiles. "You have a nice dad."

"I do!" Carter beams.

As they approach the exit an alarms sounds.

"You got to be kidding me!" Jake says under his breath.

A clerk approaches them. "Can I see your receipt, sir?"

Jake hands her the receipt and looks down at a wide-eyed Carter. "It's okay, buddy. Sometimes this happens."

The clerk matches the items in Jake's cart with the receipt. "Okay, sir, everything looks fine. Thank you."

Jake grabs the bags and grins at Carter. "Let's go home."

*

"Now it's your turn," Carter picks up Hart and places him on the bathroom counter.

Hart stares at his toothbrush, licking his lips.

Carter squeezes poultry flavored toothpaste on Hart's toothbrush. "This much?" he asks Jake.

Jake nods in amusement. "Sure."

Carter begins brushing Hart's teeth. "Oh, don't that feel so good, boy? I think he likes it...see, Hart likes it!"

"I see," Jake says. "He looks like he's enjoying it."

Carter rinses the brush. "Okay, rinse!" Carter giggles as Hart drinks from the faucet.

Jake shakes his head at Hart. "You are one strange dog."

*

"Hi, soldier!" Faye greets Drew before he even walks through the front door of the coffee house.

"Ma'am," Drew nods as he steps inside. "Just dropping off cookies."

"I test all cookies before handing them off," Faye reaches out from behind the counter. "My back is screaming at me with this big boy inside," she rubs her belly.

Drew opens the tin and holds it out toward her. "Sugar."

"How I love your sister!" Faye exclaims, taking a cookie.

"When is the baby due?"

"Six more weeks of this..." she sighs. "Pretty soon, I'm just going to roll places and give my feet a break," she laughs. "Yesterday, this guy ordered a coffee...and I was so tired I just wanted to launch it across the room instead of walking it over! But the activity keeps me occupied...I guess," Faye smiles.

"My best friend made a mouse launcher when we were over in Iraq..." Drew grins, recalling the memory as he describes it to Faye. "That might work for launching coffee."

"Did it ever catch a mouse?"

"Jasper finished it and that day it caught the mouse...the guys found it when we got back from...everything," despair fills Drew's eyes. "He was always creating something...activity alleviates the boredom over there."

"That's what Journey says. I'll place an order…one launcher, hold the mouse." Faye grins. "Have you heard of explosively formed projectiles?"

"Yeah. Very advanced and nasty. Another article you read?"

"I heard about EFP's from a veteran who came in for coffee. He wouldn't say much so I researched them…then I was asking Journey about them. He said the same thing you did with them being wicked…the pictures I saw online were awful. He keeps encouraging me to read romance books or something instead of researching how he could be killed…but we," she pats her belly, "are curious ones. We can't wait until daddy gets home."

Drew's phone rings. "I've got to take this. I'll see you later." Drew hands Faye the tin of cookies.

"Tell Nina we love her baking!" Faye grins.

A gal with empty eyes enters the coffee house. "Black, please," she calls out to Faye.

"Dad?" Drew answers the call while walking outside.

"Drew, it's your father."

That's probably where Nina gets the annoying habit of identifying herself, Drew mentally mocks the statement.

"Your mother and I are in town tonight. Nina said you're not coming over for dinner? Is this true?"

"Correct. I'm busy," with great effort, Drew prevents the curses in his mind from coming out his mouth.

"Too busy to see your parents who flew out all this way to see you both? Does this have to do with that Army nonsense?"

Where's my sign! Drew's mind screams.

"Drew, if you can't even stop by for a few minutes that will be quite disappointing."

"Add it to the list, dad. I've gotta go," Drew hangs up. His insides fume, his body pleads to destroy something. In the car, curses fly for several minutes.

*

184

Meg sips from her finger mug and stares at her unfinished painting, the knife-like pain in her head a bit less than before. She looks over at Ruger. "We just do the best we can, right? Pain may slow me down and exhaustion may paste you to the couch...but by golly, we'll keep moving forward, even if our progress can only be seen with a microscope!"

Ruger stretches and rolls onto his side.

Meg takes a deep breath. "Let's finish this," she grabs a brush and begins adding blood red stripes to the flag.

*

"No! I'm sorry! No!" screams pierce the midnight silence.

Jake runs to Carter's bedside. "Carter, you're safe!"

Carter's new pajamas are wet. His sheets are soaked with sweat and urine. "I'm sorry," Carter begins crying.

"No worries, buddy," Jake grabs the oversized t-shirt and shorts from the night before and helps Carter change clothes. He lifts him out of the bed and puts him on the ground. "I'll put on some clean ones," he pulls the sheets off the bed.

A small shiny object falls onto the ground.

Jake picks it up and sets it on the dresser. "A recorder?"

"I don't know what it is," Carter sits on the floor.

"Where did you get it from?" Jake asks.

Carter looks at Jake.

"No, you didn't, did you? Carter...from the store?"

"I'm sorry."

"Why did you steal a recorder?"

"It don't matter."

"It does matter. That's why the alarm went off when we walked out. Where did you hide it?"

"My pocket."

Jake yawns. "No more stealing, okay? Just...no more stealing. If you want something, tell me."

Carter whines, "Are you going to send me back?"

"No, but you'll return the recorder tomorrow."

Carter whispers, "You're going to tell them I stole it?"

"No, you're going to tell them you stole it."

Carter shakes his head.

"Time for bed," Jake pulls back the new blankets for Carter to crawl in. "Good night, Carter," Jake tucks him in.

Exhausted, Jake falls into his own bed.

Moments later, Jake rolls over to see Carter staring at him. "Come on in," Jake moans. "It's late."

Carter and Hart crawl into Sadie's side of the bed.

CHAPTER 30

Whatever is true, whatever is noble, whatever is right, whatever is pure, whatever is lovely, whatever is admirable—if anything is excellent or praiseworthy—think about such things.
–NIV Bible, Philippians 4:8

"I'm proud of you for being brave and returning that recorder today, Carter," Jake praises. "Okay, bubbles, bath paints, fluffy towels...and you'll be okay while I make a phone call, right?" Jake asks.

Carter nods. "I love baths."

"Music or no music?"

"I love music," Carter grins.

"You got it," Jake turns on country music. "I'll be back."

Jake rubs his eyes as he walks out of the bathroom and dials his mom's phone number. "This should be interesting."

One ring. Two rings.

"Hey, mom."

"Hi, honey!" Phoebe answers.

"I'm not sure how much time I have so I'll give you the cliff notes."

"What's going on?" concern evident in Phoebe's voice.

"This gal, who I don't know, dropped off a puppy at my door. We hit it off right away...the puppy, not the girl. I named the dog Hart. When I was at the park with Hart, I met this boy, a foster kid, named Carter. Well, long story short, his foster mom hurt him...and I found him in pretty bad shape in the park."

Jake takes a deep breath. "D called his friend who works in the foster system. She assessed that Carter could not go back to his foster home, and I...signed papers today to become his legal guardian, his permanent legal guardian, and that's why I'm calling. A social worker will be calling you to see if I'm fit to raise a child."

Silence.

Jake adds, "And Sadie had a journal. She wrote a song for me. I'm going to put some music to her lyrics, and audition for the singing competition she wanted me to try out for. She's teaching me through her journal how to, not move on, but grow from the loss...if that makes sense. You're still there, right?"

"Yes, I'm here," Phoebe says. "How old is Carter?"

"Six."

More silence.

"Mom?"

In a patient tone, Phoebe responds. "Jake, you're twenty-eight with a life ahead of you. A child changes everything."

"My life ended when Sadie left. She's where I belonged and with her gone I didn't really...care about anything...until Hart, and then Carter. And when I think of my future, they are the only certain ones I see. I'm not saying it will be easy, but I know I'm ready for whatever it brings."

"Jake, you've always followed your heart. Continue to do that. It's wonderful that Sadie wrote a song for you and I'm sure you'll do well in the competition, honey. You're very talented. I'm proud of you...I'm sure Sadie would be proud."

"Thanks," Jake lets out a sigh of relief. "I have to go. Carter is finishing his bath."

Phoebe inquires, "When will I meet my grandchild?"

"I'll call you when it's official and then the whole family can meet him. I just don't want him to meet you all then be disappointed if it does not work out."

"Okay, honey. I love you."

"Love you too, mom." Jake hangs up.

*

On the canvas, Meg adds a dab of copper paint at the top of the flag pole then scribbles the name in the bottom corner of the finished painting. *We Remember.*

*

Saturday morning, Jake awakes to a small foot in his side.

Carter and Hart are on Sadie's side of the bed again.

Jake pulls out Sadie's journal and tiptoes to the living room. He lounges on the couch and opens her book.

I'm finding we have to be strong enough to explore our weaknesses. Our strength lies in our flaws and perceived limitations. We're taught to cover them up, deny them, or avoid them. But when we really take a look at our fears, we realize they are made up. They are not truths. We have the power to change or even eliminate them. Yet, we have to take that first step in exposing them. That first step is hard, probably because we're still unsure of ourselves, still wondering if becoming vulnerable is worth the risk. Once we start, we have an audience, and quitting becomes less of an option.

"Fine," Jake says aloud. "I will start writing the music for your lyrics."

Life is a combat zone. We first must declare victory, then fight. We first must declare happiness for our lives, then live. I have an amazing life filled with beautiful friends, family, and my best friend, Jake. I'm declaring victory on the WARE project. And I'm declaring happiness for my life...from this moment on.

Jake picks up his journal and writes. *Entry #9: Declare victory, then fight. Declare happiness, then live.*

He whispers to the morning rays of sun streaming through the living room. "I wish you were here, love, but I'm slowly starting to understand."

*

Meg waves to Nina from across Sydney's Cafe.

Nina grins and leads Edison over to the table.

"Hey, little man!" Meg gives Edison a high-five.

Edison smiles and climbs up on Meg's lap.

Nina plunks into a chair. "I'm glad you called to meet for lunch. I was on my way home and wondering if I'd have to make ketchup sandwiches for lunch."

Meg's nose scrunches. "That doesn't sound good."

Nina points to a square item leaning against the adjacent table. "What is that?"

"A present for you."

"For me? Can I open it now?"

Meg nods.

"Why are you giving me a present?"

"You'll see," Meg says.

"Meg," tears fill Nina's eyes as she gazes at the painting. "Meg," she looks back at Meg. "You painted this for me? Why? It's so beautiful."

"I took pictures at the Memorial Day POW Ceremony…and one of the photos reminded me of when I heard Jasper's name."

"So you painted it…for me?"

"It's a thank you…for what you gave."

"I'm a mess," Nina wipes her eyes. "Thank you," she hugs Meg. "This means…so much."

"I'm glad you like it. Shall we eat lunch?"

Nina carefully rewraps the painting. "I'm going to take it out to my car…and then yes."

Edison watches Nina leave with the painting then looks at Meg.

Meg jokes, "I gave her a painting and she gave me you."

*

"Hey, Angela!" Jake opens the front door.

Hart races behind the living room couch as Angela walks inside.

"Hey guys! How are you doing, Carter?"

Carter shyly smiles. "Hi, Angel."

"His face looks much better, Jake. How is he doing?"

"He has some trouble sleeping, but we're able to calm him…'we' being the dog and I."

Angela looks around the house.

"Do you want a tour?" Jake asks.

"I'd especially like to see where Carter sleeps."

Carter takes her hand and guides her across the living room to his door. "This is my room."

"You have a very nice room, Carter. Jake, do you mind if I ask him some questions without you?"

"I'll make lunch."

Carter bounds out of the room. "Angel says her name is really Angela, but we can still call her Angel."

"Angel is an appropriate name for her," Jake grins. "Does Angel want to stay for lunch?"

"Thank you for the offer, Jake. Maybe another day?"

"Sure. Did we answer all your questions?"

"I have papers for you to sign and then I'm going to call your mom later today. Did you get a chance to talk with her?"

"She is expecting your call. If you need anything else just let me know. Or D. He knows everything about me."

"He is a good friend, Jake. He would do anything for you."

"He is a great guy. We've been friends for a long time."

Carter walks over to Angela as she opens the front door to leave. "If you need to see my room again…just let me know."

Jake stifles a laugh.

Angela bends down. "Thank you, Carter. I will let you know." She turns to Jake. "Thanks for letting me come over."

"You bet. Anytime."

"Have a good day, guys!" Angela waves.

A few moments later, there is a knock at the door.

Jake opens the door. "Did you forget…Oh…come in Meg."

Hart once again shoots behind the couch.

"Buenos días! Am I interrupting anything?"

"Carter and I are about to have lunch."

"Hey Carter, I'm Meg."

Carter says in a barely audible voice, "Hi."

"Wait…" Jake narrows his eyes. "Did my family send you?"

"I wanted to stop by, but they gave me another reason."

"Which one called you? My sister or my mom?"

"I can't divulge that information. It's top secret."

"Ah, my sister Beth, then."

Meg hands a bag to Carter. "I brought something for you."

"For me?" Carter reaches inside the bag and pulls out a dog kite. "Thank you!"

Jake says, "It's a kite. You run with it in the park on a windy day, and that big part, the dog, flies in the air like an airplane."

"Can I play with it outside?"

"Sure."

"Okay," Carter runs outside with the kite.

Meg's facial expression changes the moment Carter leaves.

"I'm okay, Meg."

Meg nods. "I see. I'm proud of you. You have every excuse not to bother with a kid right now, so yes, I know you're okay. In fact, I dare say, you look a bit perky."

"Then why are you so…not perky."

She sighs. "On Purpose Journey."

"What about it?"

"The troops used to respond to Sadie…but with her gone, they write to me."

Jake nods.

"Sadie was the counselor. She knew what to say when someone was pouring out their heart. She knew how to let them own their feelings. She knew how to play the social game…I don't."

"Yet," Jake says.

"The troops I've connected with are such sweet souls….one guy returned from a mission where one of the planes was shot down. Four guys died and a few were injured. This guy just wants to come home. I don't want him to die. I don't want any of them to die, but there's nothing I can do for them. I have no control."

Jake transfers lunch from plates to plastic bags. "Just be the best friend you can be with the moments you have with these people. They are not pouring out their hearts to you for you to give them some kind of out or fix their security challenges. They're telling you how they feel because you will listen. They just want someone to know their story."

Meg gives Jake a strange look. "She would have said the same thing. She would have added that being sad would not change their situation...to stop making their sad story all about me. It's about them, so keep it about them."

Jake grins. "That sounds just like Sadie."

Outside, Carter flies his kite a foot off the ground.

"Miss Meg, do you want to come to the park with us?"

"I'd love to join you both...but just to monitor your mental status for my report to your family, of course," she laughs.

"I can't believe Beth sent you over here to spy. Well, I guess I can."

"This is such a neat toy!" Carter exclaims.

"Carter," Jake says. "Let's see how high that kite can really fly!"

*

Drew answers the call. "Yeah?"

"Drew, it's Nina."

"Nina, you know I have caller ID and recognize your voice."

"Not now, Drew. It's...it's Bill..."

"What about him?"

CHAPTER 31

Cherish your visions; cherish your ideals; cherish
the music that stirs in your heart,
the beauty that forms in your mind, the loveliness
that drapes your purest thoughts,
for out of them will grow all delightful conditions,
all heavenly environment;
of these, if you will remain true to them,
your world will at last be built.
–James Allen

Three red velvet chairs face a flag draped casket.

The chaplain closes, "We do not mourn for Bill, for he has found refuge in the great harbor of eternal peace. We mourn for ourselves, for a good friend is no longer among us. We will miss his shoulder next to ours. We will miss his encouragement and counsel as we meet the storm and strife of life."

The three man rifle unit stands at a distance facing the casket. At the command of the officer in charge, they fire three volleys.

Carter crawls on Jake's lap after the first shot.

A bugler sounds Taps; the powerful, soul-moving melody rings through the crisp afternoon air.

Two members of the Coast Guard Honor Guard, in full uniform down to the white gloves and polished black shoes, raise the flag from the casket and hold it in a horizontal position, waist high over the casket, until the conclusion of Taps. The reflection of the flag dances on the top of the casket—a red, white, and blue tide washing over the cherry wood. A few feet away, wind blows a chime hanging from an old tree; the clang accompanies Taps in perfect harmony.

Carter leans back against Jake's shoulder as the flag is folded into a triangle, the red and white stripes vanishing into the blue.

Each member of the Honor Guard holds the folded flag while the other salutes.

One of the coast guardsmen walks over with the flag and presents it to Gigi. "On behalf of the President of the United States, the Commandant of the Coast Guard, and a grateful nation, please accept this flag as a symbol of our appreciation for your loved one's service to Country and the Coast Guard. God bless you, and God bless the United States of America," he salutes the flag then walks to the side of the casket.

Gigi tightly holds the flag on her lap.

Jake puts his hand on Gigi's. "We'll be right over there."

Jake and Carter walk over to the tree housing the chime, the branches of the tree spread out like a bad hair day.

As Carter stands in front of Jake watching people place flowers on the casket, Jake gives Carter a backwards hug.

Carter puts his hands up to his shoulders, resting them on top of Jake's hands.

An older man approaches them. "You knew Bill?"

Jake nods. "He was a good man."

The older man loses a tear. "He loved ya for who ya were," his voice squeaky with sadness. "Being yerself was okay by him." He looks at the casket then walks away.

Jake whispers to Carter, "I love ya for who ya are."

Carter puts his head back to look at Jake and smiles.

Gigi motions to Jake. "Thank you for coming, dear."

"It was amazing, Gigi. Bill was amazing."

"Yes he was."

"Hola," Meg touches Jake's shoulder.

Jake turns around. "Hey, Meg, Drew, Nina…"

"Hey, Jake," Drew says, placing his hand on Gigi's shoulder. "I'm sorry for your loss, ma'am."

"Thank you, dear."

Jake hugs Gigi. "I'll call you later."

Jake waves to Meg, Drew, and Nina before he and Carter walk to the far end of the cemetery.

Jake motions toward a grave. "This was my Sadie. She would have loved to meet you, Carter." Jake sits down in the grass.

Carter sits next to him. "Why did they shoot three times?"

"It's called three volleys and it's an old battlefield custom. The two battling sides would stop fighting to clear their dead from the battlefield. When they fired three volleys, or three shots, it meant the dead had been properly cared for. Then, they would resume their battle." Jake looks over toward Carter. "The three shots mean that Bill has been properly cared for, laid to rest."

"That he's safe now?"

"Right," Jake nods.

"What is Gigi going to do with the flag that man gave her?"

"She was given a memorial flag. It is only used for funeral services and since it is not a standard flag or a storm flag, it is stored in a presentation box. It was given to her from a grateful nation. Sadie would have loved that service. It was so powerful and...honorable."

*

"To Bill," Drew drinks from a full bottle of Jack as he stands next to his kitchen sink. The potion slides down his throat with a slight blissful burn.

Drew pours the rest of the bottle down the drain. "So long my steady friend, sweet golden nectar that numbs my world."

*

Jake pulls into his mom's driveway.

Phoebe opens the front door before Jake can knock. "Hi, honey!"

"Mom, this is Carter. Carter, this is..."

"I'm your Grandma Phoebe, Carter. It's nice to meet you."

Carter grins. "Hi."

Grace comes up to Jake. "Oh...my...gosh...my little brother has finally come to a family lunch?" she hugs him.

"Hey, Grace. How are the blind dates coming?"

Beth flies around the corner. "Jakey!" she hugs Jake.

Jake introduces, "Carter, this is Beth, my younger sister, and Grace, my older sister."

Beth kneels down in front of Carter. "Carter, welcome to the family. We're a goofy bunch but you'll find us fun. Would you like something to drink?"

Carter looks at Jake.

Jake nods.

Beth says, "Why don't we go look in the refrigerator and see what options we have. I need something to drink too."

Carter takes her hand as they disappear into the kitchen.

Phoebe guides Jake and Grace to the living room. "Let's sit down."

Grace interrogates in her usual fashion. "Are you okay? Are you really going to adopt him? Did you think this through?"

"Grace, I'm okay. Yes, I'm going to adopt Carter." Jake pauses for a moment. "Have you ever felt led to do something totally out of your comfort zone, and something that you didn't even know if you could do...but then found that when you started the process, that was the only time you felt a sense of peace in your life?"

"A kid, Jake? This is more crazy than peaceful."

"Carter and I are meant to be a family, Grace." He grins. "But...I know I'm crazy and that never changed."

Grace's concern shifts to acceptance. "Then we support you...and yes, you're crazy...no argument there."

"Thanks." Jake turns toward Phoebe. "Did Angela call yesterday?"

Phoebe nods. "Angela called and asked questions about who you are and if I think you're fit to be a parent. I told her 'absolutely not.'"

"Well, at least she has been warned," Grace smirks.

Jake fires back at his mom. "Very funny...but I know there's no way you'd pass up a chance to be a grandma."

When Beth returns with Carter, Carter sits on Jake's lap.

Grace asks Carter, "What did you guys do today?"

"We went to a funeral with guns and Gigi. Then we sat by Sadie. Hart did not come with us today...he's at home."

Grace turns to Jake. "Who is Hart?"

"My mystery puppy that was dropped off a few weeks ago. A blond gal in a red car dropped him off with a note, and left without saying a word. I gave up trying to figure out where he came from."

Grace asks, "Who is Gigi?"

"Sadie met Gigi's husband, Bill, when she was shipping care packages. We met Gigi at the park when she was walking with Bill. And I recently met Gigi again outside the bookstore in town. We've met every Sunday since. Bill died a few days ago. The ceremony, with military funeral honors, was today."

Beth chimes in. "What were you doing at a bookstore?"

Jake grins. "I needed a journal because I'm reading Sadie's journal and I'm trying to learn the lessons she was learning."

"What kind of lessons?" Beth asks.

"How to change your thoughts, and how changing your thoughts can change your life. Her wisdom amazes me," Jake chokes back emotions.

Phoebe comments, "Sadie was a remarkable woman, Jake."

Grace and Beth nod.

Jake takes a deep breath. "She was."

"A lot of changes," Phoebe adds.

"Changes for both of us," Jake looks at Carter. "But we're doing okay, aren't we?"

"Yep," Carter leans into Jake's shoulder.

"Let's head into the dining room for lunch," Phoebe stands.

Jake whispers to Beth, "You sent Meg to my house to spy?"

Beth suppresses a smile. "What are you talking about?"

Jake confirms, "Yeah, that's what I thought."

*

The aroma of cookies greets Drew as he walks into Nina's house.

"I know," Nina defends, "this container is bigger, but this way the veterans can have more than one cookie...and after Bill's funeral...I was in a cookie-making mood. And tell Faye I say 'Hi.'"

A look of annoyance crosses Drew's face. "She's married, Nina. And I would never steal another man's wife."

"I didn't say anything. It's just nice you have a friend."

"She's always researching and freaking out about something that could kill her husband…kind of odd in a funny way. But I see the other side of waiting for us when we're overseas."

"Lonely on both ends," Nina hands Drew the cookies.

"Thanks. You're welcome to come if you want to."

Nina's eyebrows rise. "Thanks, Drew. That's nice of you to offer but I'll stay the secret cookie baker."

"Later," Drew closes the front door.

Nina opens the cabinet and pulls out two nails and a hammer.

She carries Meg's painting from her bedroom to the living room, testing several locations to see where it fits best.

Edison watches as Nina pounds nails into the living room wall.

"There," Nina hangs the picture, adjusting it slightly so it is level. "It says 'We Remember' because we remember daddy."

"Daddy," Edison points to the flag in the window.

"That's right, honey," Nina wipes a tear from her eye. She whispers, "I'll never stop missing daddy."

*

"Hi, soldier!"

"Hey, ma'am," Drew hands Faye the container. "Here they are, freshly baked and twice as many."

"Tonight, why don't you bring them in to the veterans? They want to meet the delivery boy."

"I can do that," Drew opens the top. "Test one first?"

"You know me well, soldier. I'll take three to test."

"Read anything lately?"

"Journey got so mad at me yesterday. I told him he can tell me what to read when he's home…and until then…I'm in charge," she grins. "Of course, that will change when he gets home…I'll still be in charge," she laughs.

"More IED's?"

"Close. Directional Fragmentation Charges."

"DFC's…ah yes. Victim operated and used in Afghanistan."

"What do you mean by victim operated?" Faye asks.

"Pressure plate activated," Drew clarifies.

"Oh, yeah. Journey was saying how DFC's are like giant shotgun shells! And wicked!"

"True that. They take a large canister similar to what they used in Iraq to make EFPs, but they pack the bottom half of it with explosives then place fragmentation material on top of it, such as rocks, glass, nuts, and bolts. Then they bury it in a mud wall, or lay it on a roof aimed at the gunner's hatch on the top of the vehicles. They detonate it with a command wire with a simple switch on the end as the gunner crosses its path…it's nasty sh…stuff."

"Stuff, huh?" Faye chuckles. "I married military, soldier. I know how you all say stuff all the time," she laughs. "Oh, before you go into the meeting, Bill requested this for you from someone he knows," she points to a box. "It came yesterday."

Drew sets down the cookies and opens the box. "A guitar?"

"He said something about you playing when in Iraq?"

"I did. Haven't played since," Drew runs his hand along the soundboard of the guitar.

"Well, now you can. You should get to the meeting before it starts…or at least get the cookies there before it starts."

"You're trying to convince me to go to the meeting?"

"With Bill gone…yes, although being this pregnant…please don't make me drag you. I can barely tie my own shoes."

"At his funeral they read off his service accomplishments…"

"I wasn't able to go…" she whines. "Was it beautiful?"

"Yeah. I didn't know he had done so much. I'll attend the meeting tonight…so you can just focus on tying those shoes."

"Good. Up the stairs and you'll see the others. Oh, and you can leave the guitar behind the counter here if you want."

"Thanks," Drew sets the guitar into the box and opens the tin for Faye to take another cookie before heading up the stairs.

CHAPTER 32

Let us never accept mistakes as final; let us organize victory out of the broken ranks of failure and, despite all odds, fight on calmly, courageously, unflinchingly, serenely confident that, in the end, right living and right doing must triumph.
—William George Jordan

Jake instructs, "If the computer game does not work like it should, just read your book. I'll check on you during my second class."

"Okay," Carter excitedly stares at the computer screen.

During Jake's second class, he dashes back to his office.

Carter is on the couch with his head on his knees, crying.

"What's going on, Carter?"

"I tried and tried and kept messing up," Carter whines.

"Okay, bud, come here," Jake bends down to Carter's level. "You have two choices. You can keep trying, or you can stop playing the game and read. Which one do you want to do?"

"I want to play the game, but I can't..."

Jake holds up his hand. "You are smart and if you want to play the game, then play the game the best that you can. If you get stuck, that's okay. As you learn more, you will be able to pass those levels. Addison wants you to have fun with this game, not be upset if you cannot master it on the first day. Say this out loud, 'I can achieve anything I want to achieve because I'm brilliant.'"

"I can achieve anything I want to achieve because I'm brilliant...what does brilliant mean?"

"It means you are really smart."

"Oh, okay."

"I need to get back to my class."

Carter wipes his eyes. "I want to try again."

"Then try," Jake motions to the computer.

Within ten minutes of starting to teach, Jake hears a young voice yell, "I'm brilliant!"

Jake grins as his students look toward his office.

*

"Sgt. Manning," with slight surprise in his voice, Reiss opens his apartment door. "You should have called first. I could have made us a nice dinner…maybe even dressed up," disdain accompanies a muddy smell oozing from Reiss's apartment.

"Sgt. Cooper asked me to deliver a message."

"I don't take orders anymore. I'm out of the fuckin' Army."

Drew continues. "Cooper said he didn't fuckin' spend two weeks in your hospital room in Germany so you could piss your life away when you got back to the States."

"Nah, he spent two weeks in my room because his wife wouldn't come to Germany to…"

"Enough," Drew scolds. "You're welcome to come with me to the meeting place I go to if you want."

"AA?"

Drew shakes his head. "Still an asshole."

Reiss grins briefly before torment fills his eyes. "I remember parts of what happened that day."

"Doesn't matter."

"You should know."

"No, Reiss. It is what it is…the past. You can't go back. I can't go back. Now and the future is what matters."

"That what they teach in your special little meetings?"

Drew curses. "Find a meeting, Reiss. I've seen Cooper pissed off once…that's enough. And you smell like shit. Take a shower."

Reiss swears as Drew leaves. "Go report to daddy, Manning."

Drew makes a gesture with his hand as he walks away.

Reiss smirks. "Relay that same message to Cooper from me!"

Reiss slams the door and picks up his garbage can, tossing it into the middle of the room. "My life, is my fuckin' life!" he shouts. He grabs his car keys and storms out.

*

"Carter, I'm going to talk with Jake for a few minutes. You are welcome to play while we talk, okay?" Addison says.

Carter darts toward the library area of the classroom and lounges on the floor with a book.

Addison walks over to Jake and sits on a desk in the back of her classroom. "Carter is so intelligent. He understands complicated material but lacks some basics."

"Makes sense," Jake says. "What do you suggest?"

A sparkly pink clip holds all but two wisps of her sandy blond hair. Addison twirls a runaway strand with her finger. "With one more week of school left, I can teach him the basics during my free hour and after school."

"When can we start?"

"Tomorrow," Addison stands. "How are you doing, Jake?" she touches his arm.

"I'm...okay. How are you?" Jake follows her toward the library area of the classroom.

"I'm working on forgetting that chapter in my life," Addison's smile is bittersweet. With a tender tone she adds, "What you are doing for Carter...Sadie would have been so proud."

"Thanks. I'm new to all of this but Carter and I are doing well. Thanks for spending time with him today."

"Sure. And I'm glad he likes the computer game. Carter, it was nice to see you again," Addison smiles.

"It was nice to see you too, Miss Addy."

Before leaving the classroom, Jake glances at Carter's enlarged pockets. He whispers, "Is there anything you'd like to leave in this classroom?"

"Jake? Everything okay?" Addison asks.

"Yeah." Jake shoots Carter a look of question. He whispers again, "Return it before we leave the classroom."

Carter meanders to the toy section and empties his pockets, placing several toy cars on a blue plastic shelf.

Jake shakes his head and mouths an apology toward Addison.

Addison answers with her eyes then turns around to clean the classroom board while Carter returns the toys.

"Good job," Jake puts his hand on Carter's shoulder. "Later, Addison!"

"Bye, boys," Addison waves.

*

"Hey," Reiss walks into the On Purpose Journey office.

"Hola," Meg looks up. "How's life?"

Reiss tosses his keys and phone onto a small round table and drops into a plush chair in the corner of the room. "I just got a ticket."

"For?"

"Speeding."

"And why were you speeding?" Meg asks in her calm tone. "So excited to see me?"

"I was pissed off," Reiss sighs.

"Would you like to color a picture?"

Reiss grins. "Color?"

Meg nods and points to Edison behind a counter. "Edison was pretty upset when his mom left so he's coloring a picture for the troops overseas to deal with that emotion…and he's doing a fine job. He may be willing to share crayons with you if you want to color as well."

Reiss walks over to the coloring table.

Meg bends down next to Edison. "Will you share the crayons with Reiss?"

Edison hands Reiss a crayon and a coloring book.

"Thanks, buddy," Reiss grabs the coloring book. "I'm not going to…"

"I don't think Edison invites many others to color with him...he has a bit of a," Meg pauses, "sharing challenge right now...so I think it would be appropriate to just color one page with him...for him."

A dimple sinks Reiss's cheek. "For him," he sits on a mini chair, his legs stretched sideways.

Edison stops coloring and watches as Reiss outlines his superhero character in red before coloring in the picture.

Reiss sets aside the red crayon and picks up a blue one.

Edison picks up the red crayon and outlines his superhero character in red.

"Good job, buddy," Reiss grins. He turns toward Meg. "You're on babysitting duty?"

Meg stacks items inside care packages. "I'm trading for Nina's cookies. It's a sweet trade. Edison will sometimes even help me with care packages...so then I get help and cookies."

"Aren't there laws against that?"

"I don't discriminate. I'm a shameless user of people."

Reiss hands his finished picture to her.

Meg analyzes the picture. "Well done, Reiss. And being the shameless user I am, here you go," she hands him an empty care package box.

"Kind of weird being on this end of the process," Reiss begins filling the box. "Do you and Gunner still have meetings?"

"Yeparooney. Cinnamon rolls at Sydney's tomorrow morning."

"Cinnamon rolls sound good."

"I'll save you a seat."

Reiss sets a full box on the counter. "I have to go clean garbage off my floor."

"Sounds delightful. Well, my crayons are available any time."

Reiss laughs. "See ya, Meg."

"Adios, Reiss. See you tomorrow."

"Maybe...I'm not sure," Reiss turns back toward her before leaving. "Yeah, save me a seat. I'll be there."

*

Jake and Carter pull into the parking lot of Angela's office where a man and a boy loudly argue.

Carter stares at the boy. "Why is that man yelling at Tag?"

"People sometimes choose not to control their anger. You know that boy?"

Carter nods. "He was nice to me when Theo died." Carter waves at the boy and receives a disgusted look in return.

The man curses toward Jake and Carter. "Keep walking!"

Jake puts his hand on Carter's shoulder and directs him inside.

"Hey, Carter!" Angela's assistant, Ruby, makes snapping noises with her chewing gum. "How's my favorite guy doing?"

"Hi, Miss Ruby." Carter remains close to Jake.

Angela rushes into the lobby area. "Hey, guys! Carter, I have a few questions to ask you so you can come with me."

Carter looks back as Jake nods in encouragement.

Jake leans back in one of three navy blue thin cushioned chairs in Angela's waiting room; a car magazine stares at him from the table. *Haven't touched Candy since Sadie died*, his thoughts roll back to his conversations with Sadie about Candy.

Ruby breaks the silence. "Jake, what you're doing for Carter is great. He's a good kid."

"I agree."

"When Carter first came through this office, he was closed off and pretty beat up," Ruby pops her gum. "His mother was a drug addict. Angela makes a difference in the process of placing kids. She's not just about getting them into a foster home; she thinks they are better off waiting until the right family comes along. There are so many kids needing homes and not enough parents willing to take them in. Carter is lucky to have you."

Carter bounces out in front of Angela.

"That should do," Angela says to Jake. "Thanks for bringing him in, Jake!"

Jake nods. "You gals have a nice day."

"Will do," Angela smiles and walks back to her office.

Ruby cracks her gum. "See you guys later!"

*

Drew sits at the edge of the cemetery duck pond and allows his anger to run wild as his mind fumes. *Reiss went from former marine and a hell of a medic...to pissed off, useless, and hiding in misery.*

A duck scurries toward the edge of the pond as its intended target duck flies off.

"Chased off for now...but not gone," Drew says aloud. He wishes he had his flask for times like this...but is glad he doesn't.

CHAPTER 33

Impossible is just a big word thrown around by small men who find it easier to live in the world they've been given than to explore the power they have to change it. Impossible is not a fact.
It's an opinion. Impossible is not a declaration. It's a dare.
Impossible is potential.
Impossible is temporary. Impossible is nothing.
–Muhammad Ali

Meg looks up as Jake and Carter walk into the On Purpose Journey office. "Hola, mi amigos!"

Jake's mind states the obvious. *No baggy camouflage pants. No paint-stained shirt. No ball cap with a messy red ponytail hanging out the back.*

"You look pretty," Carter says to Meg.

"Thank you, Carter." Meg looks at Jake. "Wow, a speechless Jake after my makeover from your sisters."

"You…look…good." Jake clears his throat.

"I dig the changes they suggested."

"Yeah…I second that. How's everything going?"

"It's madness with the *Inspiration Behind the Warrior* programs Gunner and I are developing plus keeping these care packages going overseas."

Jake turns to see a familiar face walk into the room.

"Candy Man!" Reiss shakes Jake's hand.

Carter stares at Reiss's face and slides behind Jake.

"Hey, Reiss," Jake says. "What have you been up to?"

"Facial Surgeries. Driving fast. Wrecking cars. Jumping out of a plane. Screaming at doctors. Getting out of the Army."

"How is civilian life?"

"Pretty fu...awesome, man. Who is this?" Reiss looks at Carter.

"This is Carter. Carter, this is Reiss," Jake introduces.

Still partially behind Jake, Carter whispers, "Hi."

"I'm adopting him."

"Gotcha." Reiss studies Meg. "Meg...you look...hotter."

"Jake's sisters did a makeover."

"Are they hot and single?" Reiss flexes and extends his left hand several times. "I could take on two ladies...don't want anyone feeling left out."

"You're so thoughtful," Meg responds with sarcasm.

"That's me," he beams. "So Jake, how's the car?"

"Haven't worked on it for a while."

"You've been waiting for me? That's understandable, man. I don't like doing things without myself either."

Meg chuckles.

"Yeah, that's it, Reiss," Jake grins.

"I'm done with speed activities for a while...they've become boring. I'm ready to get my hands under a classic."

Jake writes down his number and address. "Come on by."

"What kind of car, again?"

"'72 Nova."

"I've got a guy that can hook you up with some spinners..."

Jake shakes his head. "Still keeping it stock, man."

"That's right, I forgot. No spinners." Reiss turns to Meg. "You ready?"

Meg says to Jake, "We're picking up some donations and I needed Reiss's muscles."

Reiss flexes his not quite bulky but not scrawny arms.

Jake laughs. "Sounds good. We'll see you guys later."

"What happened to that man's face?" Carter asks Jake.

"He was burned," Jake says as they walk to the car.

"Why?"

"He was a soldier in the Army. Some bad people tried to kill him when he was fighting for our country's freedom...but he survived. He's very strong."

"Oh," Carter nods.

*

D flashes the peace sign at Jake from Jake's front porch. "First day of summer vacation!"

"I'll be at school next week to finish paperwork but no more classes to teach. When does your soccer summer camp begin?"

"One week," D says.

Carter runs up to D and gives him a hug. "Uncle D!"

"Hey, kid. How's my favorite nephew?"

Jake unlocks his front door. "You camping out on my porch?"

"Heck yeah, do you have any hot dogs?"

"No," Jake walks inside. "But I have marshmallows."

D follows Jake inside. "Have you put music to Sadie's lyrics yet?"

Hart runs behind the couch as D walks in.

"Nope. You staying for a while?"

"Nah, I just wanted to see if you had the song ready yet. I'm going on a hot date with Angela tonight."

"Nice," Jake grins. "Tell her we say hello."

"And make the conversation about you? Nope. I'll tell her my abs of steel say hello," D lifts his shirt.

"Yeah, man, tell her that right away…it'll save you some dinner money."

"My remark isn't kid appropriate. See you later, Jake!"

"Later, D," Jake walks to the bedroom closet. Flipping the latches on the black case, he pulls out a guitar and carries it to the living room.

"I love guitars!" Carter sits on the couch.

"I'm going to create a song with lyrics Sadie wrote…so I have to mess around with different notes to come up with a tune for the song."

"Can I watch?"

"Sure," Jake nods as his fingers begin dancing with the strings.

CHAPTER 34

There are seasons, in human affairs, of inward and outward
revolution, when new depths seem to be broken up in the soul, when
new wants are unfolded in multitudes, and a new and undefined good
is thirsted for. There are periods when...to dare, is the highest wisdom.
—William Ellery Channing

S unday morning fog lounges on the streets and lawns.
Jake knocks on Gigi's front door.

"Come in, dears," Gigi's weary voice greets Jake and Carter. Her kitchen shades are closed and the drapes are pulled shut. Stuffy air hovers in the front hall.

Carter makes a face and looks at Jake. "It smells..."

Jake whispers, "Shhh...I know."

Dirty dishes line the kitchen counter.

"Would you like some tea?" Gigi opens her tea jar. "Oh dear, there's only one bag."

Jake puts his hand on Gigi's shoulder. "I have an idea and I'm hoping you'll say yes."

"Oh?"

Jake continues. "I thought it would be fun to have lunch at the bakery. My stomach has been craving hot ham since I saw their sign this morning. Care to join us for lunch?"

"That sounds nice. I have not been out since..."

"I know, Gigi. Do you mind if we stop at the store?"

"Oh, I guess I could pick up a few things myself."

"Why don't you take a minute and write down the things you need from the store. Carter can help you." Jake motions for Carter to come over and whispers, "Keep her busy. Tell her a story or ask her questions while I clean up the kitchen. Can you do that?"

Carter nods in delight with the assigned secret mission.

Gigi takes a pad of paper and disappears into the den.

Carter follows her and smiles back at Jake.

Jake fills the sink with warm water and soap, sliding each dish into the water.

Carter peeks into the kitchen twenty minutes later. "She's coming!"

"Good job, buddy. I'm done."

Gigi looks at the clean counter. "Oh, my, I cannot believe you washed my dishes, Jake. I'm sorry you had to see this," she motions across the counter.

"My friend, D, came over after Sadie died to find not only my counter a mess, but my whole house a mess. This was nothing compared to my place! But I'm starving, so let's get to the bakery before they run out of ham!"

*

"Hi, soldier!"

"Hey, ma'am," Drew grins. "I found out at the last meeting why I never see anyone walk through here to go to the meeting."

"Oh, you've been told about the secret entrance out back. Yeah, most of them prefer to use that entrance instead of coming through the coffee shop. How's life?" Faye asks.

"Okay. How are…"

"Don't ask how I'm doing…I'm huge!" Faye turns sideways.

"Cookie?" Drew holds out the tin.

"These aren't making me huge, are they?"

"No, ma'am."

Faye takes a cookie. "Oatmeal?"

"Oatmeal Raisin."

"Yum!" Faye throws back her head before taking a bite.

"How's Journey doing?"

Faye's face breaks into a smile. "He says he'll be glad when he's home because then I'll stop asking him bomb questions," she laughs. "My topic this week was HME's…know what they are?"

"Home Made Explosives," Drew nods.

"They pack one gallon jugs…these explosives weigh twenty pounds! It's insane!" her dark curls bounce in outrage.

"The largest I've seen was one hundred and forty pounds…seven jugs latched together. Sometimes they'll even put a jug of gasoline on the top."

"I read that! But why?"

"They try to set tires on fire or any fuel that is spilled from the punctured fuel tanks, and for propaganda. If they are filming it for a recruiting video they want it to look spectacular and lethal."

"Journey didn't have to go…he volunteered because he felt that was why he joined…and that he should be there. When I talk to him or read his letters I can tell he's not very happy."

"Most are not necessarily happy to be in a combat zone…having to deal with incompetence, frustration, missing family and friends. Some days, I cursed myself for making the choice I made…but you let it out and go back to doing your job."

Faye sighs. "I'm just waiting for the day when he comes home, and I run into his arms…" she puts her arms in the air. "And my belly hits him…and he goes flying…"

Drew lets out a laugh.

"I just want him home," Faye pouts.

"Right on. That's what helps a guy get through each day…you wanting him home."

A veteran walks down the stairs. "Yes!" He calls up the stairs, "Cookie Man's here!" He looks back at Drew. "We're starting in five minutes, man."

Drew nods to the veteran and holds out the tin to Faye.

"Thanks," she smiles. "Your guitar is still here."

"I forgot it last week but I'll take it home with me tonight. See you later," Drew climbs the stairs.

Faye pulls five worn note cards out of her apron pocket and flips to the last card in the stack. In a space on the card, she prints, *You wanting him home gets him through each day.* She reads the rest of the cards containing messages of encouragement then places them back into her apron pocket.

*

"I'm fuckin' hot, then I'm cold," Reiss flexes and extends his left hand as he lies in his floating circular bed and stares at the ceiling. "I want to be here, then I wish I was over there again," the darkness absorbs his words. "I remember all the faces…the pleads…what the fuck was I supposed to say but that you'd be okay?" his heart bleeds for those he couldn't save. "I lived," Reiss sighs. "And your kid has no father." Uncertainty on how to process this latest mental torment session surrounds him. "And when I see my sick face…" his phone beeps with a text message from Meg.

Forgot to tell you…Edison traded his picture for your picture and took your picture home. Haha. Nina says it's on their refrigerator. You'll just have to come in and make another one for the troops.

Reiss grins and sits on the swaying bed. "Ahhh," frustration fills his words. "It can only get better, right?"

CHAPTER 35

To affect the quality of the day, that is the highest of arts. Every man is tasked to make his life, even in its details, worthy of the contemplation of his most elevated and critical hour.
–Henry David Thoreau

J ake stares at the package on the table addressed to Sadie.
Carter stands next to Jake. "What is it?"

"I don't know."

"Do we have to take it with us?" Carter asks.

"What do you mean?"

"Do we have to take it with us to heaven to give to Sadie?"

"Let's see what's inside," Jake opens the package and pulls out a flag, a certificate, and a note.

Dear Sadie, really sorry for the delay in writing you. I got home a month ago. One of my soldiers died overseas. I wonder why the good ones have to go. You never hear about the crack addict that dies or the burglar that pays the ultimate price. Not that you can compare the two. We are about one percent of the U.S. and we have elected to put on the uniform, train, and put our lives in danger on a regular basis. Not because we have to but because we are driven or guided to do so. We don't think of the ultimate sacrifice until we are put into that situation, and most often, we never hesitate to take the final step to protect our brothers or sisters.

I guess I got off track for a minute there.

As we are special to you all, you all are in fact special to us. I brought this flag overseas, and I took this flag on every mission. The plan was to give it to someone that made an impression on me. So I wanted to send you the flag with a certificate that has every location it has been to.

I wanted you to know how much your letter and packages mean to us. The items are great but your letter, and distracting us from our own depressing environment for a minute, is especially nice. Sorry for going on so long. I just wanted you to know that you're making a difference. Sincerely, Clark Foston

Carter folds his hands. "Do we have to put it in a box like Gigi's flag?"

"This flag," Jake unfolds the flag, "is made to fly. Let's hang it outside to remind us of all of the men and women who choose to protect us. To honor them."

Carter looks at the certificate. "This flag visited all these places?"

"Only to find a home right here in Wisconsin."

"At our home?"

Jake smiles. "At our home."

*

"Hi, soldier! Here on a Friday afternoon, huh?"

"Hey, ma'am," Drew nods. "I forgot…"

"Your guitar," Faye answers. "I don't get the excitement with guys and guitars…guitars seem to just be background music. I think it would be more fun to play an instrument that takes the stage…like a saxophone or French horn."

"Background music?"

"Oooh, I hit a musical nerve, didn't I? I just think strumming a guitar would get…boring, after a while."

"Boring?"

Faye holds up her hand. "Let me start again…soldier, why do you like playing the guitar? To blend into the background?"

"Because it's boring and everyone else plays one."

"See? I knew it! Mommy is smart!" Faye pats her belly. "For real, why the guitar and not the drums, banjo, or harmonica?"

"First time I deployed there was a guitar in the chapel, so I messed around with learning how to play. But the guitar is like a little orchestra, where you can play chords, bass, and melody. And you can mess with the strings and bend, slide, hammer, palm, tap, or strum…it

216

can be boring," Drew grins, "or complicated depending on what music you want to make."

"See...now it sounds interesting," Faye smiles. "When are you going to slide, hammer, tap, or whatever else you said for us?"

"I didn't say I could do all those things...I just said one can do all that with just a boring guitar."

"You're avoiding my question, soldier."

"I'll think about it," Drew picks up the guitar and carries it toward the door.

"Can I ask you something?" Faye sprays cleaning solution and wipes the counter.

"Yeah," Drew turns around, resting the guitar box on the ground.

"Why? Why take out our guys with IED's? Control and power would seem obvious but we'll just send in more guys."

"They plan on outlasting us. They know they can't defeat our military but they can defeat the populace. If we lose enough guys, and drag the war on too long, they know the public will get louder and louder about bringing us home. They just have to outlast us. What did Journey say?"

"He was supposed to call...and didn't. I haven't heard from him for a few days so my imagination kicks up a whole bunch of possibilities."

"Things happen with lines going down or blackouts or missions and you can't reach home. Give him a week before you let that imagination of yours go wild."

Faye points her finger at Drew. "I'll give you a week before bugging you to play something on that guitar."

Drew picks up the guitar. "I'll think about it."

*

"Dang," D sits on Jake's couch digesting the tune that Jake just finished performing. "So that's the audition song?"

"That's the one," Jake nods. "It's totally her though, right? With the words?"

"Completely who Sadie was, bro. If we make it through the first audition, that will be the beginning of the school year. How's that going to work with you teaching?"

"I'm…" Jake pauses. "Taking a leave from teaching."

"Okay, bro," D processes the statement without a shred of shock. "You're thinking like a rockstar…I can roll with that. We audition first in Chicago. I brought the papers with me." D hands one of the forms to Jake while he fills out the other one. "The competition is in a month."

As D leaves he says, "That is a great song, Jake. It just keeps playing over and over in my head."

"Thanks, man."

D flashes the peace sign. "See you later!"

"Later, D!" Jake kneels and puts his guitar back into the case. Carter puts his arm on Jake's shoulder. "What's up, buddy?"

"Are you taking me back? I didn't steal anything."

"Nope, you're stuck with me," Jake latches the guitar case. "D and I are entering a singing competition. Truth is, I don't know if I'll even make it through the first audition…but if I do make it to the end, wouldn't it be fun to hear our song on television?"

"You'll sing on television?"

"Yeah. The people watching vote to keep us or we get voted off the TV show."

"On TV?"

"On TV. It's a pretty big deal to win…but that's a long way off from where we are now. Now we are just going to audition to enter the competition."

"Will I get to watch you on TV?"

"Absolutely. People vote to keep their favorite singers on the show. You'll have to vote too. You'll vote for me, right?"

"Yes!"

"That's my boy!"

*

Gunner's crooked smile appears with knowing that the question he just asked will fuel the end of today's *Inspiration Behind the Warrior* meeting.

"Speaking of words...so there I was," the medic captures the attention of the veteran group in the coffee shop. "My guys took intense WIA from an IED. QRF is on scene. I'm asked for the sitrep and being a pucker factor million I give a bloody," he puts both of his thumbs up. "Next thing he's screaming, 'Use words asshole, words!' at me."

"Damn, Gunner opened Pandora's envelope today. Airman even shit up the place," Boon hoots, his face reddens as he laughs.

The airman adds in a slow voice, "Pull trigger...gun goes boom..." he says in comical disgust. "It horrifies me Boon has kids...who sanctioned that?"

"Boon's got kids? Idiocracy in session," the medic smirks.

"Stand down boys, all our wives are eventually leavin' us for assholes without WARE," Boon taps his palms on the table.

*

Jake closes the bedtime story book. "Carter...what's in the yellow bag?"

Carter hops out of bed and pulls a worn flannel shirt out of the yellow bag. He reaches into the shirt pocket and opens his hand toward Jake. "Theo gave me this."

"A Purple Heart?" Jake asks.

"Theo said he got it because he never gave up. He said I was a good egg," Carter's eyes narrow as he giggles. "It's silly to call people eggs. He was a soldier. Like that man with the burned face."

"Reiss," Jake nods. "It's too bad Theo had to live on the streets...after serving our country."

"Theo was my best friend."

"That was nice of Theo to give you such a special gift."

"Yeah. He knew," Carter nods.

"He knew what?"

"I'd be okay," Carter lies down still looking at the medal. "Do you want to meet him?"

A question bends Jake's eyebrows. "I'd like to meet him."

"Okay. I'll show you who he is when we get to heaven. Then you can meet my mom too."

"Sounds like a plan. Good night, Carter." Jake turns off the light as Hart assumes his guard dog position near Carter's bed.

*

Reiss strolls into the kitchen still laughing at the sitcom episodes he's been watching for the last few hours.

He spins before reaching into the refrigerator for another beer. Popping the cap, he takes a drink and sets the bottle next to the latest prescription bottle he brought home.

He picks up the prescription bottle and reads the warning label. "Alcohol may intensify these drugs…heeell yeah!" he grabs the beer and meanders back to the couch. Laughter once again bubbles from him.

*

At 4 AM, Carter wakes Jake with tears in his eyes.

Jake turns on the light. "What's wrong, buddy?"

Carter cries harder.

Jake pulls him up and sits in bed with Carter in his arms. When Carter falls asleep, Jake lays him on Sadie's side of the bed, then goes back to sleep.

CHAPTER 36

Because we returned home and have lives to live, maybe it is a good idea
to live just a bit each day for those who were not as fortunate.
–Michael Orban

J ake places flowers against Sadie's grave. "Love, I still miss you,"
he whispers.

Carter looks up at Jake, smiles, and puts his hand in Jake's as they walk back to the car.

As they approach the car, Jake spots Gunner, and switches directions.

Jake introduces, "Gunner, this is Carter. Carter, this is Gunner."

"Mister...your leg!"

"Carter!" shock evident in Jake's voice.

"It's all good." Gunner turns to Carter. "Well, Carter, I was fighting overseas in a war. Do you know what a war is?"

Carter nods.

Gunner continues. "I was in an accident where I lost both my legs. This fake leg," he points to his prosthetic, "works like a real leg. Soon I'll have two fake legs."

"How's therapy going?" Jake asks.

"Little by little retraining the brain to walk."

"That's got to be rough, Gunner." Jake looks at the four grave stones in front of them. "Dang, all four of them died on September eleventh."

Questions load Carter's facial expression.

Jake replies, "September eleventh was a sad day for our country when many innocent people were killed...yet a very strong day for our country when people of all backgrounds joined together to help one another. It is an important day in history."

"Oh," Carter nods.

Gunner remains silent, hoping his lips do not betray his heart. "Carter, it was nice to meet you. Jake," Gunner shakes Jake's hand. "Take it easy."

"See you, Gunner!" Jake and Carter walk toward their car.

Gunner stares at the four graves. "Someday I'll say something, just not today."

*

Kleenex wads fill the garbage can.

Meg's eyes are red puffs of agony. Her head screams with pain from the pressure of constant tears; her heart, lies broken in a pool of loneliness. She dials Reiss's number.

"Yeah," Reiss moans. "Oh, damn, Meg, I can't help you with care packages today. It's not a good day."

"I second that," Meg says. "Are you okay?"

"Nah, yeah, just the combination of things last night that shouldn't have been combined."

"We'll reschedule, Reiss."

"Okay, see ya, Meg."

Meg ends the call as tears spill down her face. "I had to put my Ruger to sleep," she says to the empty house. "If anyone cares…and I ran out of cigarettes…if anyone cares."

*

Moonlight illuminates Meg's *We Remember* painting through the living room window.

Curled on the couch in an old flannel shirt of his, Nina whispers, "A year ago, we talked on the phone. You sounded happy…which made me happy. I told you about Edison and you told me about the palm trees. I told you about our washing machine sounding like a rocket and you told me about how you couldn't get the sand out of your clothes…so maybe," she laughs quietly, "I could launch our machine over there. I miss you. I miss talking to you. And I miss," she wipes a tear, "just having your arms around me when I'm not really sure…about life. You being overseas was hard…but you being gone is worse," she wipes another tear as it slides to her cheek. "I just miss you."

*

Jake hits the snooze on his alarm twice and rolls over. A knock at the front door awakes him.

"That face says it all." Grace walks into the house and vents to Beth, "Didn't I tell you he'd forget about this morning even though we just scheduled this yesterday?"

Beth giggles and hugs Jake. "Good morning!"

Hart hides behind the couch as the girls walk inside.

"Good morning, Beth. Has anyone fed Grace yet?" Jake grins.

"Not funny. I was up early because we were scheduled to come over. I set my alarm," agitation evident in Grace's tone.

"I set my alarm also…" Jake says. "I just turned it off twice because I felt like staying in bed."

Carter walks out in mismatched clothes and with hair styled in three directions from sleeping. "Hi Beth. Hi Grace. We're going to Sydney's for breakfast to celebrate. I love cinnamon rolls."

"What are you celebrating?" Grace asks.

"I slept in my own bed the whole night!"

"Oh, that is good news, Carter! And I agree…Sydney's cinnamon rolls are so good," Beth smiles.

"Give me ten minutes and I'll have Sadie's stuff laid out for you to look through," Jake walks toward his bedroom.

Grace says, "Do you want to keep any of it?"

Jake flashes a smile at Beth. "Well, I tried on some of the high heels, but unfortunately, my feet are too big."

Beth bursts out laughing as Grace glares at Jake.

"You can put whatever you gals don't want into the white bag. I'll drop it off at the thrift shop." Jake dials Meg's number as he walks into the bedroom.

"Hola, Jake."

"Carter and I are going to Sydney's for breakfast. Care to join us?"

"My face is puffy from crying all night and I'm in a really bad mood. Still want me to join you?"

"Absolutely. Meet in twenty minutes?"

"Grand. I'll be there."

*

"Good morning, dear!" Gigi oozes cheerful poison as she retrieves her morning paper.

Drew raises his hand with a weak greeting. "Morning."

"How's your sister, dear?"

"Fine."

"And little Edison?"

"He's fine," Drew's disdain freely flows.

"Wonderful. Pretty soon you'll have a new neighbor, dear."

"Oh yeah? You moving?"

"I am. This house is a bit big for one ol' lady," Gigi laughs. "Have a nice day, dear."

"You too," Drew slips on his running shoes as Gigi walks back into her house.

*

Meg waves when Jake and Carter walk into Sydney's Café, both wearing baseball caps.

"Meg!" Carter runs up to Meg and sits next to her.

"Hey, Carter! I like your ball cap."

"Thank you. I love my hat," Carter pats his hat.

"Carter, you can go and look at the items in the glass counter to see what you want for breakfast," Jake sits down as Carter walks to the front counter admiring the breakfast bakery. Jake says to Meg, "Grace and Beth are sorting through Sadie's clothes...I tried to and couldn't. Too many memories and...I couldn't be there. I don't know..."

"It's not about saying goodbye, Jake. It's about saying thank you for being in our world as long as she was. We were lucky..."

"True. Why were you crying last night?"

Meg bites on the end of her glasses. "I had to…" she takes a deep breath. "I had to put Ruger to sleep."

"Oh, man, I'm sorry. That had to be rough."

"Twas. So your invitation this morning was nice," Meg waves to someone behind Jake.

Jake turns around. "Gunner?! Join the party, man."

Gunner looks at Meg as he wheels himself into a spot at the table.

"My head hurts more than normal because I had to put my dog to sleep…hence my swollen eyes and bad attitude."

Compassion fills Gunner's expression.

Meg points to Jake. "Your turn."

Jake looks up from a menu. "Oh, uh, I couldn't be at my house because my sisters are going through Sadie's stuff because I couldn't, and Sadie's perfume and clothes…bring back memories…which is depressing, heartbreaking and numbs my world."

Gunner hesitates. "Uh, my wife was in a job interview in one of the towers on September eleventh. My father and mother were in the same building with my daughter going to meet mommy after her interview. They all died when the first plane hit the building. I was here…working…as an architectural engineer. They were supposed to see the city…just a little vacation."

"The four graves…" Jake whispers.

Gunner nods. "The four graves are my family. I quit my job and became a marine. Didn't think I had anything else to lose…forgot about my fuckin' legs, though," his grin bittersweet. "So I came to drown my world with cinnamon rolls as I get ready to fly out and inspire people through *Inspiration Behind the Warrior* programs."

"I don't know what to say, Gunner," Meg puts her hand on his shoulder.

"I don't either," Jake shakes his head.

"I don't need you to say anything. It is what it is. You're the first people I've told except for my guys overseas…"

"Miss Addy is here!" Carter runs to Jake. "I almost know what I want for breakfast," Carter strolls back to the counter.

Jake turns around and waves. "Hey, Addison."

Addison walks to their table. "Hi, everybody," she smiles.

225

Jake introduces Meg and Gunner to Addison.

Gunner points toward the table. "Care to join us?"

Addison touches Jake's shoulder. "I don't want to intrude."

"Not at all," Jake slides a chair up to the table.

"You're all so nice!" Addison sits down.

Sydney saunters over to their table balancing a tray of waters and coffee mugs on his belly. "Halo, my regulars," his Australian accent greets them. "Got almost the whole gang this mornin'," he slowly speaks each word as he distributes the coasters and glasses.

"D's on a date…"

Sydney's eyebrows rise. "Oh yah? Some girl finally reined him in, eh? D says you're tryin' out for a singin' competition?" he fills their mugs with coffee.

"We'll give it a shot," Jake nods.

"Well, if ya can win Sydney's cinnamon rolls you have a shot at winnin' on the tele," he winks as he leaves.

"So, how is everyone?" Addison asks.

"We were all just saying what super crappy things in our life made us come to indulge in cinnamon rolls this morning," Meg sets her menu aside. "My head hurts and my dog died."

Jake adds, "My wife died."

Gunner says, "My family died and I lost my legs."

Jake, Meg, and Gunner laugh as Addison absorbs their comments.

Addison puts her pink purse on the table. "My baby died."

"Well then," Meg says. "Join us, Addison, in the breakfast designed to eat away our sadness."

Carter bounces over to the table. "Did you tell them why we're celebrating today?" he asks Jake.

Jake shakes his head. "Why don't you tell them."

"I slept in my own bed all night!" Carter beams.

"Great job, Carter!" Gunner flashes his crooked smile.

"That's so wonderful," Addison adds.

Meg holds up her coffee cup and toasts, "To sleeping in our own beds all night!"

The group holds up their glasses and toasts.

*

"Hi, soldier," less enthusiasm in Faye's voice than normal.

"Hey, ma'am," Drew nods. "You hear from Journey?"

"Yes," an edge in her voice. "He's okay."

"Good," Drew narrows his eyes to analyze her mood before he offers to play the guitar prior to the veteran meeting tonight.

Faye waddles around wiping tables with disinfectant sprayed paper towels. "He doesn't want me talking to you anymore..." she shakes her head. "Sometimes that man messes with my mood!" She pats her belly, "And momma don't need any more moodiness!"

Drew remains silent.

"Journey says you're trying to be my man while he's gone. Says that's why you bring me cookies and say all the stuff you say...I'm not looking for a man, soldier."

"I'm not..." Drew defends.

"I know! I'm just..." Faye rolls her eyes. "He doesn't want me going out with anyone...asks me so many questions about where I'm going or where I was. And any time I'm talking to a man Journey gets all...annoying. I mean, seriously?! If he knew I looked like this...maybe he wouldn't be such a suspicious little pot of...something nasty!"

Drew stifles a grin.

She sighs. "Maybe it would be best if you just came in the back way from now on."

"Sure," Drew calmly states while his insides rage at the accusation.

"I'm sorry...he just gets all fired up about you and me and..."

"I'll come in the back way, ma'am," Drew walks out.

*

Drew pulls a new bottle of Jack out of the cupboard and sets it on his *Fuck the World* sign. Divorce papers on the counter mock him.

"Trying to be her man? How about making sure your wife doesn't go out and find her own Asshole Steve, Journey, you..." obscenities fly. Drew takes a sip from the bottle; the sweet burn coats his insides.

Drew lifts the bottle for another taste…then turns and smashes the bottle against the counter; glass and Jack paint his kitchen.

He drops the bottle neck into the garbage, steps over the glass chaos, and walks out the front door.

At the edge of the cemetery, a homeless man stands on the curb holding a sign. *Need money to refuel my rocket. Please help me go home.*

Only if you take me with you, Drew smirks to himself.

The homeless man's empty glare follows Drew as he walks past.

CHAPTER 37

The greatest achievement was at first and for a time a dream.
The oak sleeps in the acorn,
the bird waits in the egg, and in the highest vision
of the soul a waking angel stirs.
Dreams are the seedlings of realities.
–James Allen

Jake drives into the courthouse parking lot, his gut reminding him of the magnitude of this moment with a massive knot of nausea.

"Thank you for letting me stay with you. I had fun," disappointment saturates Carter's words.

"You bet," Jake nods. "Ready to go inside?"

"No," Carter grips his yellow bag and remains in the car.

"You'll be okay, buddy," Jake opens his door.

"It don't matter," Carter shakes his head as tears start falling. "Why are you giving me back?!" he pleads.

"What?" Jake sticks his head back inside the car. "Give you back? I'm not. Carter," Jake closes his door and opens the back door, sitting next to Carter on the back seat. "This hearing is to adopt you. I'm going to be your dad. After today...you'll be stuck with me...forever."

"You're not giving me back?" Carter wipes his eyes.

"No."

"Why do you want to keep me? No one wants me."

"I do. And Hart likes you too. And Hart doesn't like anyone."

"Hart likes me," Carter grins.

"I know he does," Jake nods. "And no one else is going to brush his teeth."

"Hart loves when I brush his teeth!"

"I know," Jake nods again. "You ready to go inside now?"

229

"Okay," Carter exits the car with his yellow bag.

"You can leave the yellow bag here…you'll be coming back."

Carter stares at Jake, then at his bag, then back at Jake.

"You're coming home with me, Carter."

"Okay," Carter mentally battles letting go of his bag.

Jake closes the car door. "How about I hold the bag for you while we're inside?"

"Okay," relief washes over Carter's face.

Jake and Carter walk up the courthouse stairs, Carter's hand holding Jake's while his other hand grips his yellow bag.

"How are you both doing?" Angela asks as Jake and Carter walk inside the courthouse.

Carter holds tightly to Jake's hand without saying a word.

"Just breathe," Angela instructs. "And follow me."

Carter freezes when he sees his foster mother. "Momma," he whispers in terror as he digs his fingers into Jake's hand.

Jake pulls him close. "You're okay, buddy. I'm right here."

The thought of losing Carter passes through Jake's mind. *What if the court says no?* His stomach knot tightens.

Angela holds out her hand. "Carter, it's time for us to go up front."

Carter gives Jake a hug, then takes Angela's hand. After a few steps forward with Angela, Carter runs back to Jake.

"You'll be okay, Carter," Jake kneels down.

Carter hands him the yellow bag.

Jake sets the bag on the ground and makes the heart signal with his hands.

A smile erupts across Carter's face. He returns the signal and joins Angela to walk upfront.

D puts his hand on Jake's shoulder. "Big day, huh?"

"Yeah," Jake's chest tightens with each passing minute. "I'm doing the right thing, right?"

"Yeah, bro. No doubt," D says.

"What if there is doubt?"

"There isn't. You probably just had a bad sandwich for lunch."

Jake grins. "A bad sandwich, huh? Are those quite common?"

"Very common on big days, bro. Very common," D laughs.

*

The flag's red and white stripes wave as Jake pulls into Phoebe's driveway. Jake looks at Carter. "Ready to see your family?"

Carter giggles. "Ready!"

Jake shuts the car door and begins walking toward Phoebe's front porch. "Joel?"

Bulky biceps under a gray t-shirt and khaki cargo pants outfit his grinning brother. "Wanted to be here for the big celebration," days without shaving accompany Joel's world-touring tan skin. "Mom filled me in. Congrats. You're a dad?"

"I am. How…are you?"

"Have to fly back tomorrow but tonight's about you and this boy, Carter, who I'm looking forward to meeting."

Jake introduces, "Carter, this is my brother, Joel."

"Welcome to the family, Carter." Joel motions toward the front door. "After you," Joel pats Jake on the back as they walk inside.

"I love cake," Carter says as they walk inside to the aroma of freshly baked chocolate cake.

"I love that sign," Carter points to a banner in the front hall that reads, *Welcome to our family, Carter!*

"My name is in blue!" Carter beams when he sees the cake.

Jake grins, "It's a good day, Carter."

*

Edison bounces out of the car with his toy plane and begins to run in circles in Drew's front yard, flying the plane with his hand held straight in the air and making his own interpretation of plane noises.

Nina grins as Drew opens his front door. "You forgot your cookies for Sunday's meeting!" she holds up a container of sugar cookies.

Drew opens the door a few inches and grabs the container. "I didn't go. I'll take them next time."

"Why didn't you go?" Nina asks.

"I didn't feel like it," annoyance seeps from his words.

Edison races up to Drew with his plane and attempts to fly his plane into the house.

231

"Hey, buddy," Drew stops Edison from coming inside. "Not today."

"Why aren't you opening the door and letting us in?" A look of playfulness crosses Nina's face. "You hiding a gal in there?"

"No," Drew's acidic mood worsens. "I'm busy."

"Busy with what, Drew?" Nina tries to look around him into his house.

"Projects and fixing things. Damn. Go home, Nina."

"Play outside, honey," she pulls Edison back from the front door. "Do you want to come for dinner tonight?" concern replaces her curiosity.

"Probably not," Drew sighs with slight frustration.

"Think about it, okay?" Nina pleads with her eyes.

"I'll think about it," Drew closes the door. Turning toward his kitchen, he curses at the smashed glass and the busted chair that helped him smash even more objects. "A little morning frustration makes for some big evening projects."

*

Reiss, the last of Jake's friends to leave the party, shakes Jake's hand. "You invited me because you felt sorry for me?"

"Nah, I wanted a bunch of friends here to support Carter."

"Damn, here I thought it was about me."

"You're a soldier. That's an understandable mistake."

A dimple sinks Reiss's cheek. "Glad I could help a brother out. Was thinking about coming by to see the Nova tomorrow."

"Sounds good."

"See ya, Jake."

"Later, Reiss."

Joel walks into the living room and sits across from Jake. "Nice friends."

"Yeah," Jake nods.

"How are you doing with Sadie being gone?" Joel asks.

"I'm fine. I'm trying to look at her presence in my life as a blessing. She could have been with anyone, but she chose me. It's starting to seem like there's a plan. And even though she's gone, she's still rocking my world."

"Wow…" Joel's tone is sour.

Jake tries to analyze the odd response.

"And Grace says you are trying out for a singing competition?" Joel shakes his head in disgust. "Glad to see you're doing so well. I really thought Sadie meant more to you."

Shock takes the air out of Jake's chest as anger, hatred, and grief rage inside of him. Jake storms into the kitchen.

"Jake, what's wrong?" Grace asks.

"I'm fine. We have to go, but thanks for coming today."

Grace and Beth look at one another with the same look they had after Sadie died.

Get home, I just need to get home, Jake's mind screams.

Joel wanders in to talk with Phoebe as if nothing happened.

Jake motions to Carter. "Let's go."

Carter grins, "Can we…"

"Let's go," Jake orders expressionless. Jake turns to his mom. "Thanks. We'll see you later."

"I'll get some cake for you to take home. Honey, are you okay?"

Jake glares at Joel then looks back at his mom. "I'm fine."

Tension fills the room.

On the porch Jake hears his mom say, "Aren't you going to say goodbye to your brother? He came a long way to see you."

Joel responds, "It's okay, mom. I just enjoyed being here with the family and seeing everyone again."

*

Meg quickly pulls on her pajamas, camouflage pants and a black top, before answering her phone.

"Meg, it's Nina. I wasn't sure who else to call. I'm sorry, I'm just kind of a mess and I needed to tell someone."

Meg sits on the couch. "Okay, tell me."

"I get excited when Drew seems to be coping better…but then things go back to where they used to be. He won't tell me anything…and I…I don't want to pry, but I want to make sure he doesn't do anything…you know, I just hear so much about suicides and I don't want him to…end like that."

"You think he might kill himself?" Meg asks.

"No," Nina sighs. "I don't know. I mean, I hope not. I just don't know how to help him. He won't talk to me."

"Uhhh…you're asking me to?"

"I know, it's late…I owe you big time already…for so much…"

"I doubt I'll be able to change anything, Nina."

"Everything is a mess…and I've been staring at your painting…I just wish Jasper was here."

"I'm sure Drew's fine, Nina. He probably just had a bad day…but I'll go over there." Meg hangs up and leans her head against the back of the couch. "Drama, drama, drama. And you better not be sassy to me, Drew," she tosses the warning into the air. "I'm losing precious sleep by checking on you," she puts on her coat.

*

After Jake tucks Carter into bed, the phone rings. "Hello?" he whispers.

"Jake, I…" Joel begins.

"You said enough…" anger boils at hearing Joel's voice.

"Jake…"

Jake hangs up the phone.

*

"I'm just going to keep knocking," Meg sings to a made-up tune as she knocks on Drew's front door.

"What?!" aggravation assaults Meg as Drew opens the door.

"So, you're doing well," Meg says with complete composure.

"Meg?" Drew shakes his head. "What are you doing here?"

"Your sister thinks you might try to kill yourself."

Obscenities fly from his lips with, "Nina's annoying as hell."

"You wouldn't let her into your house. You wouldn't talk to her. You didn't go to your meeting Sunday. She has a point."

"My life," his voice gets louder, "is my life. I don't..."

Meg holds up her hands. "I'm with you, man. Let me in."

"Are you wearing pajamas?" curiosity smothers Drew's anger.

"I'm supposed to be sleeping right now, but I'm here."

Drew opens his door.

Meg walks in. "Wow, you do this all on your own?"

"Yeah...well, I used a bat after the chair broke."

"Nice. So what's next?"

"Rebuild what I destroyed."

"Ah, right. And why did you destroy it?"

"Doesn't matter. And just because we had that breakfast chat doesn't mean you're my shrink or my girlfriend."

"Wait," Meg smirks. "I need a moment to recover from the shock of us not dating. You remember our conversation, right? Relationships aren't my thing. People annoy me."

"A gal at the veteran coffee house was told by her husband overseas that she can't talk to me anymore. He told her that I was flirting with her. It's total bullshit."

"Okay, so you and I aren't getting married because of her?"

Drew grins at Meg's playful sarcasm. "I was talking with Faye so she wouldn't feel the need to find some other guy to talk with...like my cheating," curses fly, "wife did. I wanted to spare Journey that shocker...and the bastard accuses me of trying to get with his overly pregnant wife."

"Did you tell Faye why you've been talking with her?"

"Nah, I got the hell out of there before I destroyed something that didn't belong to me."

"Good call...but she probably was telling you what her husband said so you could tell her what to tell him..."

"Say that again?"

"Tell Faye why you were talking to her...so she can tell her husband why you were talking to her. Then the husband won't have to be jealous and the wife won't feel like she's cheating."

"Doesn't matter anyway," Drew shrugs.

"Yeah, it actually does matter, darling. For you…for the husband…for the wife…this matter matters for everyone. And how pregnant is overly pregnant anyway?"

Drew uses his hands to show how large Faye is. "Huge. Really huge."

"Wow, her bun is busting out of her oven! Okay, so you're not going to kill yourself, right?"

A look of amusement crosses his face. "Nope."

"Grand. Then I'm going home to sleep."

"Thanks for stopping by. Did you call me darling?"

"I did," Meg turns toward him before walking out. "And instead of picking up a bat and beating the life out of your kitchen, next time you could just come and help me put together care packages…or cut up empty boxes for recycling. I could find a delightfully destructive task for you if you're in need."

"Good to know," Drew grins. "Good night."

*

Joel's accusations trail through Jake's mind erasing his option of sleeping. He reaches for Sadie's journal.

When I let go of my past and the sad stories I've held onto, almost as if they were old friends, I am free to fully love and give. Free to be who I truly am…just me. I titled my journaling notes "Journey with the Secret"…and the secret to a meaning filled journey? You can.

Having dreams, the passion-filled kind, means we can achieve them. Us being here, means we still have a purpose to fulfill. When falling down or when stuck in the deepest darkness of our own mind, how do we find the strength to get back up? Love. With all the qualities we possess and all the soul searching we do, the greatest piece of our life, the most important thing…is love. And it's not about finding love or searching for love…we are already loved by Him who created love and therefore filled with love to give.

Our struggles are not weaknesses but opportunities to see our strengths. The first step to seeing our strengths or the strengths of others...is love. Life we're given—living is our choice. Love we're given—loving is our choice.

Jake pauses to absorb her words, then writes in his journal. *Entry #10: The secret to a meaning filled journey: You can.*

CHAPTER 38

One can never consent to creep when one feels an impulse to soar.
–Helen Keller

M eg meanders down the hall in dice slippers and a bathrobe. "Joel?" she opens her front door.

"I screwed up," stress crinkles Joel's forehead.

"It's early. Really early. Like birds not even up early." Meg sighs. "Come in. Water or cheese sandwich?"

"No."

"Coffee?"

Joel walks in. "Coffee sounds great."

The coffee machine drums as Meg pulls out her finger mug and a second mug for Joel. "I'm ready to be entertained. How did you screw up?"

*

Jake awakes Carter. "Time to get up Mr. Carter Gallagher."

"I love my new name," Carter grins.

Jake sits on Carter's bed. "I was upset by something someone said last night...so I had a pity party for myself."

"What's a pity party?" Carter sits up.

"It's when you feel sorry for yourself and you choose to be sad for a while as you think about the sad things in your life."

"Oh. Do you get cake?"

"No, no cake. I want you to know that sometimes other people will try and rain on our parade...but we don't have to accept their rain. We just have to move to where the sun is shining. As I sat in bed last night, I thought about you and Hart and our friends and our family...and I realized that there is always sunshine somewhere in our lives."

The doorbell rings.

Jake opens the door. "Meg, you shouldn't have…" Jake begins to close the door.

"Jake…" Joel pushes the door open.

Hart scurries behind the couch.

Meg motions to Carter. "Put on some shoes and come outside with me."

Jake tosses Meg an acid look.

"Uh, that look, is for him," Meg calmly points to Joel. "He has especially bad behavior…but you still have your brother, Jake. Just listen to him before I transport him to the airport."

As Meg and Carter walk outside, Joel closes the door adopting a look of curiosity and shame. "Jake, I'm supposed to be at the airport right now but I'm here because you would not take my call last night."

"Go save the world, Joel," Jake folds his arms.

"You stubborn…" Joel sighs deeply. "Coming back here reminds me of Phin."

"Meg's brother dying wasn't your fault…"

"Just let me talk, Jake!"

"You have one minute."

"I didn't mean to question your love for Sadie…I know you loved her."

Jake leans against the kitchen counter. "I will always love Sadie. But she's taught me that unhappiness or happiness is a choice. And running away from your pain will never stop the pain. You have to let go of not saving Phin, and forgive whomever you blame for taking him from you."

Joel warns, "Don't get into a God conversation, man…"

"Not being able to save Phin made you go to medical school. Without that moment, you may have chosen a totally different path."

"True."

"Why did Meg drive you over here?" Jake asks.

"I've been writing to her since I left."

Jake's irritation level rises.

"Might as well get it all out…" Joel studies Jake's face. "I killed her brother, Jake…which ruined her family…and pretty much her life. I owe her…"

"If you control death, then you owe Meg."

Obscenities flow as Joel shakes his head. "I didn't say I controlled death."

"You were lifting weights, you walked out, Phin dropped a weight on his chest and died. How did you kill him?"

"Jake," exasperation spikes the edge of Joel's words. "I walked out to talk with a girl. I got back…and Phin was dead. If I would have been there, he'd be alive."

"If Phin would have waited until you returned to lift, he'd be alive. Maybe."

"You don't get it, Jake…"

"I don't get it?! My wife died! I should have been there to save her…to get help…I was too late! So, yeah, I get it! But I also get that I don't get to choose who dies…but I get to choose how I live until I do."

"That's deep," Joel stares at him then bursts out laughing.

Jake points to the door. "Your minute is up."

"Cut me some slack," Joel puts his hand on Jake's shoulder. "I get your point…I just am not used to the brotherly love thing." Joel mumbles, "I have to figure out the mess in my mind…not blame myself, blah, blah. Meg said the same thing."

Meg strums her fingers on the door and opens it an inch. "Joel? We need to leave if you want to catch your flight," she closes the door.

Joel looks at Jake with persuasive confession. "I'm sorry for yesterday…and for leaving you and mom…and for not writing…and," he looks up trying to remember any other offenses. "And for all my other bad behavior…well, not *all* of it…"

"Okay, I got it…you're sorry."

"So…" Joel's eyebrows rise.

"We're good, man. Go to the airport," Jake opens the door.

Joel hugs him. "Luv ya, bro."

"Yeah, love you too. Safe travels, man."

Joel walks outside. "I'm ready Miss Meg."

Carter runs past Jake into the house as Meg walks toward her car. "Jump in, Jack, we're going to have to fly to get you to the airport!" Meg glances back at Jake. "You okay?"

"You were writing letters?" Jake says.

"Mio myo," Meg shakes her head as she gets into her car. "Another conversation I can look forward to having."

*

"Yoo hoo, are you home?" Gigi knocks on Drew's door.

Drew opens his door, his mind spewing all sorts of mental fire at the sight of the happy woman.

"There you are!" Gigi smiles. "Since I'm moving, I have quite a few things I won't be taking with me and I was wondering if you wanted them. Mostly furniture."

"I don't think so. I just got orders this morning that I'm deploying again so I'm going to be moving out."

"Do you want to deploy again, dear?"

"It's my job."

"When are you leaving?"

"Three weeks. It made sense to live here when I was married, but…"

"I was sorry to see her leave. Such a shame."

"I finally signed the divorce papers today…doesn't matter."

"Your happiness matters. You're a nice young man."

Drew grins. "Thanks."

"Where will you live when you return home?"

"I'll put my stuff in storage and figure it out when I get back."

"How did your sister take the news?"

"Haven't told Nina. Actually, you're the first to know."

"I will keep you in my prayers," Gigi puts her wrinkled hand on Drew's forearm. "I sure do appreciate what you do for our country. Bill was in the service, as you know, and I know it's not easy seeing what you see or doing what you do. You just know that you are special and loved…no matter what…and you just come home safely, okay, dear?"

"Okay," Drew nods. "Thanks, Gigi."

"I better get back to packing my house," Gigi walks down the porch stairs. "Have a nice day!"

"You too," Drew calls out, Gigi's happy venom suddenly harmless. He closes the door and picks up the phone. "The worst part of deploying…" he dials Nina's number.

*

Jake pulls the tarp off of Candy.

Carter's eyes enlarge with excitement.

"Carter, this is Candy," Jake points to the car. "Candy, this is Carter."

"I love shiny cars!"

"I need to do a lot of work on the engine to get it running right. I've been rebuilding the engine because some of the engine parts were really old and it's been taking time to swap them out. I haven't worked on Candy for a while, but Reiss is coming over today to see the car…"

Reiss pulls into Jake's driveway and whistles as he walks up to Candy. "Hot da…" he adjusts his greeting upon seeing Carter. "Dang…hot mistress, Jake."

"Reiss, meet Candy."

"What's that?" Carter points to the leather necklace around Reiss's neck which hosts a dime-size strip of metal with two pointed ends.

"When I was in an accident overseas, this is the piece of shrapnel, or metal, they pulled out of my arm…it hit a nerve and that's why sometimes my hand goes numb." He presses his thumb against the piece of metal. "It's a souvenir…like a reminder."

"Oh," Carter nods.

"Candy Man, what are we doing for Candy?" Reiss asks Jake.

"Honing out cylinders, new pistons…and looking at getting a racing cam put in."

"Topping off the power meter," Reiss nods. "Then what are you looking at for horsepower?" Reiss inspects every inch of Candy.

"I don't know but first thing I'm going to do is put it on a dyno."

"What's a dyno?" Carter asks.

"A dyno," Jake says, "is a device which helps us calculate the horsepower of the car...tells us how powerful Candy is."

"Oh," Carter nods. "I'm going to go and get Hart so he can work with us on Candy, okay?"

Jake nods. "Sounds good."

Reiss waits for Carter to walk inside. "So no spinners, Candy Man...but what about some bad ass shoes? I saw some rims the other day that would make any grown man cry."

Jake laughs. "You're really into rims, huh?"

"Just sayin' man, don't knock 'em until you see 'em."

"Maybe. I'll look, just not sure I'll touch..."

"Maybe usually means yes sometimes." Reiss rubs his hands together. "Okay, let's power up your mistress."

*

Meg sits across from Gunner at Sydney's Café, stirring her coffee. "So next week is the week?"

"Next week is the week," Gunner takes a deep breath.

"How was the process for leg number one?" Meg asks.

Gunner straightens the napkin holder on the table. "Brutal. The first physical therapy sessions were pretty rough. It doesn't hurt to get fitted for the new leg but the process can be difficult."

"How so?" Meg stabs her last piece of cinnamon roll with her fork.

"The hard part about a new leg is the alignment. The fit has to be perfect or it throws off your posture, messes with the way you walk, and makes your back hurt. Getting it perfect can be frustrating and painful."

"How soon after will you be walking?"

"The medical team told me it depends...could be walking in three months or it could be two years before I get out of this wheelchair. But I'm sick of wheeling myself around. When I get that second leg strapped on and fit right, I will be walking."

"How do they know what kind of leg will fit you?"

"It usually takes them a week to cast the leg, order the foot, and get it all put together."

"Gunner, I'll be around to help you out," Meg stands as she sees Nina walk in the front door of the café.

"Thanks, Meg. Addison's done teaching until fall…said she plans to help me with therapy."

"Swell. Count me in as the backup."

Nina walks up to their table. "Hey, Meg. Hey, Gunner!"

"Hey, Nina." Gunner's phone rings. "Hope you both have a good time today." He answers the call, "Hey, Addison! I was just talking about you…"

CHAPTER 39

And when it is all over and the victory is yours,
and the smoke clears away and the smell of the powder is dissipated,
and you bury the friendship that died because they could not stand the
strain, and you nurse back the wounded and fainthearted who loyally
stood by you, even when doubting, then the hard years of fighting will
seem but a dream. You will stand brave, heartened, strengthened by
struggle, re-created to a new, better, and stronger life by a noble
battle, nobly waged in a noble cause.
And the price will then seem to you—nothing.
—William George Jordan

Jake is without a greeting with the exception of raised eyebrows and pursed lips as he opens his front door.

"Today is fix stuff day…and we have a stuff to fix," Meg says.

"Yeah we do," Jake leans against the doorframe. "My brother didn't write the family for years, Meg. Years. But you knew…"

"Jake, that wasn't my secret to share. I will say, however, that I encouraged Joel and downright threatened the man to write to his family."

"Threatened him?" Jake grins.

"Many mistake my kindness for weakness…"

"You lost me at kindness…"

"Are we done here? Bueno bueno? I have places to go, people to patch."

"Look at you being all peopley…"

"Aw, and look at you, making up your own word. I'm glad I taught you something." She looks at her watch. "We're good?"

"Is this the kindness thing you were talking about?"

"I'm taking that as a yes." She walks away and yells, "Adios, Jake!" with a wave of her hand.

*

"Hart!" Carter yells after dropping Hart's leash. "Hart!"

Hart bolts through the park toward a blond gal walking a little white puppy.

Carter turns toward Jake. "I'm sorry…"

Jake and Carter run after Hart.

The blond takes a knee as Hart rolls on his belly and licks her hands. She laughs and glances at Jake. "Does she like him?"

"Excuse me?" Jake asks.

"Sadie…does she like the puppy? He was perfect based on the form she filled out. I couldn't believe it…"

"Ah…you're the gal with the red car!"

"That's me. Sorry I didn't have a chance to explain that day. I was late for an appointment, but I knew Sadie would know what it was all about. You didn't answer my first question. Does she not like the dog?"

"Uh, I'm sure she would have. Sadie passed away three and a half months ago."

"Oh my gosh!" the color drains from her face. "I'm so sorry!" she sits down and pulls the white puppy onto her lap. "How did it happen? How did she…"

Carter grabs Hart's leash and toy and looks up at Jake.

Jake nods to Carter then sits down as Carter heads off to play with Hart. "A stroke. We never saw it coming. Sadie filled out a form requesting a puppy?"

"I'm from an organization called Puppy Rescue. We find homes for unwanted puppies. Sadie met Laina, who I set up with a puppy."

"I remember her talking about Laina," Jake says.

"Then Sadie came in to talk with me about her veteran program because we place half of our pups with veterans. Before she left, she added her name to the adoption list, but she wanted something very specific. Like, very specific. I was certain I'd never come across the type of puppy she wanted. And on her form, she checked that I could just drop the dog off. When I handed you the box that day I figured she would take care of explaining. I can't believe it," she shakes her head.

Jake points to the white puppy lying in her lap. "Is that puppy from the rescue?"

"We got this one at the rescue a few days ago. So far, I have not found a home for him. Know anyone that wants a puppy?" she laughs.

"I do."

A look of surprise crosses her face. "Well, he comes with a puppy pack just like your dog did. By the way, what did you name him?"

"Hart. He's afraid of most people, but a great dog."

"He was rescued from a home where he didn't have much human interaction. Hart is a great name."

"What's your name?"

"Oh, I'm Isabel. You can call me Izzy."

"Izzy, it's a pleasure to meet you. I'm Jake, and the boy running around with Hart is Carter. He's my son."

"It's nice to meet you, Jake." Izzy tickles behind the white puppy's ears, "This one loves to be cuddled."

"Thanks for dropping off Hart. He was a surprise, but it's nice to have Sadie connected to this part of my life."

"It's fun for me to see he has a great home. We don't get to see many of the dogs after they leave the rescue."

Jake looks at Carter playing with Hart. "Yeah, he has a good home."

*

Reiss shakes his head at the sight of Drew entering Sydney's Café. "If you weren't so hot, I'd be so pissed at you right now, Meg."

"Hooray for shallowness," Meg grins. "This is important."

"I'm not talking to him, Meg."

At the sight of Reiss, Drew's eyebrows sink in disappointment as he looks at Meg and stops. Meg walks over to Drew. "Nina said you're leaving and," Meg whispers something.

"Blackmail?" Drew stares at Meg with a numb expression. "Fine." He walks to the table and drops into a chair across from Reiss.

"Manning," Reiss nods, his tone cold.

"Let's just get this over with…"

"Okay," Meg instructs. "Here's how this will work. Reiss remembers parts of that day," she looks at Drew. "I know you do too. So, Reiss is going to talk," she looks at Reiss, "in a respectful way, because he respects you," she looks back at Drew. "Drew, you can say something, or not say something, but you both were there and you both lost something, and you both came home without something."

Drew smirks, "Forcing us to make up and be friends, mom?"

"You know what's on the line, Drew…" Meg warns.

"What…you're leaving? Just like that?" Reiss asks.

"Just like that," Meg nods and walks out of Sydney's Café.

Reiss breaks the silence. "How'd she threaten you?"

"No future care packages…ever. And," the corners of Drew's mouth slightly turn upward.

"And…what?"

"She'll give my parents my address overseas and tell them I want to become a doctor in a really bad way."

"Damn, that's cold," Reiss laughs. "Hot yet functions with no heart."

"I don't want to talk about Jasper."

Reiss's smile disappears.

"I don't want to talk about that day."

"Okay," Reiss stands. "Looks like those meetings have been helping you."

"Don't be an asshole."

Reiss sits back down and whispers, "I can't talk to anyone else about that day…do you know how they look at me already? Like a sorry sonofabitch who got his face blown off!"

"You were doing your job."

"Yeah, that keeps me all happy and satisfied."

"What do you want to know?"

"How I got Jas killed."

"You didn't. The fuckers who set the IED killed him."

"I just want, need, to know."

"That's all, Doc. You go there. Shit happens. If you come home, you get up each day, and…try to push that shit aside so you can deal with the shit that's waiting for you at home."

A dimple sinks Reiss's cheek. "Inspirational, Manning."

Drew stands.

Reiss nods and dials a number on his phone, whispering, "Don't die, Manning. I'll need a wingman for all the hot ladies when you get back…"

Drew shakes his head, his eyes amused. "Roger that, Doc."

*

"Ma'am," Drew walks inside the coffee house with his guitar.

"Hi," Faye's tone apologetic with a pinch of sadness.

"My wife hooked up with Asshole Steve when I was overseas because she needed someone to talk with. She left me for him when I got home…so I was talking with you…" Drew explains.

"I'm sorry," Faye waddles from behind the counter. "Journey's job and my hormones can make for some awful conversations sometimes. I heard you missed the last meeting."

"Yeah," Drew nods. "When is your husband coming home?"

"Four weeks. He better be here in four weeks. When baby gets here…someone's gonna have to take care of mommy," she laughs then tears form in her eyes.

"Ma'am?"

"Journey said that when he was boarding the chopper, he looked at the flight line and saw soldiers lined up next to two Black Hawk helicopters with their right hands raised in salute as the bodies of fallen soldiers were brought out of the aircraft in body bags," tears stream down her face. "So," her expression hardens, "if he comes home, he'll be home in four weeks."

"When he comes home, ma'am. When."

"When," Faye pushes her dark curls behind her ears. "When."

"He should come to these meetings when he gets home."

"You both can go together," Faye winks.

"I'm deploying, ma'am. I'll be gone before he gets back."

Faye stares at him in disbelief.

"It's my job."

"I know," Faye sighs. "I know. But you listen to me," she holds up her finger with ultimate authority. "Come twelve months, or however long you're over there, you come home. And the second you get home, you come here. But you come home, you hear me? You come home. And I want your address overseas the second you know it."

"Yes, ma'am."

"And you're playing me a song before you leave?" she states as a half question half demand.

A boyish grin crosses his face. "I'm playing for Junior, so he doesn't inherit his mom's opinion that guitars are boring."

*

Meg stares speechless at a lanky legs, white whiskers, black heart shaped nose pooch resting in the arms of a blond standing outside her front door.

"Interested?" Izzy grins. "Jake says you might be looking for a dog…and this dog is looking for a home."

"This is Jake's idea, huh?" Meg pets the dog. "He's ridiculously adorable."

Izzy hands her the dog. "Is that a yes, you'll adopt him?"

"Absofrickenlutely," the white puppy shakes in Meg's arms. "Oh, you're scared? You'll be okay. You're a cutie pie."

Izzy holds up a folder. "A little paperwork to fill out."

Meg pushes open her door. "Come on in."

"Any names come to mind?"

"Smith…as in Smith and Wesson."

"Firearm company?" amusement shows in Izzy's grin.

"Yep," Meg kisses Smith on the head. "Still going to let me keep him?"

"After hearing that…I don't think it would be wise for me to try prying him from your arms," Izzy spreads the paperwork on her counter. "A few signatures and Smith is yours."

*

Sorting through the mail, Jake flips to a note from overseas. A moment of memories freezes his mind. "Carter, you have a letter here…from a soldier."

"A letter? For me?" anticipation and excitement fill Carter's words. "Can you read it to me?"

"Sure," Jake bends down so Carter can follow along as he reads the note.

Dear Carter, the soldiers of the 1-128th Infantry Battalion thank you for your support. Our Red Arrow Canteen is a place where soldiers come to unwind and stock up on much needed goods. The Canteen has been a great success and this would not be possible without you and others like you. Your artwork has been a welcomed treasure for several of our guys overseas. God Bless you Sir and God Bless America. Sincerely, Sgt. Mark Spard

"Your first note from a soldier," Jake hands him the letter.

Carter happily takes the note and walks to his room. He pulls the flannel shirt out of his yellow bag, and tucks the note inside the pocket with the Purple Heart. He rolls up the shirt and places it back into the yellow bag.

Carter stares at the bag then pulls the shirt back out, removes the Purple Heart Medal and letter from the pocket, opens his top dresser drawer, and places the shirt into the drawer. He sets the letter and the medal on top of the flannel shirt and closes the drawer.

Carter turns around as Jake stands in the doorway.

"Should we throw out the yellow bag?" Jake asks.

"Okay," Carter carefully folds up the bag and hands it to Jake.

"Okay," Jake nods.

*

"A waste of two good minutes," Drew puts down his pen and rereads the note he painfully wrote.

Dear mom and dad, I'm not going back to medical school. I'm deploying again for twelve months. Please check in on Nina and Edison while I'm gone. Take care, Drew.

Drew folds the note and slides it into an envelope.

*

Jake sits on the edge of the bed and pulls out Sadie's journal, turning to her last journal entry.

On this journey, none of us truly know the plan, so we follow. We follow with hope. Hope that the direction we are going is correct and the actions we are taking are getting us to where we need to be.

We follow with faith. Faith that God will bring those into our lives that we need, and gently remove those whose journey with us has come to an end. Faith that everything we need will be provided to and for us.

We follow requesting wisdom. Wisdom to know that each day is a new day of living our life on purpose. We need not know all the details—we just need to trust the one in control of the details.

Jake takes a deep breath and closes her journal. He slowly pulls off his wedding ring. Kissing it once, he places the ring carefully into the drawer with Sadie's journal.

*

"Drew?" Nina opens the front door releasing the aroma of freshly baked cookies. "You're leaving in the morning…it's late…is everything okay?"

"You're still up," Drew walks inside. "I couldn't sleep either. Mind if I wake Edison?"

"Okay, sure…why?"

"I want to show him his daddy's dance."

"You're going to teach him Jasper's dance?" a giggle bubbles out. "I've seen you try to dance, Drew."

"I can rock the victory dance," Drew assures with a grin.

Nina turns on the living room light and yawns. "I'll get Edison, and you," her eyes sparkle in amusement, "setup for the victory dance. We'll victory dance you off…and we'll victory dance your return home."

THE END

End Notes

Chapter 2, Chapter 21 Quotes: Jordan, William George. *The Majesty of Calmness*. New York, Chicago: Fleming H. Revell Company, 1910. Bountiful, Utah: Empowered Wealth Institute, 2004. Print.

Chapter 4, Chapter 36 Quotes: Orban, Michael. *Souled Out: A Memoir of War and Peace*. Candler, NC: Silver Rings Press, 2007. All rights reserved. Printed with permission.

Chapter 10, Chapter 13, Chapter 16, Chapter 32 Quotes: Jordan, William George. *The Power of Purpose*. New York, Chicago: Fleming H. Revell Company, 1910.

Chapter 11 Quote: Trump, Donald J., with Meredith McIver. *Think Like A Champion*. New York City, New York: Vanguard Press, 2009. All rights reserved. Printed with permission.

Chapter 12, Chapter 18, Chapter 28 Quotes: Frankl, Viktor. *Man's Search for Meaning*. New York: Washington Square Press, 1963. Printed with permission.

Chapter 15 Quote: Hill, Napoleon. *Think and Grow Rich*. USA: BN Publishing, 2007. All rights reserved. Printed with permission.

Chapter 23, Chapter 25, Chapter 31, Chapter 37 Quotes: Allen, James. *As A Man Thinketh* ; (including, Morning and evening thoughts). Mineola, New York: Dover Publications, Inc., 2007. Printed with permission.

Chapter 30 Quote: THE HOLY BIBLE, NEW INTERNATIONAL VERSION®, NIV® Copyright © 1973, 1978, 1984, 2011 by Biblica, Inc.™ Used by permission. All rights reserved worldwide.

Chapter 38 Quote: Keller, Helen. *The Story of My Life* (1903).

Chapter 39 Quote: Jordan, William George. *The Power of Truth*. New York, Chicago: Fleming H. Revell Company, 1910. Bountiful, Utah: Empowered Wealth Institute, 2004. Print.

Reference Chapter 31, p. 200: "Memorial Guidebook." *The United States Coast Guard Auxiliary Memorial Guide Book*, 1 September 2006 Past Captains Association: 7. http://www.auxpdept.org/pdf/MemorialGuideBook-9-2006.pdf

Reference Chapter 31, p. 201: "Military Funeral Flag Presentation Protocol." *United States Flag Manual*, Copyright © 2008 by Jeff Seeber and the Military Salute Project: 26. http://usmhc.org/Flag.php

Photo of Mollie Voigt: Artists' Eyes Photography, Slinger, WI

About the Author

O n Memorial Day 2007, Mollie received a forwarded email from a soldier's mother. The email was from her son in Iraq. He told his mom 13 guys and gals in his group had not received anything from home their entire tour overseas so if someone wanted to do something for Memorial Day for the troops, could they please write a letter of support to boost the morale overseas. This was the first time Mollie heard of our troops being overseas without support. Morale Builder Packages and letters were sent to each soldier, yet the costs associated with the project encouraged the decision to reach out for help to obtain items for Morale Builder Packages and funds to continue sending the "boxes of love" overseas…and so was born the Mission Soldier Adoption program. As the group supported the soldiers, they quickly came to realize how many troops overseas could use help to make their deployment a bit brighter. After a few months, they expanded the program to support all branches of the U.S. Military and veterans here at home as donations from individuals and companies came in from across the globe.

Mollie began to write a self-help book in 2009 which transformed into the MOON DUSTERS novel, and marked the beginning of her career as a novelist. For more information, please visit http://www.Mollie Voigt.com

In communicating with troops overseas and speaking with veterans, we became aware of the adjustment made once a warrior returns home from combat. For these reasons, Mollie founded the non-profit organization, On Purpose Journey Inc., in 2009, which currently supports those who serve with a focus on troops and veterans. For more information on services provided and how to support our mission, please visit http://www.OnPurposeJourney.com